Praise for Han[...]

'Warm, funny, romantic and just all-round fun! This book made me feel all warm and fuzzy, I loved it!'
Olivia Beirne

'. . . perfectly playful one-liners, big-hearted romance, and characters so warm you want to curl up with them under a duvet and watch *Bridgerton* together like a couple of wine-soaked besties'
Lisa Dickenson

'I adored Doyle's relatable characters; [and] her fresh, zippy prose'
Nicole Kennedy

'Such a brilliant concept and great characters – funny, romantic and toe-curlingly awkward. I absolutely loved it!'
Tom Ellen

'Warm, witty and oh-so relatable, I couldn't put this book down'
Zara Stoneley

'Funny and heart-warming – a perfect summer read'
Rachel Parris

HANNAH DOYLE is a journalist and best-selling author who writes deliciously relatable books about love and friendship. Sponsored by coffee, she spends her days writing and running around after her twin sons in Sheffield, where she lives with her husband. Previously, Hannah worked for a celebrity magazine in London and has appeared on television and radio chatting about the hot showbiz topics of the day.

@byhannahdoyle

@byHannahDoyle

byHannahDoyle

Also by Hannah Doyle

The A to Z of Us

The Pick Up

The Spa Break

HANNAH DOYLE

HQ

ONE PLACE. MANY STORIES

An imprint of HarperCollins*Publishers* Ltd
1 London Bridge Street
London SE1 9GF

www.harpercollins.co.uk

HarperCollins*Publishers*
Macken House, 39/40 Mayor Street Upper,
Dublin 1 D01 C9W8
This edition 2025

1
First published in Great Britain by HQ,
an imprint of HarperCollins*Publishers* Ltd 2025

ISBN: 9780008651732

Printed and bound in the UK using 100% Renewable
Electricity by CPI Group (UK) Ltd

MIX
Paper | Supporting
responsible forestry
FSC™ C007454

This book contains FSC™ certified paper and other controlled sources
to ensure responsible forest management.

For more information visit: www.harpercollins.co.uk/green

For my Loughborough Lads

Chapter 1

Predictably, I've spilt coffee down my shirt already. I only know this because the train is so busy that I'm being pressed up against one of the doors and, in a bid to avoid my face nestling into somebody else's armpit, I've tilted my head down. It's afforded me a bird's-eye view of the stain. It's not even 9am! In my haste to get on this train, I sort of forgot that I'd be travelling at rush hour. At what age *will* I be able to drink a beverage without spilling some down myself? Not twenty-nine, that's for sure. The stain, I decide, looks familiar. I stare at it some more and realise that it's the exact shape of the Sydney Opera House, which is something.

As we pull into the station the horde of commuters become so eager to alight that I'm squished further into the door, legs digging into the hard lines of my suitcase, which I may have overstuffed with books for the trip. Why does rush hour turn people into monsters?

After a tediously long wait, the train doors slide open and I am unceremoniously popped out onto the platform like a slice of hot toast, a tangle of limbs and luggage.

'Sorry!' I call, pausing to rub my sore legs as people in suits sidestep my case with varying degrees of irritation across their faces. In hindsight, did I really need to wake up before dawn to catch the first train up to Newcastle? Probably not, but I was way too excited about the next seven days to show any form of restraint.

A spa break! With my two best friends!

Who cares if I'm *checks time* literally *hours* too early to check in? This is just the start of my great big escape and I intend to make the most of every last second of it.

Positively giddy, I pause to admire the station. I love train stations! (Just me? Probably.) The constant ting of announcements. The clack-clack of wheels on the track. The dramatic architecture. The . . . pigeons.

'Bugger off out the way, will you?' This huff comes from a disgruntled man in pinstripes as he barges past.

'You will not dampen my spirit!' I reply exuberantly, although I do also move out of the way, because no one wants to be the moron causing obstructions in the train station.

I roll my shoulders back and make my way, with purpose, to the taxi rank. There's a snaking queue, which I join, and while I'm there I take the opportunity to appreciate the beautiful building. Grade 1 listed! Opened by Queen Victoria in 1850!

And then I feel something wet land on my shoulder. Did someone just *waterbomb* me? I look around in shock, my shoulder suddenly very, very wet. No one looks suspicious. And, I look up to see it's not raining.

But there *is* a shady-looking pigeon flying overhead and I don't like the cut of his gib.

On inspection the wet patch is, indeed, bird poo. I glare at the pigeon, who, unbothered by my menacing gaze, has now landed and started to peck at a pile of dried vomit.

Thankfully, the queue moves quickly and I'm soon being beckoned into a shiny blue car by a man in a baseball cap shouting, 'Alreet, pet' in my direction.

'Hello!' I say cheerily as I slide into the backseat.

'Just watch that seat,' he cautions, pointing. 'My last punters were mortal.'

I follow his gaze to yet another wet patch, this time on the seat next to mine. Today is shaping up to be a total stain-fest.

'Mortal as in . . . human beings?' I'm confused.

'Totally steaming drunk,' he explains. 'I picked them up after they'd gan doon toon.'

'So that is . . .' My eyes track nervously back to the wet patch.

'Puke,' he confirms cheerfully. 'Don't you worry, pet, I've had the bleach on it. Good as new. But still a bit wet so you'd be better staying over that side. I'm Carl. Where are we going today, pet?'

For the briefest moment, I waver. Where am I going? I mean, I know the literal answer to that, it's a hotel by the coast that Stella has booked. The hotel that I can't wait to get to, but the one that secretly, somewhere in the back of my head, I'm also a little worried I'm running away to. With everything that's been going on at home, should I really be escaping right now? Covered, as I am, in both coffee and poo. Surrounded, as I am, by the smell of bleach-soaked vomit. Are these omens?

I shake off those thoughts immediately. Of course not! I need this break and omens aren't real . . . are they? No!

'Hi, Carl, I'm Jess.' I beam. 'And we're off to the Gurnard Cove hotel, please.'

Carl whistles appreciatively. 'Fancy.'

'I know!' I nod enthusiastically. 'My best friend booked it.'

Stella, with her kick-ass job in the charity sector, is so well connected that she's somehow managed to get the three of us a reservation at this insane-looking spa hotel on the coast before it's even properly open, with a huge discount. The place has its own vineyard for heaven's sake! It's all very much not the kind of holiday I would normally be able to afford. Last summer I booked a flat close to the beach at Camber Sands on the South Coast for my ex and me, only for Otis to announce when we got there that he 'hates sand'. The clue was in the title, I churlishly pointed out to him, but Otis claimed he'd been too busy working to pay

3

attention to our holiday destination beforehand. All to say: our seaside trip was mostly tarmac-based. I'd imagined walking hand in hand along the beach at sunset with the sand beneath our feet. Not sitting in Otis's car in the car park with the windows firmly shut 'admiring the view without any of the mess'.

Now that I've created a little bit of distance from my ex-boyfriend I can see how ludicrous that all was, and I stifle a giggle at the ridiculousness of Otis.

Honestly, what was I thinking?

'So, what do you do then, pet?' Carl asks as he pulls off.

'I'm a journalist,' I reply, glad for the nudge to stop thinking of the disaster that was my ex.

'I'd better watch what I say, then!' He laughs at his joke. I get this reaction *a lot*. Mention the word 'journalist' and people assume I've got my phone already recording, ready to fire off questions and take down their life story. The reality is, my job as digital editor of a small-town newspaper is less about breaking exclusives, celebrity gossip and politicians' scandals and more about interviewing local farmers about the literal price of milk.

'I'm sure you've got some stories to tell.' I smile at Carl in the rear-view mirror, resplendent with fluffy dice, and he promptly tells me all of them. I remember enough from the media law course I took to know that I categorically cannot repeat any of it, for fear of being sued for defamation. Suffice to say, hoo boy, does Carl have some good stories.

I'm bobbing along in the back, shouting out a thrilled 'no way' and 'what the heck?' every now and then as we glide out of the city and across to the coast. It seems Carl has managed to pick up every famous person who has ever set foot in the North East and every single one of them has been indiscreet. I'm obsessed.

'I had that girl with the croissants in my car just yesterday,' he says.

'No!'

'Aye!'

'Took her to Gurnard Cove too.' He smiles at me.

'Oh my gosh, *no*,' I repeat. ThatGirlWithTheCroissants (literally her exact social media handle) is a massive influencer. Naturally I follow her, along with six hundred thousand other people. She's the same age as me but she's got an amazing wardrobe, her own pastry-themed beauty brand and a ginormous following to boot. She also *loves* croissants and her USP is that there's usually something croissant-related happening in her posts. We're talking croissant-shaped earrings, her trademark stacked rings with pastries on them, sometimes she even pulls out a knitted croissant as a prop for photos. I cannot believe I'm going to be staying at the same hotel as she is! I head straight to the group chat.

You will not believe this news . . .

ThatGirlWithTheCroissants is staying at our hotel!

Em starts tapping back immediately.

I met her once

How didn't we know this?

What was she like?

Vapid LOL poor thing

Anyway who's ready for their Saturn Returns Vacation

Stella is typing . . .

😒

Must we call it that

What's wrong with spa break

Or, you know, plain old holiday

Em writes:

Don't be a naysayer Stella, this trip is all about our Saturn Returns baby!

I let out a snort.

'Y'alreet, pet?' asks Carl.

'Sorry,' I splutter. 'It's just one of my best friends is big into astrology and has decided that this trip will be all about our Saturn Return. And I, well, I guess you'd say the other friend and I aren't big believers in the zodiac.'

'What's a Saturn Return when it's at home?' asks Carl.

It's a valid question.

'Well, Carl,' I say, adopting a schoolmarm-ish tone. 'It takes Saturn around twenty-nine years to orbit the sun, which means that every twenty-nine years or so, we experience a major period of change.' If I sound like I'm reading from a fact book, it's because Em has been bombarding us with astrological concepts since we met, and grilling us on this particular phenomenon for the past few months. For such a sweet human being, she gets quite cross if we get anything wrong. 'So your Saturn Return happens when the planet lands in the same place in the sky as it was when you were born. It creates an exact snapshot of the sky on your birth day.'

'Riiiiight,' says Carl. 'So . . . ?'

'So, many people see their Saturn Return as an astrological coming of age, Carl. According to my friend Em, the three of us should all be expecting big things because we're all twenty-nine.'

'Big things, eh?'

'Yes.' I nod sagely. 'We're talking milestones, break-ups, make-ups, big career decisions, unexpected shake-ups. You name it, it could happen. If you believe in all that, obvs. Me and Stella don't, but Em is insisting that this week away will be in celebration of our Saturn Return and if it means that the three of us get to spend some much-needed time together, then I'm more than happy to go along with it.'

'Three best friends spending seven days in a posh hotel during an astrological coming of age?' Carl whistles. 'Sounds like things could get interesting.'

I'll be honest, aside from spending time with my favourites, the thing I'm most interested in is spa-ing the heck out of this break. Swimming, massages, you name it, I'm doing it. Well, sort of. I read on the website that they offer colonic irrigations but, much as I admire good digestive health, I do draw the line at having a tube stuck up my butt in the name of it.

Another message from Em (who no doubt will be all over the colonics) flashes up on my phone.

So excited to see you both later!

I'm on my way! In a cab now.

OMG yes Jessie!

I had a work thing this morning so plan to fly up later

Em, short for Emerald, was born into a family with obnoxious amounts of cash and my absolute favourite thing about her is that she's managed not to be totally silly because of it. A former wild child, Em had been kicked out of countless boarding schools by the time we met at uni. Now she's entered her businesswoman era (Em is one hundred per cent the kind of person who has eras) and has launched an incredibly successful jewellery line. Or 'selling gold trinkets to poshos', as Stella calls it.

The three of us have been best mates since first year and I love them immensely. What I don't love is that Stella, Em and I scattered ourselves across the country after graduation. Sometimes I find myself longing so hard to live in the same place as they do that my heart starts hurting and I worry that I've given myself some kind of cardiac problem. Alas, Stella is in London being important and Em has one of those glamorous careers that involves a lot of jet-setting, so she's never in the same place for more than five minutes. Meanwhile, I moved back to little old Carpston where I could be close to my folks and maybe even afford a house one day.

Stella is typing . . .

Just got on a train, shouldn't be too long.

Em is typing . . .

OK babes see you there.

Sending you both links to the app I was telling you about . . .

Download asap please!

We can't go on a Saturn Return break without a guide from the zodiac.

Imagine LOL disaster!

'Wow, she's like a dog with a bone,' I mutter as I open up the app store on something called Zodiac Girlie. Oh dear. I can practically hear Stella tutting as she sees the name of Em's app of choice. Tutting and also firing out a whole heap of expletives. Stella takes a zero-hostages approach to life and salty language is her calling card.

Zodiac Girlie promises daily horoscopes and astrological advice. Sounds . . . acceptable? They also have a 'no bs' policy which suits me just fine. Dutifully I type in my name, date of birth, time of birth (pretty sure Dad said I was born just after midnight) and away we go. Immediately I get a notification, which apparently sums up what the stars think I can expect from today in brief. In journalism, we call very short stories News in Brief, or NIBS for short, so I guess this is like my Stars in Brief.

A window opens, climb through it.

Hmm. Not sure Carl would appreciate me scrambling through the window here in the back of his alarmingly fast sports car. We're travelling at speed, after all. Still, I open it as low as I can without my long brown hair whipping itself into a frenzy and breathe.

First thing to note: it smells much better outside this vehicle. Yesterday's sick and bleach have mingled with Carl's aftershave and I'd been getting a bit of a headache. Secondly: I am nailing this Saturn Return already! Em will be thrilled that I have already achieved today's astrological goal and also, who knew it would be so simple? Third thing to note: the view.

THE VIEW!

'I can see the sea!' I squawk excitedly until I remember that I'm a grown-ass woman.

'Not far now,' Carl calls back.

I feel another swell of excitement as we drive around through a pretty coastal town where bunting has been strung up around the town square.

'Ooh, a bookshop,' I coo. 'This place looks cute!'

'This is where I live,' Carl says proudly.

'What a nice place to call home,' I reply.

'Aye, it's not too shabby. The local pub has a great whisky selection, too.'

'My friends have banned me from drinking whisky,' I confess. 'Em says it makes me lairy.'

Carl laughs at this, turning the car onto a coastal road. Fields roll by to our left and on our right, the sea. It is stunning. Shards of sunlight light up the ocean and I'm so busy staring that I almost miss the very chic and understated sign for Gurnard Cove. We turn onto a quiet road lined by trees and then I spot it. An imposing country house built of white stone, flanked by enormous stone lions, stands majestic at the end of a sweeping drive. Before it, a large circular pond with a fountain in the middle. It's the sort of home that would not go amiss in a Jane Austen novel.

I gasp.

'Aye, I know,' says Carl.

As we pull up two members of staff emerge out of nowhere and the next thing I know, my suitcase has been taken care of, I've been offered a hot towel 'after the journey' and I'm waving goodbye to dear old Carl.

Grand entrance. Marble floor. The smell of luxury and citrus in the air. As I step inside, it quickly becomes clear that things are a lot less Austen in here, and a lot more Le Corbusier. Shout-out to my architecture girlies!

There's ultra-modern furniture at every turn. And no reception desk because, I learn, guests have their own dedicated concierge service to cater for each and every whim. Imagine! I try to keep my mouth closed as I'm shown through the main atrium, wondering if it's high time I develop some whims of my own.

'Welcome to Gurnard Cove,' says the smiling woman who is currently walking me towards a large seating area filled with low tables and artfully arranged hardbacks. She's dressed in a stylish linen trouser suit and motions for me to sit on a sofa made from – best guess – cotton candy. I blink and there's a delicate cup of fresh herbal tea in my hand.

Ooh.

'Our ethos here is simple,' my guide tells me serenely. 'We're here to help you unplug from the outside world. To cleanse. To connect mind, body, soul. There's plenty to keep you busy while you're with us. A private stretch of coastline. Our kitchen garden, orchard and vineyard are all available to stroll through and sample. Maybe you'd like to take root in the woodland, or realign in our state-of-the-art gym . . . '

'Wow, there's a lot to take on board.'

'Don't worry,' she says. 'We're here to facilitate. My name is Santi and I'm here whenever you need me. If you follow this link,' she seamlessly produces an iPad with a QR code, 'we can get you set up on the hotel's WhatsApp. Each day we'll tell you what's going on and can book you into any activities you'd like. And if there's something else you'd like to try, please don't hesitate to call me.'

'Thank you!' I manage.

'Your room isn't quite ready just yet,' Santi explains. I look at my phone. Still three hours until official check-in. 'But perhaps you'd like to enjoy the gardens, or sit by our outdoor pool with a cocktail?'

Now that sounds up my street, I think gleefully.

'Pool please!'

I'm trying not to walk around with my mouth remaining wide open, but it's difficult. We move outside to a terraced area studded by huge black trellis structures, which frame a stunning view out to the sea beyond. The architecture's *amazing*, the old building in stark contrast to the modern glass and timber one which stretches out to the right.

'That's the spa,' Santi says, following my gaze. 'You'll be staying in one of our spa suites, which are beyond the spa. Breakfasts and dinners are back in the original building. But for now, our outdoor pool.'

I trot along after her, down some steps, drawing closer and closer to the cliff's edge. There, built right into the edge of the cliff, is an infinity pool which knocks the breath right out of me.

Oh my days, it is beautiful! You can swim right up to the edge! And it looks like I've got it all to myself.

'It's heated so even on cool days, of which we get many, you can enjoy a swim,' says Santi. She motions towards the sunloungers, each positioned with a view out across the coast, and I wonder if I should pinch myself to check this is actually happening. Everywhere is so luxurious! I've only been here for a matter of minutes but already, I can feel my shoulders relax. I listen to the seagulls call out in the distance. The gentle sound of waves crashing below. The glisten of the sea on this gorgeously sunny day.

And that's when I spot something – some*one* – even more beautiful than the sea view.

It turns out that I'm not alone at this pool after all.

Chapter 2

What a *wonderful* day to have eyeballs, I think to myself as I watch an extremely buff and marvellously almost-naked man step into the pool. I spin around to figure out where he came from and spot a changing room behind me. Next thing I know, he's carving his way through the cerulean blue like a knife through butter and oh my *word*. Athletic body, beautiful face, are those cheekbones for real? This dude is divine.

DIVINE.

I have never seen such an incredibly hot man in my entire life, I realise delightedly as he pauses, pushes the water off his face, then carries on swimming those strong, broad strokes.

I shade my eyes to get a better look. Although, hang on, I shouldn't really be ogling him like this, should I? I'm pretty sure he wouldn't appreciate being on the receiving end of Jessica Jones and her apparent new job title, Debauchee.

But then, I reason, surely he must get this all the time? So very pretty. Dear lord, those abs are so defined he could probably grate cheese with them. Am I dribbling? And why must I be covered in bird poo, coffee and the smells of vomit-masking-bleach while in the presence of such an impeccable human being? The thought pulls me up, and I decide that I really *must* stop staring at him.

It's probably dangerous, isn't it? Like staring at the sun. My poor, bedazzled pupils.

I absolutely will stop.

Soon.

Really soon.

Or maybe . . . five more minutes?

I slip my sunglasses down over my eyes to fully cement my newfound status as a degenerate and grab a sunlounger with a bird's-eye view of the . . . the sea, the sea. That's definitely what I'm staring at, your honour. To think that just this morning I was waking up in my little mildewed flat and now look.

I cannot wait for Em to get here so I can point him out. Powerful arms propel him forward through the water. Long, lean legs kick back. There's no splash, this guy moves effortlessly. His dark hair glistens. Droplets cling to the angles of his face.

Oh to be a droplet of water!

He's paused at one end now, catching his breath.

I try to do the same. Not easy, given that he's hoisted himself half out of the water and the sun is casting shadows across a chest cut from marble.

The five minutes is up, hotdammit, so I try to stop panting and attempt to busy myself with a copy of the hotel's magazine on the table next to my lounger. It's made of thick paper and embossed font. The words 'whole life cleanse' jump out at me and I nod enthusiastically at the mag like we're on the same page.

My enthusiasm wanes dramatically when my phone pings with a message from my ex-boyfriend, a scowl darkening my face for the first time today.

Jess, where are the teabags? xO

Oh for goodness sake! Otis should know this already. And I bet he's after *my* teabags, I think churlishly, even though I've repeatedly asked him to buy his own. Urgh, no, I refuse to think

14

about Otis right now, I decide, tossing my phone to one side. I'm on a whole life cleanse! I'm starting a brand-new chapter!

Like moths to a flame, my eyes flick back to Hot Swimmer again. It's like opening a packet of Maltesers and promising yourself you'll only have a few and the next thing you know, your hand has a mind of its own and the entire pack has been demolished.

This man is my packet of Maltesers and I would happily devour him whole.

What has got into me?

I'm not usually so lascivious, promise. Come to think of it, I can't remember the last time I felt such a strong physical attraction to someone. Maybe . . . never? Boyfriends have been and gone but the whole fireworks and fanfares and clothes being ripped off in the heat of the moment thing? Surely that's just for books and boxsets, not normal humans like me. No, I'm just pottering along in the real world, focusing on the important things, like family, saving money and my newfound appreciation for artisan sourdough.

Only now I seem to have added Hot Swimmer fantasies to my repertoire. I briefly allow myself to dream about diving into the pool and having hot, hot sex with him but then I have to stop that immediately because *imagine*. Or rather don't.

Am I sweating?

I shake my head and take a sip of the cucumber water that has materialised by my side. Fantasies are fine, right? All this imaginary pool sex can stay happily in my head, where it belongs. Because obviously, this taste sensation would never look in my direction. And even if he did, after everything that happened with Otis, I really ought to be taking a break from boys.

It just makes good sense.

A splash of water lands at my feet.

'Sorry,' comes the husky-voiced apology. He's looking right at me with piercing grey eyes.

'No worries.' I gulp, now firmly back in the fantasy. I literally wouldn't know how to handle myself if I got swept away by a man who did things like *this* to my insides by just minding his own business, swimming in a pool. Imagine if we kissed! OR MORE!

It's a battle, but I do eventually drag my eyes away and refocus on the hotel magazine. It's giving ultra luxe. I still can't believe I'm actually here and that the whole trip, food and drink included, is costing me less than that sand-free week in Camber Sands. I turn the pages and marvel at the spa, all natural wood and soft stone edges. My fingers track down the list of treatments, all included in the stay, and I vaguely wonder what 'lift rapide' entails.

'THERE'S A LIBRARY HERE?'

I shouted that out aloud. Startled, I look up to see Hot Swimmer pause and smile at me. Embarrassing.

'Wait 'til you see it,' he calls over. 'It's great. Really big.'

No stop it, Jessica.

I try to recall the art of conversation. Because I ought to reply, preferably with some actual words. Something cool and casual and normal. A cheery 'gotta love a library!' springs to mind. But I've been rendered speechless by the realisation that this is my dream man swimming before me. Physically exemplary *and* appreciates a library? If there was a jackpot for this kind of thing, he'd be the big win. Honestly, a hot library lover? And now the news that there's a library here?

Today is The One.

You know what's not The One? My face. I try to smile back at the swimmer, now that words are too difficult and all, but I fear I'm grimacing at him so I burrow further behind the magazine and will myself to calm the heck down.

Just focus on the library. And the tennis courts, the yoga studio, the natural pool, the surf shack, the stables . . . For fear of sensory overload, I snap the magazine shut.

Hurry up, Em and Stella!

My ultimate crush is back to doing laps again, and I am grateful.

I stretch out on the lounger, the sun now high in the sky, and undo the top few buttons of my shirt. Is it the weather, or am I hot for other reasons? Hard to tell.

'Can I get you anything?'

I jump, surprised by the interruption. A member of staff is standing by my side, bringing with them a waft of lavender from the plants growing around the entirety of the pool. 'Perhaps a peach margarita?' they suggest, when it becomes clear that I'm in a man-trance. 'We have some freshly picked peaches from the hotel garden that are just delicious.'

Now that does sound good. I check the time.

'It's a little early for me . . .' I waver, just as Hot Swimmer steps out of the pool and wraps a towel firmly around his tight torso. His whole body shimmers in the sunlight and I swallow, hard. I find myself with a terrible thirst. 'Oh, go on then. Yes please!'

I have stepped into my lush era (if they're good enough for Em) and I am totally okay with that. Slightly tipsy on a midday margarita, I remain glued to my sunlounger with my sunnies on, magazine truly abandoned as I enjoy the show. I've even started up a game of What Does He Do as I work my way through career options for Hot Swimmer.

I'm guessing model, with that mesmerising combination of pale eyes, dark skin and brown hair. Now that he's finished swimming, he's taken up one of the sunloungers opposite and is perched on the end, drying off in the surprisingly warm British sunshine. I wouldn't be surprised to find a photographer hidden in the bushes taking publicity shots of him for the hotel's website.

Or, option two, athlete. That body. It's not the kind that comes naturally, but then it's not the kind of frightening body-builder, veins-popping bod either. Sort of sculpted perfection, like a sexy statue.

A noise from beyond breaks my reverie and I sense instantly that Stella has arrived. My heart leaps. She's here! I watch as she marches over the top of the hill and down the stone steps towards the pool, waving at me, and I wave back, thrilled beyond words to see her.

'All right, dickhead?' she booms across the tranquil setting.

D-head? Honestly, she's coined all sorts of 'terms of endearment' in our ten years of friendship but I'm not sure I can handle this latest development. Especially in front of Hot Swimmer Who Reads.

But then it becomes clear that Stella is not talking to me.

She's talking to Hot Swimmer.

Why is she swearing at strangers in the swimming pool?

If Stella gets us kicked out before we've even checked in, I won't be best pleased.

Hang on, she's not just talking to him. She's *running towards* him.

Why is *he* a d-head?

I gawp as Stella barrels into my new crush at 100mph. She wraps her arms tightly around him and he's laughing as he hoists her up into the air and plonks her back down again.

'Stella,' he says, and even in my confusion I note that there's the hint of an accent.

Do they know each other?

I mean obviously yes, yes, they do. But *how?* And more importantly why has my best friend kept this beautiful acquaintance a secret from me for so long? Seems rude.

Stella is now ruffling his hair like one might a dog or a small child, while he bats her away with a sweet fondness. She's laughing too, and I watch her take a step back as if to soak him up. Then she turns to me.

'Jessica! Get over here!' She beckons me over from the other side of the pool.

Hot Swimmer cocks an eyebrow, clearly as surprised that Stella knows me as I was the other way round.

Right, so, I'm going over? I slip my trainers back on. Do my legs still work? I trot across the flagstone floor, not at all self-conscious to be walking towards the hottest man on the planet while a bit tipsy.

'Jesus H, Jess!' Stella calls as I get closer, pushing her own sunglasses up onto her head and looking at me admiringly. 'Your tits. YOUR TITS! I haven't seen so much of your tits in years.' It's at this point that I remember I unbuttoned the majority of my shirt in a lusty hot flush. 'You look banging.'

I am contemplating diving in the pool fully clothed until this moment can be over.

'Can we stop using the word tits?' I mutter, trying to button my shirt back up but Stella keeps swatting at my hand.

'Haven't seen the girls since uni,' she says before pulling me into a hug.

'The girls,' I snort in spite of myself. I squeeze her back, ninety-nine per cent overjoyed to see her and one per cent very much aware of the beautiful man's presence. Or is it the other way around?

'What's that?' She frowns, spotting the coffee stain.

'Coffee,' I explain, rolling my eyes at myself. 'Don't you think it looks like—'

'The Sydney Opera House,' comes that deep voice, and I fully stop in my tracks to look at him now.

'That's exactly what I thought!' I marvel.

'I'd recognise those Jørn Utzon waves anywhere,' he adds, smiling shyly at me.

Shut the front door.

'Look at this.' Stella beams as I try to compose myself. 'Two of my favourite people on the planet, bonding over being architecture nerds.'

She claps her hands together.

I'm so confused right now.

'Sorry, who . . .' I begin, thoroughly stumbling over my words. A quick glance at Hot Swimmer confirms that he's looking right at me, which makes me blush inordinate amounts.

'Jess, you remember my little brother Luke, right?'

The penny takes painfully long to drop. I literally look from him to her, out to the sea and then back from one of my oldest friends to Hot Swimmer as my pathetically confused brain processes this information.

This is Stella's *little brother* Luke?

Nooooooooooooooooooooo.

OH NO.

Surely, no?

I have fallen into an abyss of cringe and may never return. I simply can't have just spent the past hour perving over my best friend's little brother, last seen about a decade ago when he was a gangly teenager. Can I? I can. *I did.*

Goodbye, dignity, it's been nice knowing you.

I look at each of them again, the sibling similarity hitting me for the first time. The sheer height of the two of them. The sheer *beauty.* Those high cheekbones. When Stella walks into a room, everyone stops what they are doing and I have no doubt that Luke has the same effect. Stella's mum is Scottish and her African American dad left shortly after Luke was born. She never dwells much on her tough upbringing but I know that Stella cut all contact with her dad when she discovered he had another family back in Baltimore. Stella wraps an arm around her brother and beams her broad smile at him, and he reciprocates with the exact same grin.

'It's so good to have you back,' Stella's saying, walloping Luke on the back. 'My little bro, back in the UK.'

My brain scrambles for information. When *was* the last time I saw Luke? And how in hell could I not have properly *noticed* him then. I cast my mind back, and it settles on the one time we met. He could only have been about seventeen when he came to visit Stella at uni, and I think we must have exchanged a grand total of three words before Stella and Em took him out on a bar crawl. Naturally, as it was exam season, I too enjoyed a wild night of revising while eating ice cream straight from the tub.

But now that I think about it, I do remember a fleeting glimpse of this tall, skinny, shy kid. He was sweet, and polite, and definitely overwhelmed to be surrounded by older women. And, well, that's about it? He went home the following day and the next thing I'd heard, he'd moved to America on a sports scholarship.

'Jessica Jones, have you and your tits been here all morning?' Stella brings me back to the present moment with yet more unsolicited chat about my breasts.

'Um, yep!' I squeak, approx. an octave higher than normal. Notice that Luke is now pointedly looking anywhere but my 'tits'. 'We, I mean, *I* got here super early and our rooms weren't ready so they said I could hang out by the pool.' Is he embarrassed by my tits, or the fact that his sister keeps mentioning them?

'Mate.' Stella grins. 'I am SO excited for the next week. Thank Christ you're here, I've missed you.' My heart swells at this and I reach across for a snuggle. 'And you've already bumped into my surprise. Luke is here!' She claps her brother on the back again and he turns to me with a disarming smile, his gaze holding mine for a beat longer than strictly necessary. It ignites the tiniest question in my mind, like, is he thinking the same? Ha ha no, don't be ridiculous, Jess. I always have been fanciful; I blame all the books I read. But before Luke looks away, while his eyes are trained on mine, I seriously consider stepping into a parallel universe where I am bold and brave, and in that universe, I am flinging my clothes on the floor already.

Stella's still talking, *about her little brother*, and I am thankfully brought back to my senses. 'He's got a new job heading up the sports department here, haven't you, little man?'

I can't help it, the corners of my mouths twitch upwards at this. If Luke, who must be a good six-foot-five, is less than thrilled to be called 'little man' by his older sister, then he doesn't show it. He smiles softly and catches my eye again for all of one second

– which, it turns out, is all it takes to set every nerve of mine aflame – before replying: 'That's right. Couldn't stay in the States forever.'

Ah, so that's why his voice sounded familiar. Luke has the exact same Yorkshire accent as Stella, no hint of a transatlantic twang after years across the pond. Maybe if he'd said more than just a few words about the library earlier I would have cottoned on sooner.

'So you're working here now?' I finally manage.

Luke nods. 'The hotel won't properly open for another week so I'm kind of at fifty per cent capacity right now,' he's explaining.

Imagine him at one hundred per cent.

NO STOP IT.

He continues, 'We're doing a soft launch, mostly for press and celebrities—'

'And siblings,' chips in Stella.

'And siblings' friends,' he glances at me again, 'which is great because it means you will get to see it before it gets really busy.'

'We owe Luke for the ridiculous discount,' Stella tells me.

'I don't mind you owing me.' He smiles, catching my eye.

To say I feel flustered doesn't cover it.

'Wow, erm, thanks,' I begin.

'I'm kidding,' he says. 'It'll be a pleasure to have you here.'

'And considering you're not working full time yet, we can factor in some fun stuff together, right?' asks Stella.

'For sure.' Luke nods. 'I'm coaching some classes but I will definitely be around.'

I slightly stagger back at this thought, which Stella and Luke both seem to think means I've stepped back to admire the hotel.

'Beautiful, isn't it?' Luke says. 'The old house is Neoclassicism at its finest. She dates back to the late seventeen-hundreds. I love the columns, the stone, the history . . . '

'When we were kids, Luke's favourite thing was planning dream holidays where we'd jet off together and go visit places of

22

Chapter 3

We're a bit sweaty by the time we reach the hotel's helipad (sure) but it is worth it to find Em shrieking so loud on seeing us that we can hear her above the helicopter's considerable din. My heart leaps as she starts running towards us, mouthing something I can't hear, before we're tackled into a snuggle.

'Your helicopter is so windy!' I shout, holding my hair back from my eyes. 'When will the whizzy bit stop whizzing around?'

'You mean the rotor blade?' Em bellows back. 'Any minute now.'

The engine cuts, the 'rotor blade' stops, erm, rotoring and peace descends. So naturally, we fill it with as much noise of our own as possible.

'Yaaaasssssss girls.' Em jumps up and down.

'Eeeeeeek,' I call, bobbing along with her.

'AM I STILL SHOUTING?' shouts Stella.

It takes a full ten minutes for us to stop staring lovingly into each other's eyes, leaping about in excitement at the prospect of a whole week together after so long, and by the time we do, Em's luggage has been put on a golf buggy and yet another member of staff is standing nearby, politely waiting for us all to stop shrieking.

'Sorry!' I say. 'We're just very happy.'

'And we're very happy to welcome you to Gurnard Cove,' says a polite man in crisp linen. 'My name is Julian. Your room is ready, would you like to follow me?' Then he motions towards the golf buggy and I wonder at what point of the holiday will I manage to stop cooing about things. I've never been on a golf buggy before!

We hop on, Stella in the back on account of her long, long legs, me and Em up front.

'Babes, is that bird poo on your top?' Em's looking at me, perturbed. 'And also a coffee stain?'

'I had quite the journey here.' I chuckle, recounting my morning of trains and stains. Then I add: 'Taxi driver Carl gave me his number in case we want to go out exploring while we're here. I've already messaged you his contact so we all have it in case of emergencies.'

Stella checks her phone. 'Carl Vomitorium on Wheels,' she reads aloud then gives me an inquisitive look.

I nod. 'Long story. His car had dice in the mirror!'

'Did the licence plate say "Fresh"?' asks Em.

'Did you yell to the cabbie, "Yo, Holmes, smell ya later"?' Stella chips in.

'And now I'm sitting on my throne as the prince of Bel Air.' I nod happily,

Em looks around. 'We're not in Bel Air now, babes. Where actually are we?'

'It's called the North East.' Stella rolls her eyes. '*Northumberland*, Emerald.'

'Yes, I know that!' retorts Em. 'But, you know what I mean.'

'Nope,' says Stella.

'I had no idea it was so beautiful up here, is what I'm saying.'

'Ah yes, it is baffling when one gets outside the M25, isn't it?' Stella's putting on a posh accent now. Em takes this well, as she does all the jibes Stella sends her way re being a bona fide aristocrat.

'I blame the jet lag,' Em says with a yawn, her long blonde hair tumbling serenely around her pretty, pretty face.

'Where have you been?' I ask. It's genuinely impossible to keep up with Em's comings and goings.

'All over!'

'Business or pleasure?'

'Gosh, who knows, Jessie. What is business, really? Or pleasure for that matter. It's all so fluid to me,' Em says.

Stella snorts at this.

Em continues, undaunted. 'I got back from America yesterday,' she explains. 'Work meetings etc, and then I met up with some fellow cosmic enthusiasts for a crystal swap on Miami Beach.'

I hear Stella mutter 'cosmic enthusiasts' in the back and get the giggles.

Em grabs my hand, a twinkle in her eye. 'There was an American football player on the flight home.'

'And . . .' I say excitedly. Emerald *always* has goss.

'We banged. God, athletes are great in bed. Or, you know, tiny bathrooms on planes. So . . . thorough, right?'

I nod like I know what she means, when the reality is quite the contrary. Needless to say Em and I are opposite ends of the scale when it comes to pretty much everything. I mean, her entire life is thrilling and I spend a lot of time marvelling over her amazing joie de vivre. While I'm spilling drinks down myself and fielding text messages from ex-boyfriends, she's off boffing sportsmen on first-class flights back from America.

'I missed you so much.' I sigh happily.

'We're here,' Stella says as the golf buggy pulls up to a stop. 'And I'm over the soppy bastards part of this holiday. Let's go check out our room and start having some fun.'

Julian has pulled up outside a sleek wooden one-storey building with its own front door and hops off the buggy. There's a gravel path edged with saplings leading to the front door. 'You will be staying in one of our spa suites for the next week.'

'A *suite*!' I whisper.

Stella and Em bound inside, with Stella shouting expletives and Em making appreciative noises about 'the vibes'. I thank Julian, step inside and gasp. Again. I have a feeling this holiday is going to be very gaspy.

There's a hallway, for a start, where our luggage has been lined up for us next to three pairs of fluffy hotel slippers. I immediately put on a pair; so soft! We walk into a living room with bouclé sofas that look like clouds arranged around a neutral rug. There's a large mid-century dresser against one wall with a coffee machine and three Thermos flasks next to it for when we want to go out adventuring. An old-fashioned radio plays jazz. To the right, bifold windows open onto a decking area, and a plunge pool glistens in the distance.

'Is that . . . ? Do we have our own pool?' I gawp.

'All of our spa suites come with their own private bathing areas,' Julian confirms. 'We can arrange massages and treatments in-suite, too. Please message your personal concierge service with any requests.'

I try to say wow but it comes out as garbled noise.

Back inside, Julian is showing us the bedrooms. All three of them.

'One each?' I ask.

'Looks like it,' Stella says, grinning and squeezing my arm.

I thought we might be sharing a room – maybe two single beds and a third camp bed if we were lucky. I'd already happily signed myself up for sleeping on a sofa. At five-foot-three, I'm the prime candidate for sofa surfing.

I pad into the bedroom at the end of the hallway and giddily note the beautiful furnishings. The softest bed with crisp white sheets. Neutral décor with sophisticated black accents. An armchair where I'm sure I'll spend tons of time reading. Bowl of fresh fruit on a coffee table, plus a glass jug filled with iced water next to a selection of tiny chocolates. French windows open out to my own private terrace with views over the immaculately tended gardens.

'I've got my own deckchair!' I shout, mouth full of tiny chocolate.

'Have you seen the bathrooms?' Stella calls.

Bathrooms, plural?

Oh my very days, I have an en suite! Sleek, white and stocked with full-sized fancy products. What's azelaic acid when it's at home?

Julian gives us a quick demonstration of how to use all the everyday essentials I'm so totally used to in real life, like the voice-operated coffee machine, the online pillow menu and how to adjust the colour in the showers.

'Sorry, Julian, what did you just say?' I ask as he breezes through one of the bathrooms.

'These are chromotherapy showers which support our physical and spiritual journey,' Julian explains patiently. 'Choosing the right colour for your mood will make your bathing experience all the more special.'

'So true, Julian, so true.' Em nods. 'Speaking of which, my crystals are super jet-lagged and I was hoping you could organise someone to come and cleanse them for me?'

This is officially the most ridiculous thing I've heard in my entire life, and I once 'interviewed' a courgette (long story).

'Certainly, I'll get our crystal cleanser sent over here right away. She's called Gemini and she's the best in the business when it comes to recharging,' replies Julian, with a serious look on his face.

With that, Julian retreats, leaving Stella and me staring at each other, baffled.

'Okay, what the hell is a crystal cleanser and if we're saying that this hotel has one on staff, called Gemini, I'm going to have to jot this down for my future memoirs,' says Stella.

'I would pay good money for your memoirs, babes,' Em says, and I'm suddenly struck by just how good it feels to be in their presence again. Emotions plus margarita and I find myself welling

29

up at the thought of a whole week of *this*, with my favourites.

'Jessica, stop it.' Stella isn't even looking at me.

'Stop what?' I ask, swiping away a stray tear.

'If you start crying, you'll set me off too. I already said, the soppy bastards part is over.'

'How did you know?' I whisper, impressed.

'We've been best mates for ten years. That's long enough for me to sense when your emotions are about to get the better of you. And also, you cry at literally everything.'

'No I do not!' I protest.

'Remember when you tried to save a bee you found on your windowsill in halls?' Em chimes in.

'Barnard,' I sniff.

'Who calls a bee Barnard?' Stella teases, squeezing me extra tight to show she's joking.

'I spent days trying to save him. RIP Barnard.'

'You made a coffin for it out of a matchbox and then insisted we all attend the funeral,' adds Em.

'I remember that now.' Stella grins. 'I actually attended that funeral! I must have been drunk.'

'Actually you were just looking for excuses to get out of writing an essay,' I point out.

'That does sound like me.'

'Poor Barnard,' I say. 'Anyway, crying at a funeral is totally normal behaviour so I don't really see your point.'

Stella just beams down at me. 'It's so good to see you.'

I take a minute to drink her in. Stella has been doing dopamine dressing since way before it became a fashion thing and she is never not wearing at least one eye-popping colour. Today she has her hair pulled back behind a bright orange silk scarf and she's wearing a matching orange jumpsuit.

'You look like a citrus fruit.'

'So sweet and juicy.' She winks. Her eyes are the same startling grey as Luke's – whom I'm definitely not thinking about by the way – and she's wearing no make-up except for a slick of mascara across her mega-long lashes. Stella is a beguiling mix of sweetly pretty with a razor-sharp tongue and I loved her extremely from the moment we met.

I watch her stifle a yawn, and it's then that I notice my best friend looks tired, probably a result of her crazy busy job.

'Why don't we get unpacked,' I suggest. 'And, Stell, I can unpack for you too? Consider it a tiny thank you for sorting us out with this mega holiday. You can just chill out.'

Stella wavers. 'Are you sure?'

'Yes! Go relax.'

'Oh yeah, I can help too, might give your room a little vibe check while I'm in there,' offers Em.

'Erm, okay, thanks, guys. You might want to ignore the left zipped pocket of my suitcase, that's all my sex toys.'

I mutter to myself as I wheel her heavy suitcase through to her room. How many sex toys does a gal need for a week away? I brought zero.

I do appreciate a padded hanger, I think, smoothing down the last item to hang before sticking my head into the living room and finding Stella snoozing on a sofa. I grab a blanket and lay it over her, then go off to look for Em, who is sitting cross-legged in her bedroom, chanting. With everyone otherwise engaged, I decide to slip on my swimmers and get in the plunge pool.

Out on the private bathing area, there's plinky-plonky spa music playing from hidden speakers. The decking is surrounded by a neatly trimmed hedge for privacy, with large bamboo trees at the back, rustling in the gentle breeze.

So peaceful!

I get in – perfect temp – close my eyes and do not think about Luke one bit. I do not replay the way he moved through the water, or that fixing-a-towel-around-his-torso moment, or the way his gaze made me burn.

'You're welcome,' says Luke.

I snap my eyes open.

Can he read my thoughts? Where even is he?!

I hear another voice. It's pretty and tinkly and I'd recognise it anywhere thanks to my terrible habit of doomscrolling at bedtime.

'You really helped with my serve today,' the voice says. 'Like, I don't think I've played that way in ages.'

It's ThatGirlWithTheCroissants! I turn to look in the direction of the voices but the hedge is pretty solid, hiding the path or wherever they are talking. Still, curiosity gets the better of me and in seconds I'm out of the water, peeking through the bush for a better look. There she is! Walking past our spa suite with Luke in tow.

'And your serve is so strong,' Croissants carries on, reaching across and lightly touching Luke's arm. 'Must be something to do with these enormous muscles.'

I swear I see Luke step ever so slightly to the side, away from her touch. Probably wishful thinking on my part.

'Practice makes perfect,' he says in a professional tone. 'You made some great improvements today.'

'So you don't think I'm perfect already?' she asks, laughing a tinkly laugh. 'Only joking. I know I need to improve. And I can with the right motivation.'

Luke scratches the back of his head and looks down at his shoes.

So *she* was the person Luke went off to coach this afternoon.

'I will be booking in with you again, for sure,' she presses on, swishing her ponytail from side to side. Irritation prickles under my skin. 'When's your next lesson?'

'I don't have my schedule on me but let me show you back to the sports complex, and the reception desk will be able to book you in to the next class.'

'Okay,' she says. 'But I'm only booking with you.'

A flash of jealousy courses through me before I tell myself to behave. Of course Luke gets flirted with relentlessly. Just look at

32

him! And just look at Croissants. So peachy as she walks past in her cute little tennis outfit, all pleated skirt and Pilates-toned arms.

'Why are you creeping about in the bushes?' Em says loudly and I spin around. She's watching me from the door, arms folded.

'Not creeping!' I lie, laughing in as natural a way as possible to disguise the fact that I was one hundred per cent creeping in the bushes. My fake laugh needs work, I realise, while praying that Luke hasn't heard any of this.

She narrows her eyes, surveys the scene and looks at me again.

'Sure? I heard you grumbling.'

'Sure!' I squeak. 'Just, erm, bathing. That's the noise I make when bathing.'

'Right.' Em doesn't believe me, I can tell.

'Well, shall we get ready for dinner? I'm starving,' I say, searching for ways to divert her attention before I land on the perfect distraction tactic. 'Oh, hey, Em. You'll never guess what taxi driver Carl told me on the way over here. Want to hear the story of a famous musician and his secret love child who is also famous? No one knows they're related!'

'You know I do,' says Em, delighted.

A lucky escape.

Chapter 4

An hour later and with Em fully up to speed on the love child goss, she appears at my door, resplendent in a metallic silver dress and platform heels.

'Holy smokes!' I say, immediately regretting my choice of jeans and a plain white tee.

'Wear the dress is my new philosophy,' Em's saying. 'Like, there's no point keeping your favourite clothes "for best", right? What even is best? If you love it, you should wear it.'

I listen carefully and reach for some massive earrings to pep up my outfit.

'You're so wise.'

'Yes, I am.' She grins. 'Love those. Ready?'

Fresh from her power nap, Stella has changed into another killer outfit and is also raring to go, but as I grab a key card my phone starts ringing.

This is awful timing, I think, seeing that it's my editor Bryan from the *Carpston Courier*. I immediately press ignore. Not today, Satan! But eagle-eyed Stella notices.

'Work call on a Friday night?' she asks.

'Yeah, I'll, erm, call him back on Monday.'

Stella and Em exchange a look.

'It's not like you to ignore work calls, Jessie,' Em points out. She's not wrong.

'Well, it's the first night of our holiday and frankly, I refuse to be interrupted,' I hedge.

'Ooh, peppy!' Em beams. 'I like this attitude, Jessie! It's new for you.'

I bury my phone in my giant clutch bag and hustle everyone out the door.

It's just a short walk back to the main hotel, where the restaurant is, but it takes us an age because the sun is setting and Em's decided that the lighting is perfect for a photoshoot. Allegedly, our skin looks amazing. By the time we arrive, my stomach is rumbling loudly.

Stella goes to find the toilets while Em and I are shown to our seats in the grand restaurant. It's so plush. There's a huge, circular bar as you enter with a massive selection of drinks in a central column, bar staff buzzing around it shaking cocktails. Beyond that, we clack along the tiled floor past elegantly laid tables with white tablecloths, sparkling cutlery and a little velvet lamp on each table, emitting a warm glow. They've really leaned into the history of the original building in here with the décor, which screams old money.

'Shall we just get champagne?' Em suggests.

'I mean, it's all included so it would be rude not to,' I say and Em nods enthusiastically. A waiter brings a bottle over and is pouring us three flutes when Stella bursts into the restaurant.

'I HAVE WALKED THROUGH THE OPEN DOOR,' she shouts, striding past the bar and over to our table, ignoring the fact that the entire restaurant is now staring at her. Our waiter, hypnotised by this beautiful and extremely noisy woman walking towards him, keeps pouring. Champagne flows over the glass and onto his feet. He mutters apologies and, after one final longing look at Stella, scuttles off to deal with the spillage.

'Have you also lost your mind?' I ask as she sits down, triumphantly.

Stella shakes her head. 'No, Jessie, I have walked through the open door.'

I shoot Em a look, who shrugs at me.

'Emerald!' says Stella. 'You should very be pleased with me. I've just achieved exactly what Zodiac Divvie told me to do today.'

'Zodiac *Girlie*,' corrects Em, cocking her head to one side. 'And, let me get this straight, are you taking today's astrological advice from the app literally?'

Stella pulls up her phone and shows us the notification.

'Look. "Walk through an open door," it says. Mission accomplished.'

'Oh yeah, me too!' I chime in. 'Mine said something very similar, actually. About climbing through windows? I stuck my head right out of the car on the way here and I must say I really did appreciate the fresh air.'

Stella high-fives me.

Em sighs. 'Obviously both of your astrological guides for the day are actually suggesting that you should take advantage of opportunities. They mean you should be alert to chances and openings. You know it's not literal, right? Literally walking through a door and then shouting about it is not going to connect you to the cosmos, Stella.'

Stella and I share a look.

'Obviously!' Stella grins.

'You're teasing me.' Em scowls.

'Only just the tiniest bit,' I say.

'I thought you'd be pleased that I've at least downloaded the app,' Stella adds.

'And I am,' says Em. 'It's a great start even though clearly there is work to be done. But do you know what? Our Saturn Return is happening! Let's cheers to that.'

She holds up her glass and we clink them together.

'Guess what I brought,' I say, picking up my oversized clutch.

'Ooh, I love this game. Is it a spare tampon for one of us, even though you're not on your period?' asks Em.

'No wait, a packet of tissues "just in case".' Stella grins.

I pretend to huff. 'Both of those things are in here, obviously, that just makes good sense. But no.'

'Is it drugs?' muses Emerald, eyes wide. 'Because that is very off brand for you.'

'Why does everyone think I'm on drugs today?' I squeak, askance, before pulling out our university yearbook.

'I'm dead,' Stella announces, her page of the yearbook open in front of her as she snorts with laughter into her glass of wine. 'Most likely to make Forbes 30 under 30? Who wrote that?'

'We were all thinking it, Stell,' I say as our main courses arrive. 'Even back then you were so driven and determined. And just look how successful you've become.'

I'm not too hot on job titles for any industry that doesn't immediately make perfect sense to me, but Stella's basically Head of Everything at the charity she set up that looks out for single mothers from low-income backgrounds. She makes a ton of money by raising the charity's profile, fundraising, hosting events. You name it, Stella seems to do it. It makes perfect sense for her to be in this job because of Stella's own upbringing, I think, my thoughts immediately going to her mum.

'Stell, how's Jacqui?'

'Ah, Jacqui. She's actually all right at the moment,' Stella says, but there's a new tension in her voice. 'She's been sober for about a year now. Luke and I are so used to her falling off the wagon that I almost can't feel upbeat about that, but, you know, I will because I know that every day she doesn't drink is a massive achievement for her and another step forward.'

I'm so relieved to hear that Jacqui is in a good place but I also feel on edge, and it's not just because Stella doesn't sound upbeat.

Stell had the hardest time growing up trying to be a mother to her own mum, and to her little brother, while Jacqui would be away drinking for days at a time. They have a difficult relationship to this day, and Stella feels a lot of anger towards her mum for not being present.

When we met at uni, Stella told some of us about her mum's past struggles with alcohol but in our first year, she'd got herself clean. And I suppose that I thought that was going to be it. I was so naive, but I hadn't known anyone struggling with alcoholism before that. Then in our second year, Jacqui fell off the wagon so badly that she ended up in rehab.

I blame myself for that.

Jacqui had come round to our flat when Stella was out and she'd asked me for money, and I didn't stop to think. What an idiot! I just handed over the £10 note I had in my wallet and I actually thought I was being really mature, lending money to my friend's mum. I have replayed that moment so many times since, so angry with my past self for being so foolish. I should have been suspicious. Why had she popped round asking for money? Why did I hand over a tenner to a woman I *knew* had issues with alcohol in the past, without at least asking questions first?

But the fact is, I didn't think. Three days later, Stella told me her mum had relapsed. She'd been off grid for three days straight until Stella found Jacqui unconscious at home in a pool of her own vomit. The look on Stella's face when she broke the news to us. Harrowing. Like all her hope had been crushed. I've gone to tell her about it so many times but Stella never wants to dwell on her mum, so I've never been able to admit what happened. I still feel like I need to do it. I need to apologise to my best friend.

'Son of Hades.' Emerald interrupts my thoughts with a dramatic whisper. 'Is that Dita Ortiz?'

Stella and I follow her gaze to a woman being escorted into the dining room.

'Oh my god, yes!' I hiss back. 'She looks even more incredible in real life.'

Dita Ortiz may well be one of the biggest stars on the planet.

'Have you seen her latest film? She spends the entire time with her hands all over Paul Mescal. I'm literally so jealous.'

'No! Is it worth a watch?'

'Mescal gets naked and there's nothing meh-scal about that.' Emerald grins.

I laugh. 'I can't believe she's here.'

'And looking so beautiful. If I look that good when I'm approaching fifty then I can die happy,' Stella says.

Stella's not wrong. As Dita walks slowly through the restaurant, she gives off this glow. Her skin shines. Her hair is pulled up in a sexy chignon. Her lips are burgundy red to match the red velvet suit she's wearing with nothing underneath – well, that's what it seems – what a look!

'She's got the sexiest accent too,' adds Stella.

'Isn't she half German, half Spanish?' I ask.

'Yup.' Em nods.

'She's been in so many amazing films.'

'Nothing more amazing than her own private life,' Em says admiringly. 'She's my inspiration. She's dated literally everybody!'

'I definitely would,' Stella purrs.

'Do you think she's staying here?'

'Well, Luke did mention the hotel's soft launch,' Stella reminds me. 'It's all celebrities and influencers here this week. And us!'

Oh yes, *Croissants*.

'Shall we see what the yearbook had to say about me?' Em asks, flicking through to her page and then starting to laugh. 'Omg, most likely to get a criminal record? I'd forgotten that, how rude!'

'You *did* take the wheels off your course tutor's car because he gave you a low grade in first year,' Stella reminds us as I chortle.

Em cracks up at the memory. 'And then he pulled all the boys on my course into his office to try and figure out who'd done it, because the idea that it might have been a woman didn't cross his tiny misogynistic mind, remember?'

'You had tyres in your room in halls for weeks.' I laugh.

Em's dad is a Formula One enthusiast and the family had spent a season on tour with McLaren. Naturally Em didn't just sit on the sidelines being all glam, she actually became quite the car mechanic as a result. It's one of the many reasons why I love her.

'Your turn, Jessie.' Em hands me the book, and I feel my stomach flip. It's been ages since we looked through this old thing. As I flick through the pages I am amazed again at how the photographs we chose are so hilarious, the hairstyles and outfits looking like a style moodboard from ten years ago. So much shiny lipgloss! I find my page and a much younger me stares back, a happy smile on my face. The page is graffitied in large, looping handwriting by Stella and Em, allowing not much space for our wider group of uni friends.

I scan to the bottom of the page.

'Most likely to . . . own a bookshop,' I read aloud. I didn't really have to read the yearbook to know it. After years slogging away in the *Courier* newsroom, I haven't forgotten my teenage dream. I've always imagined running my own bookstore with a café serving good coffee (essential), little reading nooks (welcoming), and the whole place would smell like well-thumbed books (like a home from home). Bliss.

'Yes! You wanted somewhere people could go to let their imaginations run wild, right? You were always jotting down some story or other of your own, too,' says Stella. 'Living in a dream world where everyone had secret, thrilling alter-egos. What happened to the bookshop, Jess?'

'Yeah, and how's work, babes? You've not mentioned it yet . . .'

Eek. My stomach lurches at the thought of work. We're only on day one of our holiday and there's plenty of time to talk about it all with the girls. Right now, I just want a blissful night of not thinking about the *Carpston Courier*.

'Oh fine,' I say breezily. 'You're always teasing me about telling the same stories over and over again anyway and there are way more important things to catch up on tonight . . . '

Em looks thoughtful. 'I do love the one about the giant marrow at the town fete, though. We're not really teasing, Jessie.'

'Nah, it's cool. Reporting for a small-town newspaper isn't nearly as thrilling as what you guys do,' I say with a shrug. 'And you're right, the bookshop dream still looms large. I did actually ask Bryan if I could become books editor for the *Courier* a while back. Built a whole page for the website to show him what it would look like and everything.'

'Omg yes, I can see you writing book reviews.' Em beams.

'Me too! But he didn't go for it so . . . '

'Why's Bryan always cock-blocking your great ideas?' Stella asks, brows furrowed.

'Anyway,' I rally, sliding the yearbook back into my bag. 'Work can wait. How's Fran, Stell?'

Stella lets out a low, slow sigh and tiny alarm bells ring in my mind.

'Okay,' she replies, which is the most tepid thing I've ever heard Stella say. I reach across the table and grab her hand, concerned. 'A bit mad at me right now.'

'Why?' Em reaches over and grabs Stella's other hand.

'Work's been so manic recently and I've been getting a lot of flack from Fran about the long hours, but I think it's about more than just me working late. We're at a bit of a crossroads.' She takes a deep breath. 'Basically Fran wants to be a mum, and she thinks we should start considering our options right now. And I'm undecided.'

'Oh Stell, that's a tough one,' I say.

'Do you mean undecided about kids, or undecided about Fran?' Em asks.

'Oh kids, for sure. Fran is definitely my person.'

'Phew,' I whistle. Stella and Fran have the dream relationship as far as I can see. So *together* but also not in each other's pockets.

41

A joy to be around. 'You guys are adorable.'

'I suppose we are quite cute.' Stella grins. 'And I've never met a woman who wears jeans and a tank top so bloody well.'

'I totally agree,' Em says. 'On the jeans and tank thing, but also on the fact that you guys seem to have a great relationship. I've been thinking about relationships a lot recently and I think what works for you two is that you're actually not two peas in a pod. You've both got your own stuff going on, your own likes and dislikes.'

'Yes!' I chip in. 'Exactly that.'

'She definitely puts up with my crap. Like when I missed our three-year anniversary because of work.' Stella winces. 'Oh, and by the way, thank you for texting Fran that night, Jess. She really appreciated it.'

'Oh, no prob. So does this mean you two are arguing a lot?' I ask, worried.

'We're not arguing, but we are definitely in a constant state of disagreement. She'd have a baby yesterday if she could. It started last Christmas, when Fran became an auntie, and suddenly cradling this baby in her arms changed her entire outlook. I mean, I've always known that she wanted kids but since then there's been this urgency to it. She keeps sending me links to sperm donor clinics.'

'Fran's the same age as us, right?' says Em. 'Classic Saturn Return behaviour!'

Stella looks a bit exasperated by this so I step in. 'And you're not sure if motherhood is for you?'

I watch my best friend exhale, clearly in turmoil about it. 'How are you meant to know? When is the right time? It's a lot.'

'It is a lot.'

'And I think my own upbringing hasn't helped. If I'm going to try and be a mum one day then I'm going to want to absolutely ace it.'

'Of course you are.' I smile fondly.

'I can't be doing a shit job like Jacqui. I'd want to give it my all and at the moment, I give my all to work. How do you find a balance?'

I shake my head. I've no idea.

'Parenting is a two-way street, babes,' Em says sagely. 'You share the load, right? So maybe there will be times when you have to prioritise work, and that will be okay, because Fran can take the parenting lead. And sometimes it will be the other way round.'

Stella mulls this over. 'Sometimes, Emerald, you are quite wise.'

'I totally know.'

'Let's keep talking about this,' I say. 'Because it's not nice to feel burdened by a big decision on your own. If we can help in any way . . . '

'Just being together is helping,' Stella replies. 'I love you two. What's going on with your love life, Em? Did you bang that rugby player you messaged us about?'

'Which one?'

'How many have there been?' I splutter.

'Maybe two? Or was it three?' she says, looking skywards for the answer. 'I forget, but there's nothing big to report in the romance department from me.'

'What, not dating another Henry?' Stella smirks.

I snort. Em has a history of dating only men called Henry, or occasionally Harry.

'Oh ha ha.' Em rolls her eyes. 'Come to think of it, one of the rugby players was called Harry.'

'Course he was.' Stella chuckles. 'We've lost count of how many Hens and Hazzas you've smashed.'

'Oh god, same.' Em smiles cheerfully. 'The amount of times I've sexted the wrong Henry. But not anymore, my friends! I've actually done quite a bit of soul-searching about relationships of late. It's all part of my Saturn Return no doubt, we all come to big crossroads at this time of our life.'

'Do we?'

'Don't be such a Debbie Doubter, Stella.' Em pokes her. 'You can't argue with the alignment of the planets.'

'Well, no, but you can argue with whether it has an impact on your own life.'

Em scrapes the last of her plate clean then waves her hands at the rest of us. 'Saturn is a fascinating planet. She's associated with time, and she symbolises hard work and accolades but she can also be harsh and unforgiving. There's no coincidence that we're all approaching major crossroads in our lives with Saturn back to her original spot in our skies. This is a time of radical metamorphosis for us, babes. We're learning lessons, sometimes the hard way, as we transform into true adulthood. Speaking of big things, how's Orgasmic Otis, Jessie?'

I almost choke on my seabass.

'Oh for fuck's sake, Em!' Stella tuts, slamming her cutlery down on her plate. 'They broke up months ago!'

'Oh my god, *what*? I'm so sorry!'

I'm busy insisting that she must not apologise while Stella asks: 'Do you not read your messages on the group chat, Emerald?'

Em looks terribly guilty. 'Life has been so hectic and I may have skimmed through some and oh no! Jess, you poor thing! Are you okay?'

I brush this away. 'I'm honestly fine, Em, seriously,' I insist before I start chuckling at Em's nickname for my greengrocer ex. Otis owns a fruit and veg shop in town called Organic Otis and when we got together Em took it and ran with it. 'I'd totally forgotten you called him Orgasmic Otis.'

'Physical connections are so important,' Em muses. 'Are you still getting your orgasms in, Jessie, post-split? They're, like, vital for positive mental attitude.'

I look around to make sure no one can hear this embarrassing line of chat.

'Um, well, it's not like . . . He never really made me . . . I didn't . . . ' I splutter, flustered.

'Don't tell me he never made you come?' barks Stella, so loud that actual Dita Ortiz has turned to listen to us. I cringe from my toes up.

'Shh! And . . . no, not really. Poor Otis.'

'POOR OTIS?' Stella is practically booming now. 'Are you kidding me? All this time I thought, okay, the man's a total dullard, but our Jess likes him so he must be doing something right. Maybe he comes alive in the bedroom, I thought. And now you tell us this? Honestly, Jess! You dated for, what, almost a year? And he never . . . in all that time . . . '

It's not often Stella is lost for words but it appears that we have finally found what makes her speechless. My lacklustre sex life.

'Do you want to come to a sex party?' offers Em. 'Because I'm hosting one in a couple of months.'

'Erm,' I squeak.

'Of course she doesn't,' replies Stella. 'She'd combust in embarrassment.'

'So, hang on, when did you break up?'

I recount the whole sorry tale for Em's benefit. How I'd been increasingly concerned that there had to be more to my romantic life than Otis, a man who once ranked aubergines above me on his scale of affection. How whatever bit of spark we had very much went once I realised that he could spend entire mealtimes telling me about the specific soil profile for a good carrot crop (neutral to slightly acidic, in case you were wondering) and yet not manage to ask one tiny question about my day. How I woke up one day and couldn't for the life of me remember why we were together in the first place.

'So I broke up with him,' I wrap up. 'It was awful, Em. Dramatically awful. He kept clutching at his chest and shouting: "The heartache!" I did feel bad.'

Stella tuts. Em's mouth is hanging open.

'You know what, Jess? I'm proud of you for doing that. It takes guts to see something for what it really is, and even more guts to break free. Omg, did you kick him out and throw his clothes out the window? Send him packing with gusto?'

'You can take your vegetables and stick it!' chips in Stella, grinning.

'Ha yes. Stick that cucumber where the sun doesn't shine!' Em laughs.

'Beet(root) it, Otis.'

'Oh good one.' Em grins. 'It's *bean* good but I'll *pea* happier once you've moved out.'

They're laughing so hard at their own jokes, with Stella punching Em lightly on the shoulder because she's so impressed with the vegetable puns, that they almost don't hear what I have to say next.

'Well, guys, funny story . . . ' I begin, still chuckling. 'He's actually still in my flat!'

Chapter 5

Well that went down like a lead balloon, I realise, watching Stella's and Em's faces fall as they immediately stop laughing to process my news.

'Sorry what?' Stella blinks. 'For a minute there I thought you said Otis, your ex-boyfriend, is still living in your flat. That you pay for.'

'Mmm,' says Em, frowning. 'You know that saying "he's living rent free in my head"? You're not meant to take that literally, Jessie. Especially when you've ended the relationship.'

'Okay, well, don't be cross,' I say to them, trying to see the situation from the outside. 'He *is* still in my flat but only because I felt so sorry for the poor guy. He's been so heartbroken! And I sort of haven't? Which makes me feel even worse. I'm forever finding him poring over old photos of us on his laptop. Once I got back from work and he was reading poems about heartbreak aloud and having a little cry.'

'What a drip.' Stella tuts.

'Poor Otis,' I mutter.

'Mate, he's not poor! He's taking advantage of your beautiful kind nature!'

I wince. 'It seemed like the charitable thing to do when we

first split up. I said he could stay just for the first few days while he got himself sorted.'

'And that was two months ago!' says Stella, balking.

'I know! I do see that he needs to move out because it's just weird now. I keep sending him links to possible flats to rent and he keeps ignoring me. When we first broke up, I tried to implement a food-labelling system but he just eats all my food and drinks all my tea. It's like he just won't *listen*.'

'Mate, this is not okay. We need to get Otis out,' Stella says.

'Totally,' I agree. 'And when I get back to Carpston I'm going to have a strong word with him.'

Stella and Em glance at each other and I get a feeling I'm about to be ganged up on. I gird my loins.

'Oh no,' Em says, sloshing some more wine into all of our glasses. 'You're going to kick him out now.'

'Now?' I echo, wine buzz very much crashing and burning.

'Yes.' Stella nods, like Em just had a brilliant idea. 'Excellent.'

'Now?' I repeat. 'Guys, I'm not going back to Carpston tonight. It took me hours to get here and it's so pretty at this hotel and I'm not sure Carl's sicky cab will have dried out yet and to be honest, I've had quite a few drinks now. Who's to say I won't be the next mortal customer vomiting all over his taxi?'

'There's a lot to unpack here,' says Stella. 'But let's focus on the main point. Who said anything about going back to Carpston?'

'Yeah, just call him,' Em says like this is the simplest thing in the world.

'What, do it *on the phone*?' I ask, horrified. 'That seems a bit cruel, no? Surely this kind of delicate conversation should be had face to face.'

'Dude! I'd drop him a WhatsApp if it were me.' Stella chuckles.

'I once ended a relationship during an Instagram live.' Em grins.

'You guys are brutal!' I'm trying not to smile back for propriety's sake.

'Actually, Jessie, you're just not brutal enough. We're not even talking about ending a relationship here, you've already done that. Now you've just got to clean up the mess.'

'I *am* fed up with mess,' I concede, briefly feeling sorry for myself. Honestly, today has been a stain-fest and now I'm being pressed into clearing up emotional stains too? It feels like a lot!

'You need to seal the deal,' Stella says sharply. 'Look at it through his eyes. Allowing him to stay in your flat is like you've left the relationship on life support, it's no wonder he's clinging on.'

'So true.' Em nods. 'It's time to unplug the ventilator, Jessie.'

I chew my bottom lip. 'Do we have to make this sound like I'm about to kill Otis? I feel bad enough as it is!'

'RIP Otis.' Em presses her hands together in prayer.

'It's been . . . quite dull knowing you,' Stella chips in solemnly, her eyes lighting up as she sees Em grabbing my bag.

'Oh my god, stop!' I snort, trying to get my bag back. But Em's arms are too long and she's already hidden it behind her chair.

'Em, what are you doing?' I ask, attempting stern. She pulls my phone out of the bag and brandishes it at me, eyes gleaming.

'No!' I yelp.

'Yes, Emerald!' Stella claps, egging her on.

'You wouldn't,' I say, even though I know that she very much would. At least she can't open it without face recognition. I'm about to smugly announce the spanner in their works when Stella points over Em's shoulder and gasps.

'Oh my god, WHAT is Dita doing?' she says, gawping.

I turn to stare. The next thing I know, Em has shoved my own phone into my face while I stare gormlessly at a woman who is doing nothing more thrilling than eating her dinner. The phone is unlocked. *Damn it.*

'Emerald!' I wail as she high-fives Stella. 'Stella! Stop ganging up on me.'

But my pleas fall on deaf ears.

'It's for your own good,' Stella insists.

'It's ringing,' Em says.

OH NO.

'At least let me go somewhere more private!' I hiss.

Em puts it on speakerphone and leans in to listen.

'Hey, Jess.' Otis picks up quickly, his voice broadcast around our table.

Stella blows a silent raspberry and Em sticks her thumbs down. I try not to look.

'Hi, Otis,' I say, desperately trying to gather my wits and speak in my firmest voice at the same time. 'I wanted to—'

'I found the teabags,' he interrupts, as if his inability to make a brew has been at the forefront of my mind since his earlier text. 'You're going to need to buy some more, we're almost out. Actually, Jess, while I've got you, do we have a plunger? I've blocked the loo again. Bit of bother with my digestive system.'

Stella mimes being sick. Em wrinkles her delicate nose. I look around me to make sure that no other hotel guests are listening in to this. It's so embarrassing.

'It's in the cupboard next to the bathroom,' I reply automatically. And then I see that I'm getting hard stares from my best friends. I take a deep breath.

'Otis, I need to talk to you about our living arrangements.'

Em shoots me an encouraging thumbs-up.

'Sure, sure,' mutters Otis, and I can hear him opening a cupboard and then opening a door and then . . . plunging. He is actually plunging in the background while I'm talking to him.

'I think, you know, that it's been a while and . . . After everything . . . So . . . ' I keep changing tack, trying and failing to make a sentence. Em hands me a fresh flute of champagne and makes a *neck that* motion. I do as I'm told. The bubbles tickle my throat, the alcohol hits my bloodstream.

'I guess what I'm saying is . . . '

Stella drums her fingernails on the crisp white tablecloth.

'Oof, that was a big one,' puffs Otis amid more plunging noises, his voice echoey in my bathroom. 'Actually, Jess, could you ring the landlord? I think we could do with a plumber coming out to take a look at this. Oh hang on, I've broken the plunger. You'll need to pick up a new one.'

And that, my friends, is the final straw.

'Otis, *we* could not do with the plumber coming out. The problem in my flat is not the toilet, it is you.'

'Listen, Jess, you know I have to eat a lot of raw veg as part of my job. I can't sell a new crop of PSB at Organic Otis before sampling it, can I?'

PSB? mouths a confused-looking Stella.

'Purple sprouting broccoli,' I reply. Stella yawns in response and I almost laugh before I realise that Otis has started waxing lyrical about vegetables.

'PSB is actually great for my gut microbiome. And I know it means I have some bathroom issues but—'

'OTIS. Let me stop you right there,' I almost shout. Stella and Em look impressed as they stare at me, wide-eyed, while I wag my finger at my phone. 'I am no longer interested in your digestive system. I mean, I can't say I was much even when we were together but that's not the point. What I am interested in, is you moving out of my flat. It's been months when it was meant to be days. We're not together anymore and I want to be able to move on, properly.'

I take a breath, my cheeks flushed with the exertion of being so tipsy and frank.

Em is clapping. Stella looks impressed.

We crane our heads towards my phone, awaiting a response from Otis.

He sniffs. 'Wow, okay. There's no need to be so rude.'

I mouth the word 'rude' at the girls, confused. Stella sticks her middle finger up at my phone.

'Are you sure that's really what you want?'

'Of course it's what she really wants, you vegetable-loving sponger!' Stella shouts.

I clear my throat. 'Erm, sorry about that.'

'Was that Stella? Am I on speakerphone?' Otis's voice sounds trembly.

'Look,' I say. 'This will be better for both of us. A chance for us both to really move on. I hate to see you moping around the flat, Otis, and I truly think this will be good for you.'

'I'm not moping.' He sounds affronted now. 'You can't blame a man for mourning the loss of his future. I thought we'd be together forever. Organic Otis and Organic Jess. Maybe we'd even make some little organic babies together.'

I hear a whispered 'eww' coming from Emerald.

'I never wanted to be part of the greengrocers though, Otis. You'll find your, erm, organic other half. It's just not me. And now, I really need you to move out of my flat so that I can get on with the rest of my life.'

'Have you met someone else, is that what this is?'

My mind flickers to Luke and then I have a good giggle at myself for even entertaining that as an idea. And it's actually quite nice to giggle when I'm doing something that I've been dreading for months.

'No,' I say, with a bit more confidence. 'I'm just starting a new chapter and I can't do that until you've moved out.'

The girls look really pleased with me, Em's got her head titled to one side and Stella's smiling proudly in my direction.

'Fine.' Otis sniffs. 'I'll start looking. I'll be out by the end of the month.'

'No.' I shake my head. 'You'll be out by the end of the week. I do not want to get back from this holiday and find you still in my flat, Otis.'

Stella's so happy with this she does a double thumbs-up, which makes me feel glowy on the inside.

'A week!' Otis says. 'How am I going to find somewhere in seven days?'

The girls are shaking their heads at my phone now.

'You've already had two months!' Even I'm feeling a bit shouty now. This man is ridiculous! 'And you do have your mum and dad to fall back on.'

Otis sighs. 'The last time I lived with my parents, mum kept wanting to know what time I wanted dinner. And she insists on cooking stodgy pies all the time so it's really claustrophobic and not very nourishing at the same time. It's a lot for me personally, you know.'

All of us are exasperated now. What a selfish human being he is.

'Honestly Otis, you're a lot for me personally right now,' I hit back. 'If you do end up going back to your mum and dads, do me a favour and try to be a little bit less of a douche while you're there?'

My best friends are delighted. I've never been so blunt in my life.

'You'll be out by the end of the week,' I add.

There's a petulant silence down the line.

'I want your word,' I say firmly as the girls quietly cheer me on.

'You know what, Jess, that's fine with me. I'll be out by the end of the week. I can't stay somewhere I'm not wanted. But I'm taking the air fryer.'

And with that, he hangs up.

The girls high-five me.

'I have no words for that bell-end,' Stella says. 'Other than, good riddance!'

'Yes,' adds Em. 'And well done, Jessie, you really stood your ground. I'm so impressed.'

'Thanks,' I say, 'but I think I'm having palpitations! Standing up for yourself is hard. I could not have done that without you two by my side. I mean, I know you basically bullied me into it but I do feel much better now, if a little sweaty.'

Stella beams at me fondly as the puddings arrive, three slices of glistening tarte tatin with a scoop of brown sugar ice cream.

'Next time, you're aiming higher,' Stella says.

'I don't think anything could get better than this,' I reply, after one delicious mouthful of tarte.

'I'm not talking about the food.' Stella grins at me good-naturedly. 'I'm saying no more boring, boring dudes for you.'

'He wasn't *that* bad,' I try to protest.

Em pulls a face. 'Jessie, you're a shining star. Stella's right, you could and should do so much better.'

'Yep. All these "sensible" boyfriends,' Stella says. 'You've only ever dated mediocre men. It's like you actively seek out partners who have decent jobs and zero banter because you think they'll offer you stability and what they really offer is no orgasms in a year.' (Ouch.) 'Aren't you tired of it? Besides, look at you right now! You seem like you're in such a good place, Jessie.'

'Yes,' chips in Em. 'You've definitely stepped into your more confident era. Old Jess would never have given Otis the heave-ho like that.'

'I mean, you did literally force me into that,' I point out with a smile. 'But you're right, I guess I am embracing life more at the moment. The Confident Era. I mean, I like the sound of it.'

'It's working wonders already. And for your next trick, I think you should start looking for love in new places. And by that I mean anywhere other than Carpston's Tedious Men Society.'

'Hey!' I chuckle.

'Get out there with your newfound confidence,' Stella urges. 'Who knows what will happen?'

'Hey, everyone,' says Luke, appearing at our table. I drop my spoon in shock at his arrival, and it clatters onto my plate, which is definitely really smooth of me.

'Little bro!' Stella cheers.

'Hey, Luke!' Em grins.

Startled, and with my mouth full of tarte, I opt for a really cool thumbs-up and die a small amount inside.

'Join us?' Stella asks.

'I can't.' Luke shakes his head, shifting from one foot to another.

'The Pilates instructor's doing her first candlelight class tonight and I'd promise I'd go to help out, think she's a bit nervous. Do you guys want to come to the class?'

He looks round the table hopefully, softly clicking the fingers on his right hand while he smiles at us all.

'Hell no, I think we're a bit too drunk and full for Pilates right now.' Stella pats her belly, to my acute relief.

'Oh, okay,' Luke says, trying not to look crestfallen.

'Oh you are sweet,' Em says. 'We will definitely do some active things with you tomorrow though, right, guys?' She looks around expectantly and I have a large sip of champagne in response.

'I'd like that.' Luke smiles that smile right at me and I can't help myself. My eyes grow wide. My pupils dilate. I just know that I look like a rabbit in some very sexy headlights and I can't do anything about it!

'Brillo pad,' I say once I've swallowed.

Stella gives me a sympathetic look. 'Don't mind Jess, she's got a lot on her plate. Maybe Pilates would be good for you tonight? Work out some of the stresses of the day?'

'NO, GOD NO,' I shout, too hasty. I pull it back with a gentle giggle. 'I'm, erm, way too full for Pilates but thank you, Luke.'

'No problem. Next time, I hope. See you all soon.'

As he makes his way back out of the restaurant, two things become clear. One: my inappropriate crush has not diminished in any which way. Two: Emerald is staring at me, wide-eyed. And her face has lit up like a Christmas tree.

'Jessica, I need your help,' she says, almost pantomime-like. 'With my . . . period.'

'There are spare tampons in my bag, which you still have by the way. Help yourself.'

'Nope,' she says, eyes trained on me. 'This is going to be a two-man job.'

'Jesus H.' Stella grimaces. 'Sounds bad, Em. If you don't need me, I might head back to our suite? Quite knackered tbh.'

'You go for it.' Em's addressing Stella but still staring right at me, eyes narrowed with suspicion. 'See you back there, babes.'

I'm under the spotlight.

And I fear I've been rumbled.

Chapter 6

I'm being marched through the hotel lobby like a naughty child off to see the headmistress. For someone so delicate-looking, Emerald has a vice-like grip and her fingers are wrapped tightly around my wrist.

'Em!' I protest, trying to keep up as she gallops through the lobby. 'What are we doing? And do we have to do it so quickly? I've got a stitch.'

My heels clatter across the marble floor as we sidestep other guests who are moving at a much more serene pace.

'Here we are,' Em says, pushing open the heavy oak door of the toilets. Then, I kid you not, she cases the joint, as if looking for spies hiding in each cubicle.

'Why are you being so weird?' I puff, trying to catch my breath.

Only when she's satisfied that we are alone does Em spin back round to me, a look of positive jubilation on her face like she's just met Taylor Swift. She's picked up a scent, I can tell, and now I am going to have to throw her off it.

Play stupid, Jess. What crush?!

'You've got something to tell me,' she says.

'Yes,' I agree solemnly. 'I too need the toilet on account of *my* period.'

'No, you don't. This is something much bigger.'

I shift uncomfortably from foot to foot. Em's mouth hangs open expectantly, the beginnings of a smile twitching at her lips. 'Something much . . . *sexier*.'

Her eyes grow wider.

'Spill,' she insists, leaning against a sink.

She definitely knows.

I shake my head.

'You've got this all wrong,' I say.

Em shakes hers right back, delighted. 'OH MY GOD!'

Argh! So much for throwing her off the scent. I'm shaking my head so hard I feel a bit dizzy. I hold my hands up for good measure. 'No, stop it,' I say as firmly as possible.

Em pushes herself off from the sink and cups my face in her hands like a proud parent. My cheeks are squished together and she's so close that I can see every inch of her gobsmacked *and* thrilled expression. Meanwhile I'm wondering if humans can hibernate – a few months in a cosy cubby hole should be all it takes to get over the embarrassment of your best friend discovering that you have a pathetic crush on your other best friend's little brother, right?

Em starts pawing at my arm.

'You fancy Luke,' she announces.

'No I do not!' I try to sound shocked and confused by such an outlandish claim.

'Nice try.' She folds her arms. 'I don't blame you, Jess. He has certainly . . . matured since we last saw him.' She winks at me. 'I do not remember him looking like a Dolce and Gabbana model when he came to visit us at uni. So chiselled! So fit! I mean, I'd eat him alive so he's definitely not my type. Too sweet, possibly too serious. But oh my days, perfect for you. I can definitely see the appeal. So spill.'

I shake my head, even though I know the jig is up.

'Don't make me threaten you, Jessica Jones.'

'What are you going to do, steal all my bras?'

'That's actually a great idea,' Em says thoughtfully. 'But no, it's going to be way worse than an inadequately supported bust. I've been waiting for the right moment to tell you this because I knew you'd be gassed about it. While I was in the States, I went to a party with the entire cast of *Selling Sunset*.'

I gasp. That show is my favourite.

'I know how much you love those crazy beautiful real estate agents and their crazy beautiful lives.' Em has folded her arms and looks like an evil genius. 'But, alas, if you don't come clean about this cute crush, to your beloved best friend Emerald, then I may just have to keep all the gossip from that party to myself.'

She arches an eyebrow at me.

I waver.

'And let's just say there were multiple arguments, two break-ups and one drink splashed across somebody's face.'

It's the final straw, goddammit. She knows I'm powerless when it comes to *Selling Sunset* intel.

'All right, Columbo.' I sigh. 'Or should I say Col-Em-bo.'

At this point another guest walks in so we both turn to the sinks and start washing our hands to make it look like we're not just in the loos having a heart to heart. 'Is it that obvious?' I ask.

Em giggles, delighted. 'It's written all over your sweet face. You've always been an absolutely atrocious liar, Jessie.'

'Do you think Stell knows?'

'I don't think it would even cross her mind. I mean, Luke's her little brother after all . . .'

'Blurgh,' I reply. 'It's just a crush. I actually think I've got a hold of it already. I just didn't expect to see him looking so—'

'Smashable?' Em offers.

I swallow.

'I didn't even recognise Luke at first. There's no way I'd have entertained those thoughts if I knew who he was. But, Em, he was in the pool swimming and he looked so fit and I was thinking of new beginnings and . . . '

Em and I look at each other in the spotless mirrors. Somehow looking at her reflection rather than face to face takes the edge off ever so slightly.

'Right, so you're saying you wouldn't have fancied him if you knew who he was?' Em sounds dubious.

'Absolutely.' I nod enthusiastically.

Em snorts. 'I'm pretty sure it doesn't work like that.'

'Well, it doesn't really matter either way because I've got a handle on it now.'

Em does not look like she believes me. 'Are you sure about that? Your aura is off-the-scale lusty and auras don't lie.'

'Really?' I ask, staring at my reflection in the mirror. I can't see any aura. 'Hey, aura, will you please get a grip? Stop looking lusty, you're giving the game away!'

Em laughs. 'No, Jessie's aura, you keep doing you! I love that you're working it for Luke.'

'Are we sure it's my aura and not just the sea air?'

'Don't listen to her,' Em whispers, still directing her attention to the space around my head. Then she wraps an arm around me and asks: 'Jess, would it be that big a deal if you did like Luke?'

'Our best friend's little brother?' I squawk.

'You keep saying that like it's a bad thing.'

'Of course it's a bad thing! Or have you forgotten about the pact?'

This, Emerald finds hilarious.

'Oh Jess, that was years ago! You can't still be worried about that now?'

'But we made a promise, Em! Promises cannot be broken. And there was a very good reason for the pact.'

Em fluffs up her hair and reapplies lipstick. 'It all started when I had a massive crush on James, right?'

James, my own big brother, became the subject of Emerald's adulation after she came to visit me during our first Christmas break from uni.

'That's right. And, no offence, Em, because I love you dearly, but I did find your mooning over James a smidge excruciating. Do you remember how you kept coming up with excuses to come round when you knew he'd be in the house? And how excited you got when he remembered your name that time you came to visit in the holidays? And how you graffitied your uni notebook with "Emerald hearts James".'

I pause to catch my breath.

'Omg I'd forgotten that.' Em cackles. 'Why was I so cringe back then?'

'You weren't cringe,' I insist. 'It's only natural. It's just quite awkward when your best mate fancies your brother.'

'And then Stella had a thing for Sapphire,' Em recalls. The Bay children are all named after gemstones, although her brother Malachite goes by Mal these days.

'Yes! And how did that make you feel?' I ask.

She cocks her head to one side. 'Bit cringe,' she concedes.

'See! And that's why we made a promise not to hook up with each other's siblings, out of respect for our friendship.'

'Yes but, Jess, we were teenagers then. Teenagers! Life has moved on to the tune of a decade now. And we can trust our feelings. We're not just idiots with raging hormones.' And then she looks at herself fondly in the mirror and says, 'Well, not all the time anyway.'

'A promise is a promise,' I insist. 'And anyway, it doesn't actually matter. It's not like anything could ever happen between us.'

'Why on earth not?'

'Have you *seen* him, Em?! And look at me.' I motion towards my reflection. 'We're not exactly in the same league.'

'No, absolutely not,' Em says, suddenly quite cross. She turns to face me and grabs me by the shoulders. 'I'm not having that. You, Jessica Jones, are the catch of the day. The month. The century. DO YOU HEAR ME?'

Em doesn't shout very often but when she does, it is loud. The toilet flushes and the guest scurries out, alarmed.

Em and I share a look that says: *What about washing your hands! Ew!*

Then Em gives me a little shake. 'You are wonderful. Kind, considerate, caring. Always, always putting other people's needs before your own. Sweet as a nut. And funny. And so incredibly beautiful, like a brown-haired rose.'

'A brown-haired rose?' I echo with a grin. 'It doesn't *sound* great.'

'You know what I mean,' Em insists, 'And yet you never stop apologising for yourself, as if your very being is an inconvenience, which couldn't be further from the truth. You are the brightest star, Jessica Jones, and if I hear you say that you are "hardly a catch" ever again you will have me and the full force of my cosmic connection to deal with. Understood?'

I've been stunned into silence.

'UNDERSTOOD?'

'Yes, Em, sorry. Wait, sorry, I'm actually not sorry,' I add as an afterthought.

Em looks very pleased at this. 'Good,' she says, leading us out of the bathroom and back to our room. 'So, what are you going to do about it?'

'Do about it?' I repeat.

'Maybe spend some more time with Luke, see if the feeling is mutual? I mean, he'd be quite mad not to fancy you.'

'Oh hell no! No, no. No. Absolutely not. I'm already over it, Em, it was just a little crush.'

'All right, Jennifer Paige. I used to love belting out that song at the one club at uni. My favourite night of the week was Cheese Night? Do you faint every time you touch? Has he even touched you yet?'

'Obviously not! I've just spent the whole day perving over him and that's that.'

Em thinks on this. 'So, hang on. We've established that you are a catch and Luke would be lucky to have you. We've established that the pact is a thing of the past. What's stopping you from making a move, Jess?'

'We haven't actually established either of those things,' I reply. 'We didn't even think about Luke when we made up the pact because he was a shy seventeen-year-old who was leaving the country. So I would definitely need to see how Stella felt before, you know, anything big happened.' This thought makes me laugh so hard my sides hurt. 'Em, as if anything big is going to happen anyway. Why am I even talking about this? I've literally only just got Otis out of my flat, months after we broke up, and there's a lot of other stuff going on—'

'Like what?'

'Just life, you know. Anyway, Luke is a complication too far.'

'I can see that you really like him.' Em frowns.

'Don't look so sad!' I pull her into a hug as we walk through the beautifully manicured grounds. 'It's fine. A little crush will probably be good for me, and besides, I can't trust my own judgement when it comes to actually dating anyone. I've always dated solid options, right? And they never work out.'

'Solid options?' It's Em's turn to laugh now. 'The only thing solid about Otis is what we just heard him trying to remove from your toilet, babes. Which is proof that you have terrible taste in men. Appalling. Otis is just the cherry on the cake. I was trying out my first throuple when you started dating that absolute drip at uni, what was his name?'

'Tim,' I supply.

'That's it! He wasn't the most thrilling, was he?' she says gently. 'I mean, he was studying micro-economics for a start.'

'I'm sure that's actually a very useful course. Although he did work out how often we should hang out in percentages so as not to disturb his optimal studying time,' I concede, giggling at the memory. 'Tim was kind of intense.'

'Mmm. And then there was that guy from work?'

'Oh boy, Richie,' I say. 'In my defence, Richie seemed like a good idea at the time. He was a journalist too and I thought we made a good team. But then he stole one of my feature ideas, repackaged it as his own and used it to bag a job at a much bigger daily newspaper.'

Emerald tuts. 'Not cool. He took advantage of you. They all have in their own way. Maybe you're worried about your feelings towards Luke because he actually is a good guy. Never mind sensible options, how about listening to your gut for a change?'

'Hmm,' I say, pouting. '"Terrible taste in men" seems a bit much. Anyway, you need to calm down, Cupid. I'm very happy as I am right now. And besides, I tried listening to my gut the other day and do you know what happened?'

Em's all ears.

'I bought a Peppermint Aero instead of my usual Dairy Milk and it was such a letdown. Never doing that again.'

'I have never heard such a load of utter ridiculousness and I was once a member of a zodiac embroidery circle.' Em laughs, shaking me by the shoulders.

'What's that?'

'Oh, we made zodiac patches to sew onto bags and clothes. The plan was to sell them on Etsy but none of us could actually sew for shit so we all just ended up microdosing and trying to communicate with the fairy realm. Anyway, stop trying to distract me. I am not going to let you get away with this Luke thing, Jessie. Because he could be the perfect start to your Saturn Return.'

Chapter 7

The next morning, I wake up feeling surprisingly fresh after all of yesterday's excitement. It's our first full day at the hotel and these bedsheets alone justify the journey. I feel like I've been tucked up in a polar bear's pocket, the cotton is so soft and cosy. A very decadent start to the day! I roll over to check my phone, which is lit up with today's Stars in Brief notification from Zodiac Girlie.

Water gives way to emotional depth.

So . . . I should have a shower? Go swimming? And emerge . . . deeper? Probably not, given Em's reaction to Stella's door-walking escapades last night. There's a rap on my bedroom door and Emerald bounds in, pulling open the curtains and bouncing up and down on the end of my bed. She's wearing a silk dressing gown, her blonde hair piled up on top of her head in a topknot. I smile sleepily at the sight of her.

'Morning!' She beams.

'You're very perky already.'

'It's 6am, Jessie, time to have at it.'

'Hmm. No chance of a lie-in, today?'

'In the words of the great oracle Bon Jovi, you can sleep when you're dead, babes. I have plans for you!'

I push myself up into a seated position and rub my eyes.

'Sounds ominous.'

'If by ominous, you mean dreamy, then you are correct.' Em grins. 'So, I couldn't help but notice that Stell looked totally knackered when we got here yesterday. Like, super drained. In need of some serious pep.'

I nod. 'Poor thing, the Fran situation sounds really tough.'

'I know. It's this kind of stuff that confirms I'm on the right track, to be quite honest with you.'

'You mean, with not seeing anyone right now?'

Em nods. 'Casual is just fine by me. I can't imagine what it would be like to get into a relationship with someone and then have to make decisions together. Especially the whole kids thing. I mean, ew.'

'You've always been so sure that you don't want kids.'

'That was confirmed when I was babysitting my nephew the other day. As you know, he's only four. I was tucking him into bed when he looked me straight in the eye and he said: "Auntie Em, the children in the corner don't like you very much." We were literally in his bedroom, Jessie. I even turned around to check, there were no children there. At least, none that I could see.' She shudders.

'Oh my god.' I chuckle. 'That's actually horrifying.'

'I know! He was totally cool about it and I could not sleep. Anyway, back to my plan. I've organised for Stella to enjoy an early morning cardio and ice bath session to give her a boost.' Em grins. 'And you're next.'

'What?' Despite the perfect ambient temperatures in our suite, talk of cardio and an ice bath has me shivering in my pyjamas.

'Yes! Lycra Leon has flown in for one day only and, long story short, I've pulled some strings and got you both booked in for a one-to-one session with him.'

'Emerald,' I say sternly. 'Who on *earth* is Lycra Leon?'

'He's a big deal, babes. He trains loads of names and his ethos is something like, sweat it out then freeze to death?'

'No.' I shake my head.

Em presses on. 'Well, that's not verbatim but you'll see what I mean. High-intensity cardio followed by a plunge in a freezing cold pool is meant to be so good for you.'

'STELLA.' I bypass Em and call through to our friend's room. I don't want to 'freeze to death' on day one of my holiday. 'Stella! Help me?'

'She's gone already. I woke her up just after five. She's having her cardio and ice experience as we speak.' Em is so pleased with this that she claps. I scowl.

'Thank you for being so thoughtful,' I begin. 'But I'm really looking forward to lounging around this morning.'

'Not an option.'

'But—'

'Babes, it's Lycra Leon. You literally cannot get into his classes, ever. You should be thanking me.'

'Let's not get ahead of ourselves,' I grumble. 'So are you booked in after me?'

'Oh ha ha, no. Cardio and ice is really not my bag.'

'But it's not mine either! My bag is a tote filled with books, Emerald. Not a sweaty gym bag filled with ruddy weights and ice and whatnot.'

Em pats my hand and throws me one of the hotel's embossed robes. 'I might just order some breakfast in our room while I wait for you guys to finish up. Now, come on, chop chop! You can't go to cardio in your pyjamas, Jessie.'

Honestly.

'I'm g-going to k-kill Emerald.' Stella's teeth are chattering and she's huddled under a towel, harangued. I rub her arms to warm her up while a sense of dread fills my soul. We're both in one of the spa's lounge areas, gentle music and calming essential oils

67

filling the room. It would all be very relaxing if I weren't facing my own impending doom.

'Was it a little bit good?' I ask hopefully, wrapping my towelling robe around my workout clothes.

'No, it was not,' she snaps. 'Em woke me up at 5am for a start. She literally skipped into my room, the weirdo. And then I got here and met Lycra Leon – don't get me started on how much Lycra he is wearing – and he is brutal. The cardio is so intense you think you might be sick and then, right about the time where you want to pass out with the effort, the training stops and he literally pushes you into an ice bath. It's awful, Jess. At least you brought your robe though. Right, I'm going down to breakfast to warm up.'

I bite my lip nervously. This was not what I had in mind. I don't mind exercise, per se. Bit of Pilates. The occasional run. Swimming is my favourite, I'm pretty good at it. And I love baths! My ideal evening involves lighting candles in the bathroom and then chucking a Lush bath bomb into the tub before settling in with a good book. A cold bath, on the other hand . . .

'Jessica Jones?' The man addressing me now is in a head-to-toe hot-pink Lycra onesie. Stella whispers 'good luck' before skipping off to the warm embrace of a breakfast buffet.

My tummy rumbles. I am resigned to my fate.

'I'm so sorry to do this,' Lycra Leon bustles over, 'but I'm going to have to cancel our session. One of the hotel guests is an HNWI and is insisting on a session with me right now. My hands are tied.'

'What's an HNWI?' I ask, very grateful to whatever that is for getting me off the hook.

'A High Net Worth Individual.'

'Ooh is it Dita Ortiz?' I ask excitedly. 'We saw her at dinner last night.'

'Well, I couldn't possibly say.' He gives me a look that tells me I am absolutely right.

'Oh my god, is she here?' I spin around, wondering if I might catch a glimpse of the superstar in the hotel spa.

'Often with HNWIs we find that they prefer to exercise in the comfort of their own private surroundings, so I will be taking the experience to her suite.'

'Of course.' I nod. Why walk to the spa when you're rich and famous, when the spa will come to you? How fabulous!

The man who made Stella almost pass out is now apologising profusely to me and I haven't the heart to tell him I'm genuinely relieved not to be taking part in his morning of horror, so I make some half-assed 'never mind' noises instead.

Tragically, Santi walks past at this precise moment and she is now frowning into her hotel iPad. 'Oh now, this will not do. I can't have Miss Jones without some form of activity this morning.'

'Really, it's totally fine,' I insist, but it falls on deaf ears.

'Ah, here.' She taps the iPad. 'I have the perfect replacement for you.'

'Is it waffles for breakfast?' I ask hopefully.

Leon clutches at his imaginary pearls like I just swore.

'Breakfast will still be open by the time you're done.' Santi smiles. 'But first, you get to be our first ever guest to try out one of our water sports offerings.'

Water sports? The woman is now gently but firmly ushering me down a glass corridor dotted with stone statues of elephants. Oh man. Just when I'd got my hopes up. A full English is calling my name.

'You really don't need to, I'm more than happy—' I'm still trying to get out of it but no one, apparently, is listening. A door swings open and, terrifyingly, I find myself in a changing room filled with wetsuits.

AND ALSO LUKE.

IN A WETSUIT.

Sweet saints alive.

Do not, whatever you do, stare at . . . *things*, Jessica. I plead with my eyeballs to drag themselves up and away from Luke's—

'Luke here heads up our sports facilities at Gurnard Cove,' explains Santi.

'Yep, hello, we've met,' I sort of squeak.

'Fantastic,' Santi replies.

'Yeah, we go way back.' Luke grins, his face lighting up. 'Hey, Jess!'

'In that case, you already know that you're in very capable hands,' Santi says to me, so now all I'm thinking about is Luke's capable hands.

'My first water sports guest. Here,' says Luke and his very tight wetsuit, handing me a wetsuit of my own to put on as Santi leaves. 'Have you tried paddleboarding before?' he asks, all enthusiasm.

I shake my head. 'No. I love to swim but water sports have always felt a bit too . . . adventurous?'

Luke must sense that I'm nervous because he sounds super reassuring when he says: 'Ah, you'll be great. Paddleboarding is a lot of fun and it's a pretty gentle introduction to water sports. Plus I'll be by your side the whole time, so you've nothing to worry about.'

I don't know how to reply to that so I just say: 'Right-o!'

'Right-o,' Luke echoes, corners of his lips tugging into that smile. 'Do you want to get changed and I'll meet you out front?'

I mean, the answer is most definitely no. But I'm here now, through no fault of my own, so I guess I might as well embrace it, I think, pulling on the suit. Would I have chosen a rubber onesie for my first hang-out with Luke? No, I would not. But I catch my reflection in the changing room mirror on my way out and decide that I *almost* look like a cool surfer.

Luke is a bundle of pent-up energy, bounding along as we follow a boardwalk leading from the spa, past a clearing in the thicket, to the edge of a cliff. He keeps up a constant stream of talk about paddleboarding as we walk. We reach stone steps which descend towards the bay below and I pause at the top, looking out at the shimmering blue sea beyond. It is a stunning day, the sun climbing high in the sky already, just a few clouds skittering past. And it's warm, too. After a relentless winter, it feels wonderful to have the sun kissing my cheeks again.

A throat clears and I realise that Luke is waiting, halfway down the steps, while I bask in the sunshine like a sunflower. My wetsuit and I squeak down to join him and once we're on the beach, Luke makes his way to a wooden shack with the hotel's logo on it.

'Welcome to the beach!' he says. 'Once we're up and running, this coffee shack is going to be constantly manned so guests can come and grab a drink before they bathe, swim, surf, whatever.'

'It's so pretty.'

'But for now, I'm afraid you're going to have to put up with me making you a coffee. Flat white, okay?'

'Oh yes, please.' I follow him inside as he sets to work on the commercial-sized coffee machine. It hisses and splutters into life, and I watch as Luke focuses on measuring out the coffee grounds and pouring milk into the frother. His strong jaw is set as he moves carefully, with precision, his cheekbones like peaks I want to ski down. And I'd like to ask him where he learned to make coffee like that but I can see that he's concentrating and I don't want to break the spell.

The smell of fresh coffee fills the air and I breathe in appreciatively.

'It's the best smell, right?' Luke asks, and I realise he's glanced up to look at me.

'My favourite.'

He nods, and when he's finished he hands me a cup, before leaning back against the work surface to enjoy his own coffee.

'Thanks. That's really good,' I say appreciatively.

'Really?' He looks adorably pleased with this compliment. 'I've been practising.'

'You were pretty devoted to making that coffee. You were really 'paying attention.'

'Was it that obvious?' Luke smiles.

'Your brow was furrowed and you had this intent look on your face.'

'Please tell me my tongue wasn't hanging out as well?' he asks, which makes me laugh. 'Because I used to do that at school and I got royally picked on for it.'

'Oh no! If even you got picked on at school then there is literally no hope for the rest of us,' I blurt out.

'Even me?' Luke repeats, looking confused.

Me and my big mouth. 'I mean, you know, you're, erm, obviously a good-looking guy, that's all. And good-looking people don't usually have a hard time at school.'

Luke holds my gaze for a moment. 'Oh. Well, thanks I suppose. But I'm going to insist that you never, ever look at any of Stella's old family photos because if you saw what I used to look like, you would definitely change your mind on that.'

'Oh really?'

'Hell yes,' he says, shaking his head. 'We're talking terrible teeth, trousers too short for my legs, the whole nine yards.'

I chuckle. 'Ah, the old ugly duckling backstory.'

'Come on, you must have some old photos that need to be kept under lock and key too. Unless, wait, maybe you're one of the few lucky ones who have always been beautiful. I bet that's it, right?'

This comment catches me completely off-guard. I look down for a moment but then gather and manage to think of a way to reply.

'My parents are big into photo albums. They put together a new one every year when my brother and I were growing up. And when I was about nine, I insisted on cutting my own hair to create a fringe, but obviously I did a really bad job.'

'Because you were nine?' Luke asks, with this gorgeous amused look on his face.

'Yes! Strangely I was not a professional hairdresser aged nine.

But that wasn't even the whole story. I used massive kitchen scissors for the job.'

Luke winces.

'So I went way too short with the fringe and then hacked off a load around the sides too. When I was done, it looked like I was wearing a brown helmet. And it took ages to grow out, so when we are talking photos, I can tell you that in one particular album I look a lot like a young Darth Vader.'

Luke barks out a laugh.

'I'm going to need to see those photos, Jess,' he insists.

'Never.' I grin back.

At this point both of us seem to realise that we've long finished our coffees and should probably get on with what we came here to do. Luke fetches two paddleboards from the back of the hut and then turns his whole attention back to me, the full glare of the sun.

'Are you ready?'

'If by ready you mean a bit jittery from the coffee and quite nervous re water sports then, yes, Luke, ready as I'll ever be.'

'I've got you, Jess.' Luke smiles, picking up his paddle and beckoning me to follow him down to the water's edge, looking every inch the delicious surfy hunk. Caffeine courses through my veins as I watch him set up my board on the sand, explaining that we'll practise getting into position on land first. Then he asks me to kneel down and you can only imagine where my mind wanders to at this request.

I am a disgrace. It wouldn't be so bad if he was just good-looking, like a piece of art I could admire from afar. But thanks to our little coffee break it turns out I now find myself charmed by him too, wanting to know more about him, queuing up a thousand questions in my mind.

Still, I repeat the words 'Stella's little brother' over and over in my mind to try and quell the inappropriate thoughts. Being on all fours is definitely not helping the frisk factor.

73

'May I?' asks Luke, demonstrating that he'd like to help me get into a better position using his hands.

Dear mother of mercy.

'Sure,' I manage, and the next thing I know, his hands are on my hips and, well, off to hell I go. Just point me in the right direction, pals.

'So,' I say, in a bid to distract myself. 'Lovely day we're having!'

Yes, that's it, just make conversation like a normal person.

Luke catches my eye and I realise I was wrong. His eyes aren't just any old grey. They're flint and foggy mornings and flecked with gold.

Just, whatever you do, don't gasp.

'Are you okay?' Luke frowns suddenly.

I just gasped. For heaven's sake!

Right, that is it. I have absolutely got to stop this. Poor Luke is here to do his job and I am here to have a break with my best friends. I am also an adult female who will be turning thirty later this year. I refuse to be turned into a jabbering wreck by this unexpected crush. All I need to do is get a handle on the situation.

I take an actual deep breath and steady my thoughts. I've got this.

'How long has it been since we last saw each other?' Luke's asking. 'What, ten years?'

'About that.' I nod. 'You've been in America most of that time, right?'

Luke makes an 'mmm-hmm' noise as he concentrates on my posture, encouraging me to stand. 'Both feet facing forward,' he instructs. 'I've been away a long time. It feels really good to be home.'

'Being away from family is hard,' I say, with some shred of understanding. Luke shoots me a curious look as if to ask: *You get it?*

'I can relate a little bit,' I explain. 'My mum and dad left just a few weeks ago. I was there one Sunday for lunch and they

74

announced that they'd sold our family home and were off to travel the world for a year.'

'Did they take the Darth Vader album with them?'

'Shut up.' I laugh.

'Just teasing,' he says, his face straightening up again. 'Seriously though, that must have felt like a lot, all at once?'

'It really did.' I nod. 'They flew to Australia last week and I miss them so much already, but I'm also so happy that they're off on this amazing adventure. I've been thinking about them a lot recently. This trip of theirs, it's helped me to realise that I've probably been a bit overprotective of them.'

'How so?'

'You know how families are,' I say. 'A lot of stuff happened when I was younger and I basically spent my late teens and early twenties wanting to be the best daughter for them. Let's just say my older brother James was a pain in the ass. But, I don't know, now they've gone off on this incredible trip, it's really put things into perspective for me. Maybe I've been a bit over-cautious with some stuff?'

Luke nods thoughtfully. 'You know that they're in a good place, and now you feel like you can focus on what *you* want?'

'Exactly that!' I reply, impressed by how astute Luke is. How he just seems to get me. 'Anyway, sorry. I don't know why I'm telling you this. I haven't even mentioned it to the girls yet. You're really easy to talk to. I'm guessing you developed your excellent listening skills during the ugly duckling years,' I tease.

Luke shakes his head at me, a playful smile on his face. 'Wow. Did the Darth Vader years help you develop your ability to take the piss out of people?'

'I'm not normally like this, I promise.' I laugh.

'Oh, so it's my fault?'

'Yes, Luke, it is one hundred per cent your fault. You know I'll be asking Stella for evidence of those pictures as soon as we finish up here, right?'

'Not if I get to her first.'

'Then she'll have to choose, best friend or brother. Pretty sure she'll pick me.'

'I admire your confidence,' Luke says. '*Misplaced* confidence, but still. In the meantime, I'm going to have to get in touch with your parents so they can point me in the direction of your family photo albums.'

'I'd like to see you try.' I grin.

'Parents love me.' Luke shrugs.

'I bet they do.'

'Are you doing okay though, now that they've gone off on this trip?' he asks.

I let out a long, low exhale. 'I miss them a lot, but definitely. Anyway, we were meant to be talking about you coming back home,' I prompt.

'Well, I missed Stella like mad while I was away, and Mum, but I kept pretty busy.'

'With the tennis?'

'That's right.' He smiles encouragingly at me when I get my posture right. 'I started out on a tennis scholarship at college over there. I was competing at tournament level . . . ' He pauses, shakes his head. 'Big dreams of winning Wimbledon one day,' he adds wryly. 'But I injured my ankle pretty badly and at first, thought surgery might mean I could get back to full fitness, but it kept flaring up every time I was back on court. In the end I had to stop competing.'

'That's so sad. I'm really sorry to hear that, Luke.'

He flashes me a brief look, shading his eyes from the sun with his hand.

'Thanks. I was gutted for a long while but I couldn't just sit around feeling sorry for myself, and I'd already built up a bit of a name for myself on the tennis circuit so coaching others came pretty quickly after that.'

'What made you come back?'

Luke looks up to the sky as he considers this. 'A couple of things,' he says vaguely. 'I guess the driving reason was a combination of missing my sister and this job coming up at the right time. I get to head up the sports department here and I'm going to really enjoy working across lots of different sports for a change. You have a strong core,' he adds, catching me by surprise.

'Oh, um, thanks! I don't think I've ever had my core praised before.'

'I find that hard to believe,' Luke says, suddenly looking a bit flustered, as if he didn't mean to say that out loud. 'Right, are you ready?'

'There won't be any sharks, will there?'

'Off the coast of Northumberland?' he asks playfully. 'I think we're good.'

'Right. Okay. Ready as I'll ever be.'

'I'm actually doing it!' I shout, thrilled that I've managed to keep my balance as we paddle out on the water. Luke's keeping a watchful eye, never far behind as I get more adventurous and move farther out to sea.

'You're doing great,' he calls over. 'Keep the paddle moving in a sweeping C shape to turn.'

I move my paddle to turn the board, now facing back towards the beach, and let out a happy sigh at the stunning view of the coastline, the grand hotel and modern spa nestled just beyond the clifftop. This place is so beautiful. I'd had my reservations about going paddleboarding on the North Sea in the middle of May, and it does still seem like a frankly bonkers thing to be doing first thing on a Saturday morning, but it is glorious.

After a while, Luke paddles closer to me. 'Jess, the wind has just started to pick up so I'm afraid we need to head back.'

'Oh no!' I call back, crestfallen. 'I don't want to stop yet.'

Luke smiles at this, and I see that he's one of those teachers who just loves to see his students thrive. It's very endearing.

'The paddleboards aren't going anywhere and we can get you booked in for another session, but we need to get back before it turns too rough. Follow me?'

I spin myself round for one last look out over the sea and that's when a gust of wind absolutely batters my body.

'Kneel down, Jess!' Luke calls.

I try to kneel, remembering everything that Luke taught me about safety before we even got in the water. But I'm a rookie on the board and it's not as easy as it looks. I feel a sudden sense of panic taking over. I thought I'd got this but I haven't. I'm still standing, my body acting like the sail of a boat, when another gust of wind knocks me clean off my feet. The next thing I know, I'm underwater. The cold hits my lungs and I flail about, fighting to get my head back above the surface, gripped by fear.

Strong arms circle around me.

I'm being pulled up.

I drag in a huge gulp of air, coughing and spluttering as Luke treads water with me still in his arms.

'I've got you,' he says, and it's so reassuring that the rising panic starts to ebb away. 'Deep breaths.'

His hair is slick with water now and he's watching me intently as I inhale. I feel the firmness of his hands around me and I realise that I must have grabbed onto his upper arms as I was trying to get some air.

Luke helps manoeuvre me back onto the board, which I flop onto like a fish out of water.

I splutter, lying flat on my face, as Luke guides me and the board back to shore. 'God, sorry.'

'Please don't apologise,' Luke says, looking suddenly on edge. 'I should have got you back in sooner. I could kick myself.'

'What? Don't blame yourself. It was all on me. I was having so much fun,' I insist, feeling deflated and a smidge embarrassed to be dragged back to shore after basically capsizing myself.

But there's a fire burning in Luke's eyes and I can see that he's upset about what just happened. We're wading out of the shallow water now, and he's shaking his head.

'I'm the professional here. I can't believe I put you in danger like that.'

'You didn't! I just panicked, that's all. I do that a lot. The other day I panicked when I got into gear before the traffic light turned green and I convinced myself I was going to get arrested for traffic crimes.'

Luke's features soften at this, then he looks from me back out to sea.

'We've done countless risk assessments on this part of the cove already but I've never seen the wind pick up so suddenly before. I'm going to have to have a team meeting about this, we can't offer paddleboarding to guests if we put them at risk. I'm really sorry, Jess.'

Poor Luke looks so dejected and I feel an instant desire to put the smile back on his face, so I skip across the sand to prove that I'm absolutely fine. 'Look!' I call over. 'Totally fine!'

His brows are still furrowed but at least his lips are twitching into a smile now.

'I'd like to take you to the hotel doctor for a quick check-up,' he calls as I skip back.

'Luke,' I say as firmly as possible. 'There is absolutely no need to do that. Please don't look so worried. I just fell in the sea, that's literally it.'

He does not look convinced.

'Jess, you're shivering.'

He runs over to the hut, grabs a dry robe and sprints back with it, draping it across my body. 'Let's get you out of that wetsuit,' he adds.

Then he rakes a hand through his hair and looks away, mortified.

'I mean . . .'

'It's fine,' I insist. 'I totally get what you mean.'

'Hot chocolate,' he says suddenly, like he's struck upon a great idea. 'I'll make us some of those while you get changed. There are towels in the changing room at the back of the shack, and loads of spare dry robes.'

Luke insists on staying with me for a bit, just to make sure I'm not in shock. Little does he know that the only thing causing me to be in shock around here is him. So now he's set up deckchairs on the sand, mugs of hot chocolate on a table between them and . . .

'Ooh what's that?' I ask.

'The kitchen sent down some pastries for us,' Luke says, mirroring my smile. 'We've got banana bread, Swedish buns and chocolate brioche with pistachio crème pat.'

I whistle as I pad over in my second dry robe of the day, feeling much better to have warmed up.

'Well, now you're just tempting me,' I say, and when Luke does this half-embarrassed laugh I realise that probably didn't quite come out right. At least he's smiling again, I decide, inordinately pleased that his spirits have lifted.

I take a bite of bun and let out a moan of delight.

Luke clears his throat.

It's probably the combination of sugar, coffee and the incident but I find I cannot sit still. I'm full of beans, and when I spot a shell near the base of my deckchair, I leap up and start looking for more.

Luke watches me.

'You definitely seem better,' he says as I pad from shell to shell, stashing them in one of the robe's pockets. I've a handful by the time I head back to our spot, pulling them out and arranging them on the table.

'You have a lot of energy,' observes Luke.

I nod, stopping for another sip of chocolate.

'Meanwhile, you're just chilling out on a deckchair,' I tease. 'And getting paid for it.'

He lets out a low rumble of laughter.

'So far this job definitely has its perks,' he says, looking right at me, which makes my stomach flip. He doesn't . . . He can't . . . Nah! So fanciful, Jess.

'I'm usually the one jumping all over the place,' Luke is saying, now casting his gaze out to sea. 'Racing from one thing to the next. Today's the first time I've felt still in a while, actually.'

'Always on the go?'

'Yes,' he says, those grey eyes tracking back to me again. Out here they match the colour of the waves as they roll in, which is not a little mesmerising. I fold myself into a deckchair as Luke leans forward in his, looking like he's about to say something.

'I got diagnosed with ADHD shortly before I came back to the UK,' he says, shooting me a sidelong look. 'It's funny, I haven't even told Stella about it yet but for some reason . . . ' He pauses again, and I can't get a read on the way he's looking at me. 'I don't usually . . . '

'Maybe it was my near death experience back there?' I suggest.

'Are we really calling it that?' Luke says, laughing.

'Absolutely. My life flashed before my eyes,' I reply solemnly.

'In the two seconds you were underwater?' He grins. 'Wow.'

That makes me laugh before I straighten up. 'So, how come you haven't spoken to Stella about the ADHD yet?'

Luke sucks in his breath. 'I haven't spoken to *anyone* about it yet, until now. Usually I'll be looking out to sea and thinking of all the things I could be doing with my time, or going into hyper-organisation mode, but being here with you . . . ' He stops again, shakes his head. 'I'm weirdly calm. You're strangely calming, Jess.'

'Erm, thanks?' I chuckle. 'I should have that printed on business cards. Jessica Jones: Strangely Calming.'

Luke laughs softly. 'Plus it feels easy to talk to you. You know how big sisters can be. I'm worried that Stella will go straight into overprotective mode. The way you said you felt about your folks.'

'Stella's always going to look out for you.'

'Yeah, she's been amazing. I don't know what I'd have done without her when my pro career was crumbling. She was on the phone every day, coaching me through it, offering words of advice, just being there. And I know how much you supported her, too, Jess. During everything that happened to Mum.'

'It's just what best friends do.' I shrug. 'So, how did you feel when you got the diagnosis?'

'Honestly? Relieved. It made everything fit together, like a jigsaw puzzle. Now all the behaviours that I thought made me different, make sense. I can get hyper-focused on things. Seeing you race around collecting shells, I thought, it's normally me doing that. But today, here with you, I feel still.' He tracks his eyes over to mine, like he's trying to figure something out. 'I'm probably over-sharing, sorry. As you said, I am meant to be working.'

'Oh wait, no, Luke, I didn't mean it like that!' I say hurriedly. 'I was just teasing. I'm really grateful that you felt you could share it with me and I know Stella will want to be there for you, too.'

'I know.' Luke nods. 'I will talk to her. There are a few things I need to talk to her about, actually. It's just . . . you know what she's like.'

I chuckle. 'Bit loud?'

'So loud. It's a wonder I ever spoke growing up, she was always answering for me,' he says fondly before his face clouds over. 'But, you know, Stella had to grow up pretty quickly. Even before Dad left, before things started to go wrong for Mum, she was an old soul. You know those photos we've been talking about? Mum had one hanging on the wall at home, it's a picture of me and Stella when we were little, from before Dad left. He used to insist that we should go to church on Sundays, which I always thought was ironic given the life choices he made. Anyway, Mum used to dress us up in the most ridiculous outfits for church, which made us look like miniature middle-aged people. I'd be in a little corduroy suit and bow tie at three years old and Stella would be wearing some flowery dress, like we were from the Victorian era.'

'That's actually a very cute image.'

'You try telling that to the toddler who looked like he was off to chair a meeting.' He laughs. 'I remember feeling like all the other kids my age were out at the playground, getting messy and having fun. Mum would get so cross if I got mud on my Sunday best, too. And then suddenly she didn't really care anymore. It was Stella who'd be fretting about the grass stains on my trousers, not Mum.'

I have to fight the urge to reach out and grab his hand.

We fall silent again as the sun makes a comeback, bathing the beach in golden light. Luke adjusts his wetsuit accordingly, so he's now sitting opposite me with it unzipped all the way down past his chest. And I am doing an excellent job at neither staring nor thinking unacceptable thoughts, because my recent brush with death (no sure) has confirmed that I should follow this path of being wise and sensible. Life is dramatic enough without adding a totally unattainable crush.

'This place reminds me of seaside holidays when I was little,' I say. 'We used to go to Devon – me and my brother, with my mum and dad – and then life sort of took over. I don't live close enough to just pop to the seaside. You forget how much you've missed something until you experience it again.'

Luke watches me closely as I talk and I get this unshakeable impression that he actually is interested in me. And I don't think I've had that before. Otis always looked like he was waiting for me to stop talking so he could have his turn. Like he was just humouring me. How come I never realised that before? And now Luke wants to listen to what I have to say. Is he like this with everyone? God, how exhausting to be so open and borderline flirty all the time!

'You're so right,' he says with a curious look on his face. 'I think that's why I'm happy to be back in the UK.'

'You just missed it?'

'Exactly.' He nods, checking his watch and sighing. 'Oh man, I lost track of time. I'm really sorry, Jess, but I'm going to have to head off. I've another class shortly. If you feel in any way weird, or worried about what happened, you come find me, okay? Or the hotel doctor.'

'Yes, boss,' I promise, doing my best Girl Guides salute. 'I was just joking about the whole brush with death thing, by the way.'

'I know.' He smiles, saluting me right back as he gets up to go. 'But still, I don't want anything bad happening to you. Not on my watch.'

Chapter 8

'What the hell, Jessie? Did you and Lycra Leon *smash*?! Let me look at you,' Emerald demands the minute I get back to our suite, pulling me inside and steering me onto a sofa in the living room. I collapse onto it, exhausted.

'Excuse me?' I ask, stretching my feet out to Stella and nudging her with my toe. She's reading one of the actual newspapers the hotel delivers to our room every morning, and I feel very proud of her.

Stella looks up from her paper and beams at me.

'Keeping print journalism alive, especially for you,' Stella says, jiggling the paper up and down.

Em, on the other hand, is having none of our newspaper chat.

'Just look at her, Stell,' Em says, waving a hand in my direction. 'You are positively glowing, Jessie! I know Lycra Leon is good because he comes highly recommended but there's only so much a cardio and cold bath sesh can do. And you, Jessica Jones, look like you've just been banging.'

'Well, I definitely have not,' I object.

'I did not get straight-man vibes from Lycra Leon,' Stella chimes in. 'Jess, do you have some secret moves to turn gay men straight that we didn't know about?'

Both of my best friends are finding this hilarious, winking at each other like absolute children.

'You know very well I have no moves,' I protest. 'I didn't turn Lycra Leon and I certainly haven't been doing any banging. Or "smashing" for that matter. Honestly, you two! Actually, Leon had to cancel our session.'

Em presses her fingers against my forehead and closes her eyes.

'What are you doing?' I ask warily.

'Communicating with your aura. It's giving big sexual energy.' She pulls back, looking impressed.

'Wait, have you been flirting, like I told you to last night?' Stella asks, paper abandoned, picking up my legs and sliding under them so she can get a closer look at me on the sofa.

Oh lordy.

'Of course not!' I insist, bit high-pitched, swatting Em's aura hands away and giving her a look which pleads *don't pull at this thread!*

Em does not pick up on my message one bit.

'Something's different,' she presses, squatting down to get a better look. So now both best friends are right up in my grill.

'You come back looking rejuvenated – in a sexual way – and expect us to believe you haven't spent the entire morning orgasming? I'm so pleased for you, Jessie. We should all be harnessing the power of the female orgasm,' Em adds, patting my hand. Then she springs up and wafts over to the collection of freshly cleansed crystals she's arranged on the writing desk. 'It must be the love crystals. I'm so glad I packed them. Citrine, for pleasure, and black tourmaline, for bringing us back to our bodies. Well done, my beauties! Clearly they are working a charm already. Jess, I'm so happy you are enjoying the ripe pleasures of intimacy again.'

'Honestly, guys!' I stutter. 'Ripe pleasures? I really haven't—'

'If you weren't smashing Lycra Leon, then who was it?' Stella interrupts.

'For goodness sake!' I say at top volume.

'What's got your knickers in a twist?' Stella grins.

'Or rather, *who*?' Em asks, eyes twinkling. And then it dawns on her. 'Oh,' she says like she's just figured it out.

'*Oh* what?' Stella frowns.

'OH MY GOD,' I shout. Em can't drop me in it now! I really do not want Stella finding out I've spent the past twenty-four hours lusting after her younger brother. I can't even begin to think what it might do to our friendship.

'Oh, as in, it must be that footballer, right?' Em wiggles her eyebrows at me.

'Erm, yes, that is right,' I say, going along with it. 'Spotted him this morning.'

'What footballer?'

'Perry Carver, plays in the first league,' says Em.

'You mean *Premier League*,' says Stella, rolling her eyes.

'Sure, sure,' Em says dismissively. 'Anyway, he's here. Haven't you seen him?'

Stella narrows her eyes. 'I didn't know you liked football, Jessie?'

I feel terrible for fibbing. I can't speak.

Em steps in to rescue me. 'It's not the game, babes, it's the player. He's cute.'

'So, were you flirting with footballers all morning?' Stella looks as confused as I feel.

I'm going to have to come clean about this morning's beach trip with Luke. And if that whole scenario wasn't awkward enough, these two have now unknowingly implied that I spent the morning Doing Things with Stella's little brother. Talk about uncomfortable.

'I ended up going paddleboarding with Luke,' I say rapidly, fingers balled into fists, before muttering something about how perhaps the sea breeze had given my skin a boost. 'I, erm, passed Terry on his way to the gym.'

'*Perry*.' Em shoots me a look.

'Perry! Obviously. He's so cute,' I say, no actual clue what this man looks like. 'But, erm, it's just a crush and I would never act on it.'

'Oh.' Stella looks disappointed. 'For a while there I thought we might have some exciting romantic developments for you, Jess.'

Then she goes back to her paper. Em moves behind Stella on the sofa, beaming at me, and makes unmentionable symbols involving her hands. I give her a wide-eyed *stop it* look and she bites her lip, now pressing her fingers together in a heart shape. I leave the room.

I can think of worse places for a pedicure. We're sat three in a row, each of us on a padded chair tilted all the way back, a view of the Japanese garden through the glass wall in front of us.

There's a smell of nail polish in the air, mixed with the hotel's now familiar scent, and I relax into my chair as the pedicurist gets to work, allowing my eyes to close and my mind to wander.

'So, how was paddleboarding with Luke?' asks Em, giving me a knowing look.

I glare back at her. Honestly.

'Fine thanks,' I reply, attempting breezy. 'Well, actually, it's not as easy as it looks and I ended up in the sea.'

Stella, on the other side of Em, snorts at this. 'Oh mate.'

'I know. Luke had to fish me out.'

Em's head twists back to look at me again and her face is lit up with this new titbit. She is thrilled. I can just tell that she's about to very unsubtly ask for more information so I decide to head her off at the pass.

'Actually, I could do with your advice, Em,' I say. 'About my stars.'

She peers at me suspiciously. She knows what I'm doing.

'Go on,' she says, interest nevertheless piqued.

'So, my Zodiac Girlie said: "Water gives way to emotional depth" this morning. And I don't know what that means.'

'Ooh interesting.' Em claps. 'I think that this means you're going to have real capacity for empathy and connection today.'

'So, not just falling in the sea and freaking out then?' asks Stella. 'Because that could also be—'

'Like I said,' Em interrupts with a sigh, 'we're not taking these *literally*, babes. Have you felt like you've been able to connect emotionally with someone today, Jessie?' She raises her eyebrow at me, triumphantly. Damn it!

I think back to this morning with Luke, how I shared stuff about my parents and how he opened up about his ADHD. We might have known each other for years in the sense that we've been aware of each other's existence, but we only really reconnected yesterday. And yet, already, I feel like I could share anything with Luke, which is unsettling.

'Erm, I mean . . . '

'She's been hanging out with Luke and he's about as open as a closed book.' Stella chortles.

I wonder why I got a different version of Luke to the one his sister sees. I also think that I have *got* to move this conversation on.

'Nice colour, Stell,' I say, watching her pedicurist layer on a hot pink.

'Thank you, beauty.' She grins. 'I'm feeling so summery with this gorgeous weather. What are you going for?'

I gently stick out my right foot, halfway through a coat of deepest red.

'Ooh! Nice.'

'Mm, very sexy.' Em looks at me.

'So what did your astrology app have to say this morning, Stell?'

'Oh lord, hang on,' she replies, pulling out her phone. 'Here. "Focus on the twin flame in your synastry." I mean, that's just a collection of words, right? It literally does not make sense. What is synastry? Sinister, more like.'

Stella makes a *ba-doom-chh* noise and I start chortling until Em gives me A Look.

'Actually, Stella,' she says sternly, 'this is perfect for you right now. Obviously. The stars know what they are talking about.

89

Synastry is another word for astrological relationships and your twin flame means the other half of your soul. Your stars are telling you to focus on matters of the heart, babes.'

'Hmm,' says Stella. 'Why didn't it just say that, then? Why does it need to sound so woo woo?'

'Is there anything "woo woo" in the suggestion that you look at your relationship?' Em asks, a little sharply.

'I guess I could call Fran, just to check in,' Stella concedes.

'Now that is a good idea,' I concur. 'She'll want to know how you're doing.'

'Poor thing. I've left her at home dealing with our faulty washing machine while I bugger off on a spa break with you two.'

'Just let her know how much you love her,' I suggest.

'Yes! And that you don't take her for granted,' adds Em.

'I will. As soon as we're done here.'

Em looks thrilled. 'See!' She smiles. 'My girls are finally getting in tune with the stars. I'm so proud of you both!'

'Well, let's not get ahead of ourselves,' Stella grunts as our WhatsApps buzz in unison. It's the hotel's concierge service, listing all the activities on offer for the rest of the day.

'Ooh, I might do a sound bath at 3pm,' muses Em. 'Will you guys come too?'

'Hard no,' says Stella.

'Are you still sulking after I booked you in with Lycra Leon this morning, babes? Because you've got to admit, you do seem so very refreshed.'

'You'd be refreshed if you were plunged into an ice bath pre-6am.' Stella tuts.

'Yeah, I think I'll give the sound bath a miss too,' I say, mostly because I do not know what that is. 'After my brush with death—'

'Are we really calling it that?' Em cocks an eyebrow.

'Must everyone pooh-pooh my near death experience?' I huff, exasperated. 'After my *brush with death*, I'd like to relax this afternoon. And look, there's a garden party later. Live band, champagne on the lawn, followed by a sit-down meal. That sounds great!'

'I'm definitely up for that,' agrees Stella.

We've got a university playlist on Spotify and have crowded into Em's room, where instead of unpacking she seems to have thrown her belongings all over the place. I had to move a bra from the window seat to sit down.

There's make-up and clothes everywhere and, at Em's insistence, I've got so much mascara on that my eyelashes feel heavy. I swear that every time I blink, I'm causing a cyclone somewhere across the globe.

Stella's the first to get dressed, stepping into a hot-pink jumpsuit to match her new nails. And with Em's 'wear your wardrobe' mantra in the back of my mind, I decide I might as well chuck my best dress on too. No time like the present and all that! It's a bronze off-the-shoulder dress that makes me feel quite glamorous. Meanwhile, Em opts for a skin-tight sequinned catsuit. Imagine being the kind of woman who not only owns sequinned catsuits but also has opportunities to wear them, I marvel.

'Before we go, we need jewels,' Em says, opening up a small trunk in the corner of her room. 'Behold!'

Stella and I both make cooing noises as the trunk opens and a kaleidoscope of colour sparkles from within.

'It's like a treasure chest!' I say.

'A lot of this is my new collection,' Em says. 'It's not out yet but I thought we could have a play around with some of the bits this week?'

'Play around' and 'bits' aren't words I would naturally team with the sheer amount of gold, diamonds and gemstones dazzling my eyes, but there we are.

'Jessie, this for you,' she says, pulling out a long necklace that matches the colour of my dress. 'That's tiger eye,' she adds, nodding at the gem. 'Perfs for balance. And Stell, here.' Stella is handed a beautiful gold ring with a pink gem inside. 'Rose quartz.

Emotional healing.'

Stella tolerates this pretty well, I'd say, while I fix the necklace in place and look in the mirror. 'God, it's beautiful! Thank you, Em. What are you going for?'

'Thought this diamond tiara might work?'

'No sure.' I nod as she places an actual crown on her own head.

'Subtle, right?' Em grins.

'You look dreamy.'

The garden party is being held out at the front of the hotel, where just yesterday I was toppling out of Carl's vomitorium on wheels. The large central pond in the middle of the driveway has been filled with candles floating in white paper bags. On one side of the drive is a great bank of tables and chairs, strewn with flower arrangements, with festoon lights looping from tree to tree.

'This is not low key,' Stella murmurs as we arrive.

'The tiara was the right choice,' Em confirms, more to herself than the rest of us.

'Is this just a thing they do here?' I wonder. A member of staff overhears and explains that Saturday nights will be garden party nights all through the summer. *Imagine.* Very glamorous people mill about and a brass band strikes up with oom-pah-pah versions of popular songs, so naturally it's not long before the three of us are in a circle, singing to each other with huge smiles on our faces and champagnes in our hands. I feel a little fizz of delight running through me. To be here, with them? My cup runneth over.

After a rousing rendition of Daft Punk's 'Get Lucky', the band take a break and guests are shepherded over to take our seats for supper. And that's when I spot him. Not in sports clothes, or wetsuit, or swimwear. But everyday clothes. A dark green linen shirt. Smart trousers. Honestly, how does he manage to look handsome in everything?

Em, taking the seat next to mine, gives me a nudge. 'Go say hi!'

'I will do no such thing,' I whisper, nodding pointedly towards Stella on the other side of the table.

'LUKE!' Em shouts over. 'Come join us!'

His face lights up when he sees us and he's walking over when something deeply traumatising happens.

Luke is accosted. By ThatGirlWithTheCroissants.

'Omg, what's she doing?' asks Em as the three of us stare over at Luke. Croissants has strolled right up to him and now she's got her hands on his chest! I can't look. I stare down at my menu in a stupor.

'Pretty sure that's harassment in the workplace,' Stella fumes, instantly flipping into overprotective big-sister mode. I glance back over and Luke seems to be managing the situation well. He's friendly but professional as Croissants obviously flirts with him. She's wearing a cute polka dot mini dress which makes her legs look a mile long, her blonde hair pulled back into a ponytail tied with a matching polka dot bow.

'She looks like a Dalmatian,' Em says uncharitably.

'She looks stunning.' I sigh.

'Why has she got her hands all over my little brother?'

'Hate to tell you this, babes, but your bro *is* super hot,' says Em.

'Mate,' Stella says, a distinct note of don't-be-gross in her voice.

'Oh come on!' Em continues. 'You Washingtons have got some insane genes, Stella. I mean, look at you.'

Stella pretends to fluff her hair. 'Fine, whatever, let's just not use the words "your bro" and "super hot" in the same sentence ever again please. It gives me the ick. Almost as much as watching that influencer flirt the living daylights out of him. Honestly, this happens all the time. I genuinely feel for Luke.'

Argh. Dagger to the heart. It's as I suspected, of course, but it's never great to hear that the man you like can't move for attention. Downheartedly, I cast my eyes back to Luke and Croissants.

'What's her actual name?' I ask, wishing my hair looked that sleek.

'No one knows.' Em leans in. 'It's a whole subcategory on the internet. She's a total mystery.'

Croissants is pressing her hands together and tilting her head down as she talks to him, which makes it look like she's asking him for something. Maybe a date? Luke is obviously the kind of man who gets asked out a lot. Here we are at a spa hotel full of hot influencers, celebrities and crazy rich people, and Stella says he can barely move for being flirted with. He literally just got here and already he's been cornered by a beautiful, successful influencer.

I bet Croissants doesn't have to scrub mould off the windowsills in her flat every winter. I bet Croissants doesn't eat an entire packet of biscuits at the end of a long day at work. Come to think of it, I bet Croissants doesn't even have long days at work. I've followed her for a while now and it seems to me that she spends most of her time gadding about on holiday and then making content so she can write the trip off for tax purposes. And it strikes me now that this environment is normal for her. Not a once-in-a-lifetime trip to a super luxe hotel like it is for me. This is just standard, flirting with Luke is just standard. I know I'm not meant to be jealous, I should be cheering her on for her obvious successes, right? But right now I can't help but feel a smidge envious.

'You okay, Jess? You've gone a bit . . . puffy,' Stella points out, and I note that I've balled my fists together in a huff. I'm doing Croissants a disservice, no doubt. Just because I don't command £20k per Instagram post doesn't mean I should be so dismissive, right? I bet she works super hard and deserves everything she gets and FOR THE LOVE OF GOD, CROISSANTS, GET YOUR HANDS OFF MY LUKE!

Except, v much not *my* Luke.

'I've had enough of this,' Stella says, which is fair because it starts to look increasingly as if Luke would like to escape. 'I'm going over.'

'Amazing,' whispers Em as we both watch Stella stalk with

purpose over to her put-upon little brother. 'Stella's off to Luke's defence. You can totally tell that she basically raised him. Good luck, Croissants, that's what I say! Jessie, you okay, babe?'

'Oh, you know, fine.' I sigh. 'Could do with getting over this crush, but other than that, just peachy!'

Em tuts at me like I've said the wrong thing.

'What? Look at him! Stella said herself that this "always happens".'

'I think it's you who needs to look at him, Jessie. He doesn't exactly look thrilled about the being chatted up thing, does he? So what if it happens all the time.'

'But—'

'Anyway, how *did* you two get on at paddleboarding?' she asks.

And I can't help but break into a smile.

'Knew it.' Em grins. 'Spill.'

'He's such a good listener, and he's got this kind of intensity to him when he's concentrating on something, and I felt like I could open up to him, but then he's also got this really light, fun side and he was teasing me about some stuff and I ended up joining in because it felt like we had this connection.' I pause to take a breath, notice that Emerald has clasped her hands together in excitement. 'But obviously not that kind of connection,' I qualify.

'Nope, don't you dare. I know you're about to say that you don't stand a chance and I do not want to hear it, Jessie. That's a whole heap of BS and also, so unhelpful to think of yourself in that way. So you can stop it. All right?'

'You're quite bossy when you want to be.'

'It's great, isn't it? Yikes, looks like Stella's sent Croissants packing.'

We watch as the influencer scuttles off with her tail between her legs, Stella turning to talk to Luke now. They're not that far away but not close enough for us to hear what they're saying.

Huge sharing plates of delicious-looking things are brought to the table and Em and I hungrily fill our plates, loading Stella's too.

95

I track my gaze back to the siblings and spot that Stella's waving at me, trying to get my attention. Then when she catches my eye she points dramatically to another section of the table, pumping her eyebrows up and down as she does so. Luke and I follow her gaze and I see that she's pointing out some dude in a polo shirt and chinos.

'What's she doing?' I ask.

'OMG, that's Perry Carver,' says Em.

'Who?'

'The footballer we pretended you fancy!' Em sounds exasperated. 'Look like you know what she's on about!'

'Oh god,' I whisper, pumping my brows right back because that's all I can think of in response. I watch Luke's gaze settle on the footballer, and then come back to me to see my response. Then he does this little nod thing, like he's understood something. Like he thinks I fancy someone else. OH GOD. I'd race over but I can't because he's with Stella and so . . . how did this get so complicated already? It's the first full day here! Also, there's obviously no point because it's not like I've lost my chance with Luke. I know Em means well but let's face it, I was never in with a chance. The crush, my feelings. They are not mutual.

I watch as Luke says something to Stella and then walks off, leaving me longing to spend more time in his company. I have to stop myself from getting up and going after him. Which is ridiculous, I know. But I just get the feeling that I have somehow been responsible for him leaving.

'There's something up with that kid,' Stella says when she gets back and starts tucking into her food.

'Oh?' says Em.

'He's keeping something from me, I can tell. I wonder if it's the move back here. His tennis career ended a few years ago now but I wonder if moving back to the UK has brought it all back for him. You know, like it's definitely not happening now?'

'Could be,' I say, feeling bad that I know about the ADHD

96

diagnosis, which I'm guessing is what's really on his mind. 'You should try and get some proper time with him, Stell, while we're here.'

'I will. Somewhere Croissants can't find us. When I went over just now she introduced herself to me as a taste-maker, you guys,' Stella says, pulling a face. 'What a twat.'

Chapter 9

By Sunday morning I'm starting to feel like I truly exist in this blissful spa world. I'm vaguely concerned that I'm becoming a total lush. I've even grown used to being handed refreshing drinks after a swim and warm hand towels after a long walk around the hotel's grounds. It's so lovely here and I know it's not the real world, but I am v much appreciating a break from all that.

I'm the first to wake up, so I slip a hotel robe around myself and go to investigate.

I can see Stella's got her bedroom light on so I knock on her door and potter in. She's still in bed, her hair wrapped up in a silk scarf on top of her head.

'Come in.' She pats the bed and I tuck myself in next to her. 'I'm just texting Fran.'

'Oh, let me give you some space then,' I say.

'Don't go!' she says, grabbing my arm and pulling me back. 'I'm literally reminding her to add some collagen powder to our next beauty subscription order.'

'You're so grown up,' I point out. 'Like beauty subscriptions, collagen . . . '

'I like that those are the things you think make me a grown-up, rather than, I don't know, a mortgage.'

'Well, that too,' I add, burrowing up alongside her. 'Stell, can I ask you a question?'

'Always.'

'When you first met, how did Fran make you feel?'

'Alive,' Stella says, instantly. 'She was like my own personal oxygen source. Not in a creepy I-can't-breathe-without-you way, but in a headrushy, I-feel-amazing-around-you way. Does that make sense?'

'Yes.' I sigh dreamily. 'So did you just know that she was the one for you?'

'I'm a bit too pragmatic to believe in The One. I feel like that's way too much pressure, particularly when you start dating someone. How can we ever know we've found "the one" when we haven't met all the humans on the planet? But I do believe in deep connections and I felt that with Fran. Plus, you know, I fancied her so much I could barely string a sentence together when we first met.'

I laugh at this. 'You got tongue-tied? I cannot imagine that!'

'It was so bad. The shite I was spouting, Jessie, I'm genuinely surprised she ever agreed to a second date. Why d'you ask?'

I stretch my legs out under the duvet. 'Just curious really. I've not experienced that before.'

(Until now.)

'There's time for all of that still.' Stella squeezes my hand reassuringly. 'You definitely seem like you're in a good place now, Jessie.'

'I do?'

'Yes! Very . . . zesty!'

'Zesty?' I laugh.

'You've got this joie de vivre going on and I know it's amazing here, but it can't just be this hotel. And obviously my sparkling company.' She grins. 'Don't tell Em I said this, but it does seem to me like you're maybe starting a new chapter.'

I pretend to gasp. 'Zodiac Girlie's finally got you,' I tease.

'It has not,' she insists. 'You know what I mean.'

'I do, Stell. I think finally kicking Otis out of my flat has made a huge difference too. I feel a lot lighter about that whole thing now, and that's all thanks to you.'

'You know how much I love to take credit for things but honestly, that was all you. I just helped you give him that final little shove.'

'Room for a third?' Em peers around the door.

Stella and I scooch up so Em can fit in too.

'Look, we've made a little Jessie sandwich,' Em observes.

'This reminds me of Sundays when we lived together in the flat at uni,' I say happily.

'*Friends* re-runs and a fry-up.' Stella nods.

'Jessie was always cooking those veggie sausages that smelt revolting,' Em chips in.

'Oi!' I laugh. 'You managed to eat enough of them.'

'That's because Emerald cannot cook for shit,' Stella points out.

'I'm actually much better now, guys.' Em beams proudly. 'I learned how to make dhal on a yoga retreat in India and I am totally excellent at it.'

'Isn't dhal just lentils?' Stella asks.

Em shakes her head knowingly. 'There's so much more to it. You have to cook the spices just right, and make this thing called a *tarka*. I am going to cook it for you one day, babes. Anyway, I remember that after watching *Friends* Jess would insist that we all go to the library on Sunday afternoons because she was worried that we weren't doing enough studying.'

'It's basically down to me that you guys got your degrees.'

'Totally,' agrees Em. 'So shall we do classic Sunday vibes today?'

'Vibes.' Stella rolls her eyes. 'But yes. We could even order room service tonight?'

'I mean, it has been a huge faff getting dressed for dinner these past two nights.' I grin.

'I know, so much effort.' Em laughs. 'I'm totally game for that.

I was thinking about trying out the canyoning course today.'

'What's that?' I yawn.

'I don't know.' She shrugs. 'Climbing up stuff with ropes? I think there's water involved?'

'Hmm. I found paddleboarding a struggle so I'm afraid it's a pass from me.'

'But Luke's leading the course.' Em winks at me.

I turn to give her a stern look.

'Why d'you say it like that?' Stella asks.

My look turns frantic.

'Because he's your bro,' Emerald fibs seamlessly, her angel face belying her ulterior motives. 'And you were literally saying last night that you want to spend time with him.'

'Very true,' Stella conceded. 'God, I love that we're finally living in the same place for the first time in years. Will you sign me up, too, Em?'

'Sure. You coming, Jess?' She pumps her eyebrows at me.

I glare at her. 'It all sounds a bit too adventurous. And besides, you guys reminded me about going to the library on a Sunday. There's one here at Gurnard Cove which I still haven't checked out—'

'A travesty!' Stella warbles in mock dismay.

'So I'm going to go and curl up with a good book,' I press on, ignoring her. 'We've been so busy I haven't had a chance to get any reading done yet.'

'That's because Emerald keeps forcing us to do things,' Stella points out.

'Which is very sweet,' I say, not wanting to offend Em.

'So Stell and I are canyoning, Jessie's being a premium geek, and we'll all reconvene back here for a sofa supper?'

'Perfect! Except for the geek bit,' I say, getting up to leave.

'Wait!' shouts Em. 'Quick Zodiac Girlie update before you go.'

I open up the app and show her my Stars in Brief.

Turn your face to the truth.

'I got "Wealth comes from within".' Stella shrugs, while Em nods knowingly.

Oh my god, the library! It is the stuff that dreams are made of. The room is lit by a mahogany glow from well-placed table lamps, the low thrum of silence filling the room. There are cosy reading nooks as far as the eye can see, each with its own sidetable stocked with old-fashioned board games. And the smell! That comforting scent of well-thumbed books plus a serious dose of arôme de luxury hotel. I breathe in and allow myself a brief fantasy that one day, I'll be so successful that I will have a library just like this in my own home. Imagine.

As for the actual books, there are so many that I almost don't know where to start. Almost. Ten minutes in and I've flopped happily onto a high-backed leather chair with a tower of tomes balancing on the table next to me.

I take care to be quiet, not wanting to disturb any other book-worms getting their library fix, but it quickly becomes clear that I'm alone in here. I guess most of the guests are out doing more adventurous things, like Em and Stella, or making the most of the beautiful weather, or at the spa.

Well, this feels heavenly to me.

'Can I offer you a drink?' A member of staff appears, and I wonder if they've been hiding between the bookshelves this entire time.

'Yes please!' I reply, opting for a mint tea and settling in to read. I flick through the newspaper first, then get started on a crime novel I've been itching to read and then, because my brain wants a little break from all the murdering, I crack open a book on art history, deciding that it would be very cultured of me to expand my mind while at Gurnard Cove.

I'm several chapters in and fully versed on prehistoric cave paintings when I pause for a sip of mint tea and close my eyes, just for a second.

'Are you asleep?' comes a voice from outside my subconscious.

'No!' I say, jolting myself awake and rubbing my eyes. 'Well, maybe.'

A woman comes into focus in front of me.

Well, not any old woman. Dita Ortiz, Hollywood superstar.

'Oh my word,' I whisper, wondering if I should curtsey or, like, avert my gaze? I get up then, unsure what I'm doing, and immediately sit back down. Shouldn't she be followed by paparazzi and flashing lights at all times?

Dita Ortiz has a book tucked under her arm and is giving me a look.

'I'm so sorry,' I say. 'Would you like this seat?' I scramble to get up again, remembering how Lycra Leon had been summoned to her suite to provide his regime of doom direct to Dita. That must be it. I'm in her seat. I must move!

'No, no.' She chuckles. 'Please sit.'

I freeze on the spot, still half asleep after dropping off in my pursuit of knowledge, which leaves me in a weird semi-standing pose, hovering above my chair.

'Sit,' Dita instructs more firmly.

I do as I'm told. And even though I have no clue as to why Dita Ortiz is engaging little old me in conversation, I pause to take her in. She's immaculate. Rosebud lips, dark bushy brows and kohl-lined eyes. She looks every inch a natural, if incredibly beautiful, woman in her fifties. Dita's been a screen siren for decades and I can totally see why.

'I am alone,' she says, eyes dancing furtively from left to right. This is not strictly accurate, because another hotel guest is quietly reading in another corner of the room now. And besides, for the life of me I can't figure out why she's telling me this. Does Dita think we're in a spy movie and this is our chance to have a discussion away from the prying eyes of the FBI or similar? I glance around in case there are hidden cameras.

'But now I find you,' she says, eyes twinkling. Okay, not a

spy movie. She thinks we're in a romcom. This is a tragic turn of events. Poor Dita Ortiz must be suffering from some kind of syndrome. Maybe she's acted in so many films that she now believes her entire life is being played out on camera?

She's looking at me expectantly.

'Here I am,' I say, flummoxed.

'I see your pile of crime books. My favourite. So now we talk.'

She likes crime fiction too?

'Oh great! Have you read this one? It's by a not-so-well-known author but really doesn't get the recognition it deserves.' I smile, handing over the book. 'And actually, this one's great too. The twist at the end? I did not see it coming.'

'You know the genre,' Dita says approvingly. 'I am very keen to star in a crime thriller myself, but I am always cast as the siren.'

This is baffling, because Dita seems like the kind of woman who gets what she wants.

'You would be amazing as the lead in this one,' I say, hopping up and pulling another off the shelf.

'I will read it,' Dita says. 'You are very helpful.'

'Oh, thank you!'

'I am Spanish and German. A woman of Europe. In Europe, we talk to people, we communicate. In England, no one talks. I got on your tube the other day.'

'My *tube*?'

'Your underground tube.'

'Oh! *The* tube. In London?' Not *my* tube, whatever that might be. The idea of Dita Ortiz riding the Piccadilly line is so bizarre I find myself chuckling quietly.

'Sí, sí. And no one said a thing, to anyone! Even people travelling together spoke in hushed voices. It's bizarre, no?'

'Well, I guess . . . ' I hedge.

'It *is* bizarre,' she insists, and it is very clear that I must agree with her immediately.

'Yes, sorry about, um, us.' Why am I apologising to Dita Ortiz

104

on behalf of all British people for our reserved nature? What is *happening* today?

'You know . . . ' Dita says, now beckoning me over to her own corner of the library with her new collection of crime novels. I scramble to pick up all my books, balance the mint tea on top, and hurry after her. 'I have been here all weekend and not one person, apart from hotel staff, has engaged me in proper conversation. They only want selfies! I do the selfies and hope, maybe this time, some interesting conversation will follow. What is your name?'

'Jessica,' I supply dutifully.

'Jessica,' she repeats, the J sounding like a Y in her rich Spanish accent. 'Do you think some interesting conversation has followed?'

'I'm going for no?'

'Exactly right,' she says, wide-eyed, as she folds herself elegantly into a chair and beckons for me to do the same. 'It's rude, no?'

'Well, erm, it might be because you're so very famous?' And also a terrifying powerhouse of a woman, I don't add.

'It's rude.'

'No, yes, sorry, you're absolutely right.'

Don't argue with Dita, Jess!

'So today I find you, asleep in front of your book, and I think, here is a woman I will make conversation with. Now, continue.'

Continue? Dita Ortiz wants me to make conversation outside of the realm of crime fiction. Right, let's think.

I clear my throat. 'Did you know that the earliest example of figurative art can be traced back to a cave drawing of three pigs in Indonesia?' I heave open the book and hold up a picture for her to admire.

Dita takes the book from my hand and throws it on the floor.

I gasp. Poor book. I reach to pick it up, give it a reassuring pat and put it back on my stack.

'No,' she says. 'This book, on the other hand, is interesting.' Then she hands me a hardback with a crude drawing of a penis on the front. 'It's all about sex. You will like it.'

I mean, I'm not sure that I will but we have definitely moved beyond the point where I dare to disagree with Dita.

'Thank you so much,' I whimper, sliding it to the bottom of my pile for decency's sake.

Dita is watching me closely, which is unnerving. 'You know, Yessica, you remind me of my daughter.'

'I do?'

'She is also a terrible prude.'

Wow. I can't decide if I'm captivated by this woman or quite offended.

'I'm not sure I'm a prude, per se,' I suggest, clean forgetting about my decision not to disagree with Dita. I look at her now and discover that she is currently taking a small bell out of her handbag. She rings it once. A member of staff arrives immediately.

'We will drink two Barbadillo Reliquia,' Dita instructs. They scurry off.

'This bell comes everywhere with me,' she explains. 'I find that no matter where I am in the world, if I ring it, someone will turn up to bring me things.'

I can't say I'm surprised by this. 'That sounds . . . very useful.'

'Now, where was I? Ah yes, the problem with my daughter Conchita. She did not live up to her full potential.'

'I'm sorry to hear that,' I say. 'But maybe there's still time? What is she doing now?'

'She is dead.'

'Oh my gosh! I'm so sorry, Dita. That is tragic.'

'Well, dead to me,' Dita concedes as our drinks arrive.

'Oh. That's very sad, still.'

'Well, not really dead to me,' Dita continues. 'We see each other very often and I love her fiercely. But her behaviour can be disappointing.'

I suppose it should come as no surprise that a woman who has made a career out of drama is, in fact, deeply dramatic. Dita takes a sip of her drink and I give mine a sniff, unsure what she

106

ordered because I was flummoxed by all the Spanish-sounding words. The liquid is thick, the colour of cinnamon and spice. I take a sniff. Ooh, sherry! Sometimes Mum will suggest a 'cheeky sherry' before a game of cards. In fact I'd probably be round at Mum and Dad's right now if it weren't for this spa break, or their massive world adventure.

'Drink,' Dita orders, and I note she's already finished hers.

I do as I'm told, trying not to wince at the taste and the time of day. It's not even lunch! Again!

'Good. Now, tell me more about your life, Yessica.'

'Oh, okay! Well, I'm a journalist, sort of,' I begin. 'I've worked on a regional newspaper in Carpston.'

'Craps Town?'

'*Carpston*,' I try to enunciate. 'And I'm on holiday with my two best friends. We met at uni and we hardly ever get to see each other now, because we all live in different places. Also Em and Stella have really impressive jobs, which mean they're both super busy and Em's always all over the place with her work.'

'And what is your ambition?' Dita asks, ringing the bell again.

'Oof,' I say, struggling to put the words together.

'You always dreamed of being a journalist?' she presses.

'Well . . . no, actually. When I was younger I assumed I would work with books somehow. Maybe even owning a bookshop one day.'

'Ah yes, like in *Notting Hill*. Very British.'

'Oh I love that film!'

'Humph,' Dita says, tilting her head to one side. She looks displeased. Then, very slowly and with a distinct eyeroll, she says: 'Yulia Roberts.'

'Julia Roberts?' I whisper. 'You don't like her?'

'It is a long story.' She shrugs.

I am desperate for Dita to spill the tea on whatever kicked off between her and Julia. 'Did she get a part you wanted?'

'Of course not!'

'Did she say something about you in the press, then?' I ask.

'She probably talks about me plenty, many people do. No, this is about Yulia and Hugh.'

'Hugh *Grant*?' I squeak. But just when I'm about to press for more details, Dita cuts me off.

'So, continue. Why don't you own a bookshop if this is your dream?'

'Well, it just hasn't been that simple. I suppose the problem is that I needed a stable job when I finished uni for various reasons – mostly I wanted to be close to my parents – and I knew that if I moved back to Carpston I might be able to save enough money for a mortgage by the time I turned thirty if I really worked at it. And when I got home there was an internship going.'

'At this Craps Town newspaper?'

'*Carpston*, yes. And I worked my way up the ladder there. I do still get my book fix by volunteering at the local charity bookshop, and I once tried to persuade my annoying editor to let me review books for the paper, but that's another story. It's funny, I have thought more about owning a bookshop these past few days than I have in ages.'

Dita considers this, then says: 'And you have a partner at home?'

I shake my head and pull a face. 'There's an ex-boyfriend. He's only just moved out of my flat even though we broke up months ago.'

At least, I hope he's moved out.

'Tsk.'

'I know, it's ridiculous. My friend Em says I have terrible taste in men.'

'She is right?'

'Looking back, none of them have been great.'

'You go for the wrong type?'

'I thought I went for the right type! I guess I gravitate towards sensible men with good prospects. But that doesn't seem to be

108

working out for me. I'm actually thinking about cleansing men from my life for a while, just like Gurnard Cove's whole life cleanse ethos. You know, just give myself a break. Hit refresh and all that.'

Dita starts to laugh and it soon becomes clear that she can't stop. The next thing I know she's howling with laughter. I'm not sure why, but I wait patiently for her to stop, necking my second sherry in the interim.

'Aye, aye, aye.' She chuckles. 'What nonsense. You know, Yessica, I once fell into the same trap as you.'

'You did?' And also, *what trap?*

'In my twenties, I seemed to bounce from one bad decision to another when it came to lovers. What felt right at the time was wrong. You know when your judgement is clouded by passion?'

She looks expectantly at me, and I have to explain that I have never dated anyone in a cloud of passion. 'I've never felt like that before.'

'This is so tragically sad for you.' Dita frowns. 'A woman needs passion, Yessica.'

I think about Luke and then mentally slap myself about the chops.

'But weren't you saying that passion was the problem in your twenties?'

'I thought it was! So I stopped dating. I was in the middle of one of my hot girl summers, in Paris on location, and I did not date one single person. Not even Clooney and especially not DiCaprio.'

I gasp again. Today's trip to the library is *way* juicier than I thought it would be.

'Instead, I replaced sex with painting.'

'That doesn't sound so bad. Isn't painting meant to be very therapeutic?'

'Yessica, I sucked at painting. I spent a whole summer in Paris cooped up in my apartment, painting very bad pictures of bowls of fruit. What a waste! My body was the best it had ever been and I squandered it.'

'It sounds like you're being very hard on yourself,' I suggest.

'No. Want to hear the worst of it? I got arrested!'

'For painting?'

'Yes! Well, sort of. I started stealing the paints, Yessica, and I got caught. Thankfully I was able to charm the police and I only spent an hour or so in the cell. Now, do you understand my cautionary tale?'

'Absolutely.' I nod, totally engrossed. 'Do not steal.'

'No!' Dita cackles. 'Not that. Do not ever cleanse passion from your life. It is essential, like breathing. Without it, you will end up the owner of many bad paintings and a criminal record, Yessica. I was trying to find passion in the painting, but it was not enough. And then I tried to find passion in stealing. But I should have just enjoyed the passion I already had, inside me. I should not have denied it to myself. For myself.'

'Wow,' I reply. 'That's very wise. Thank you for the advice.'

'I can see that you are not taking it on board,' Dita says, watching me. 'But one day, you will realise that life should be full, and rich. It should be about encouraging experiences, not denying yourself. Sí?'

'Sí.' I nod obediently. 'Absolutely, yes.'

'Good.' Dita also nods. 'Now we are friends and we will go to lunch.'

'And *that* is how I ended up having Sunday lunch with a Hollywood superstar,' I tell Em and Stella later as they perch, agog, on the edge of a wooden bench in the sauna.

'Stuff like this never happens to us!' Stella gawps. 'Well, except you, Em. You're always hanging out with celebrities. Didn't you say something about a pop star the other day?'

'Yes, you know Tina, the K-pop star? She's asked me to design her jewellery for her next world tour. But Dita Ortiz? She's acting royalty,' Em says, eyes wide. 'It's so exciting, Jessie! What did she eat? How does she maintain those cheekbones? And what is it really like at the Oscars?'

'Funnily enough I did not get round to asking about her specific cheekbone regime.' I chuckle, shifting on the boiling hot bench. 'But she ordered grilled fish and steamed vegetables, which was not on the menu, and then spent a long time telling me about how annoying billionaires are, as if I could totally relate. She thinks Bezos's yacht is tacky.'

'Oh my god, this is too good.' Stella leans in.

We're all sweating now. When I got back from lunch I found the girls semi-paralysed on the sofas after canyoning. 'Everything hurts!' wailed Em. 'I can't chuffing move,' said Stella. Not wanting them to develop an injury after all the scrambling around, I messaged Santi, my concierge, for advice. That's just how I roll these days. She suggested some time in the sauna would help to soothe their tired muscles, so here we are, like three jacket potatoes in a microwave.

'So you two are, like, besties now?' Em asks.

'Ha ha! Besties is a stretch but Dita did announce that we're friends and I definitely wasn't in a position to argue. It's mad, isn't it?'

'You'll be jetting off to Hollywood next,' says Stella before mopping her brow. 'Look at me, disgustingly sweaty but a lot less achy, thanks to you, Jess. You're always so good at looking after us.'

'Isn't she?' Em pats me with a hot hand. 'Our 'lil mum, always reminding us to hydrate after a night out.'

'And checking we get home safe,' Stella adds.

'Remember when we lived together and you'd insist that we brush our teeth and remove at least some of our make-up before bed?'

'And then make us breakfast the next day.'

'And don't forget the vitamins!'

'Oh yes, the vitamins!' Stella is beaming now. 'I especially like it when you remind us to take our vitamin D through the winter months. It makes me feel loved.'

'I know, what would you do without me?' I grin. It's all true but I can't help but feel like I've become a smidge, well, boring. Having lunch with a woman who has been proposed to on a Gulfstream twice, by two separate people, confirmed what I already knew before I came on this trip. It's high time I started enjoying life. Spending the whole lunch listening to mind-blowing stories and coming up with very few of my own in riposte was definitely motivating.

But also, when *did* I become the mother of the group?

'Oh Jessie! You look sad, please don't be sad. We're only teasing you just the tiniest bit and your nurturing nature is one of the most beautiful things about you.'

Suddenly I have two sticky pairs of arms around me. Then Stella grabs my cheeks and peers into my face.

'Emerald, you've upset Jess,' she says crossly.

'I have not! You started it,' Em retorts.

'Did not.'

'There will be no fighting at this luxury spa hotel,' I insist.

'I personally love that you look after us, Jess. I would not be without your messages about vitamins.'

'Absolutely,' Em agrees, pulling her beachy blonde waves up into a wet bun on the top of her head.

'You still look sad.' Stella still has my face in her hands so the whole interrogation feels a bit intense. Plus my cheeks are squished forward so my voice comes out funny.

'I'b jus won-er-ib,' I say.

Stella lets go of my face and motions for me to continue.

'Thanks,' I say, massaging my cheeks. 'I'm just wondering when this happened. Was I always like this?'

Stella and Emerald exchange looks.

'What?'

'Well,' begins Stella carefully, 'you definitely seemed more laissez-faire in first year.'

Em nods. 'Yeah. We just put it down to your course, and how in second year things got much harder, work wise, so we figured you wanted to buckle down.'

'You started coming out less and staying in more, and all power to you. You did bloody well. And that seems about the time that you also started being our little mother hen, gathering us in and taking us under your wing.'

'Yes! I definitely felt like the sloppier I got, the more measured you were.'

'You weren't sloppy, Em,' I say, defensive on her behalf.

'Jessie, I once had a three-way with two members of university staff. And it was, like, mid-morning. After a lecture. We weren't even drunk or high.'

Stella snorts at this memory.

'See!' I say. 'This is exactly what I mean. You guys always have amazing stories to tell and I have nothing.'

'But babes, we are different personalities, right? You're just not a three-way kind of gal. You like—'

'Mediocre sex with melancholy greengrocers?' Stella butts in.

'I was going to say *stability*,' Em says pointedly. 'That's just who you are, Jessie. And to be honest, the three-way was kind of lame. Just an awful lot of waiting around tbh. I would not recommend.'

I laugh at this, while a bead of sweat rolls down my forehead. 'Well, not anymore, guys. I really feel like I'm ready to make some changes.'

'Get it, girl,' says Em.

'How come?' Stella asks.

'Well, my parents have sold the family home for a start.'

'What?' screeches Em.

'This is major news!' Stella whistles. 'Pandy love that place.'

I chuckle fondly at her nickname for my parents, Pamela and Andy.

'Why are you only just telling us?'

'Em, we've been here two days and we have not stopped talking.

There's been a lot to cover! Anyway, wait until you hear this,' I say. 'They've sold up and gone on a grown-up gap year, so they're travelling the world for the next twelve months. Apparently, my Auntie Trish had got them both worried about sniper's alley—'

'Wait, what's sniper's alley?' Em interjects.

'Dad says that Auntie Trish has been in a total tizz about their age. Apparently, she told Mum that now they're in their mid-sixties, they're all basically sitting ducks, just waiting to be shot down by some horrific medical condition or other.'

'Jeez.' Stella exhales.

'Pandy are in great health but it obviously spooked Mum. The next thing I know there's a For Sale sign outside the house and they'd booked first-class flights to Australia.'

'First class!' Stella whistles. 'Love that for them.'

'I know. Dad was thrilled because where I grew up has become the trendy part of town since "back in his day", so they did really well on the sale. I'm so pleased for them. They worked so hard all their lives for me and James. They deserve this.'

Em's face darkens and Stella looks decidedly awkward at the mention of my errant older brother, who had a huge falling-out with Mum and Dad years ago. They were estranged for a long while and when he cut all ties, Mum took it particularly badly. It was all pretty awful, and one of the main reasons I moved back to Carpston after uni was to be there for them.

'How is James?' asks Stella.

'Oh fine. A bit less of a crap son now, he's been getting in touch with the folks more. Them going away just proves that Mum and Dad are in really good places now. The other day they sent me a picture of Dad snuggling this cute little marsupial in Western Aus and it literally looked like it was smiling.'

'Good for Pandy. It must have been tough for you though, Jessie. Saying goodbye to the family home and your folks all in one go.'

My chin wobbles the tiniest bit, because it *was* tough and it all happened so quickly. One minute I was going round to theirs for our weekly Sunday sherry and the next, they were off.

'I miss them like crazy but the fact that they're doing this fills me with so much joy.'

'All the more reason to enjoy this adventure of ours.' Em grins.

'Can we do that by getting out of this sauna?' Stella puffs. 'It's been hours.'

'It's been ten minutes, babes,' Em says, rolling her eyes.

Chapter 10

Later, we scatter on loungers by the indoor pool and I think on what my friends said. They're right. Back when we first met, I was definitely more carefree. Not in an oh-she's-totally-changed type of way, but certainly less worried about stuff. More relaxed. Em was right when she assumed that I came back for second year ready to focus on my studies. With that and the stuff going on with James, I *did* feel like I ought to be the child who could focus on getting good grades and making my parents proud. It's also, I realise, the summer when Stella's mum had her relapse. When she started drinking again because I facilitated her. And I saw the devastation and destruction it caused Stella and her family. How Luke left the country to escape from it all. How Stella was back to square one, nursing the mother who should have been caring for her.

I saw how fragile life could be, how easily the status quo could turn, and it just made sense to focus on things like solid careers and saving for houses and dating sensible men. With families proving so tricky, I sought out equilibrium and stability elsewhere. I would get a 'proper' job rather than moon after some flighty dream of being a bookshop owner. I would head back home to be close to my parents. It's like I've needed to prove that I can make good decisions as a result of that very, very bad one. And if Stella's mum couldn't look after her, because of what I did, then I sure as heck would be the one to look after my friends.

The fact is, this has been playing on my mind for years now. I have to tell Stella the truth about what happened and now that we're finally together, I sense that now is my chance.

'Stell?' I say, a bag of nerves as the three of us walk back to our suite together.

'Jessie,' she replies.

'Can we talk?'

'Sure,' she says, plonking herself down on a bench. Em and I sit down either side of her.

'Okay, I did a really, really bad thing back at uni,' I say, shakily looking at my best friends. 'I've been carrying it around ever since and I realise that the guilt's going to eat me alive if I don't face up to it, head on.'

'Knew I brought these for a reason,' Em says, pulling some mini bottles of champagne out of her bag. 'Got them from our minibar,' she explains as she opens all three and hands them out. 'Do continue. And Jessie, whatever you have to say, we're here for you okay?'

I accept my drink and give her a watery smile.

'A confessional!' Stella looks thrilled. 'Did you rack up a huge debt in unreturned library books? Or, let me guess, did you actually stay up past midnight the night before an exam one time?'

'Stell, come on now.' Emerald has a mock frown on her face. 'Maybe Jessie was running some kind of black market dissertation writing service the whole time, making a criminal fortune off the students who couldn't be arsed to write their own?'

'I'm being serious!' I protest while they attempt to rearrange their faces and motion for me to continue. 'It's about your mum, Stell.' I wobble. 'It's . . . it's *my* fault that she's been struggling with alcohol for all these years.'

Stella snorts, which I was not expecting. 'How on earth is it your fault?'

I take a deep breath, and then it all comes tumbling out.

'Remember before the start of second year when we moved into our flat together?'

'Oh yes, I had those dreadful cowboy boots that I insisted on wearing with everything.'

'I actually loved those,' Em says charitably. 'They were so . . . busy.'

'They had pictures of horses' heads stitched into the sides,' Stella recalls.

Em starts giggling. 'Yes! And wasn't there a slogan, too?'

'Giddy up,' honks Stella.

We're veering drastically off topic. I give my friends a look.

'Oh sorry, you were telling me how it's your fault that my mum is an alcoholic, which is definitely a normal and sensible thing for a person to think. Do continue,' Stella says, just shy of rolling her eyes.

'Stella, *please*,' I say, willing her to take this seriously. 'It *is* my fault. Your mum was sober when we met, remember? She'd battled so hard to get herself clean and all first year you were so happy about it.'

Stella's face clouds over and I feel a stab of pain for putting her through this. She never likes to dwell on Jacqui. Is it selfish of me for bringing her up? Something inside me insists that I have to tell my friend the truth, that she deserves to know, even though I feel horrible for confronting it.

'And then she fell spectacularly off the wagon again at the start of second year. Yes, I remember, Jess,' she says. 'I found her. At home, in a mess, after a three-day bender.'

'Because she'd come round to our flat,' I explain. 'You were both out. I'd only met your mum once before that, when we packed up after first year. This time she knocked on the door and she was so sweet and friendly and I didn't *think*, Stell.'

'What do you mean?'

'She asked to borrow some money,' I say, the shame of it making me feel sick. 'She said she'd come into town to pick up a housewarming gift for you, but she'd forgotten her purse. She'd left it at home. I remember her saying "silly me!" But she'd come all the way in and didn't want to waste the journey and could I lend her some money and I did it, Stell. I did it.' I hold my head in my hands as the painful memories come flooding back.

'I remember apologising because I only had a tenner on me and I wasn't sure if that was enough. And I remember that she didn't say anything after that, she just took the money and hurried off. And then three days later, when you came back from your mum's, I just knew. I started it up again. It was my fault, Stella. And I am so, so sorry. All the rubbish you have been through since . . .'

I run out of words, furiously blinking back the tears that are pooling in my eyes as I look down at my lap, too ashamed to meet Stella's gaze. This could be it, I realise. Our friendship could be over. She has every right to hate me for what I did. The thought of losing my best friend makes me feel hollow and I end up clinging on to the bench to steady myself.

There's silence.

An excruciatingly long silence.

Two fellow hotel guests stroll serenely by in towelling robes, talking excitedly about the vitamin drips they're off to try. My eyes track down to the little bottle in my hand, a stark reminder of what I did, before I look over at Stella.

Her eyes are like saucers, her mouth hanging open.

She looks from me to Emerald and back again.

And then.

'AH HA HAAAAAAAAAAAAAAAAAAAAAAAAA,' she splutters. It's a guttural noise that seems to come right up from her core. 'OH MY GOD. I'm sorry, I . . . Wait, no. I can't speak.'

She holds her hands up to her face and I watch in astonishment as her shoulders start to shake.

Is she *laughing*?

She can't be. I'm not sure quite what reaction I was expecting, but it was definitely going to be anger-adjacent. And here she is slapping her hand down on her knees so hard some fizz bubbles out of her bottle.

She's delirious. She's so utterly cross that she's having one of those inappropriate laughter moments, you know, when you get the giggles at the world's worst time.

Em and I exchange looks.

I wait nervously for Stella to calm down and then read me the riot act.

'HA HA HA.' She reaches out and grabs my hand. 'Oh, JESS! I love you and sorry, I shouldn't be laughing, but you really have outdone yourself this time.'

'Stell, I know it's a lot to take in. And I really am so incredibly sorry. If I could travel back in time and have a word with my past self, I would tell her not to be so completely foolish. I wish I could so much. All the heartache . . . ' I clam up, tears threatening to spill again but it's not for me to do the crying now. It's not my moment. I bite down on my lip and wait.

Stella finally stops howling.

'Ooh!' She clutches her belly. 'I haven't laughed that hard in ages.'

She takes a long sip of her drink and then fixes me with a firm stare.

Here it comes.

'Jessica, do you seriously think you are responsible for Jacqui's problems?'

I shrug.

'Christ on a bike, mate. You're not. Tenner or no tenner, it's not your fault. Mum would have found that money from somewhere else if she hadn't got it from you. When she's on a mission, there's no stopping her. I remember that time incredibly well, because you're right, she'd been doing so well before that. Even now I keep notes in my diary on her sobriety, or lack thereof. And it wasn't you who started that spiral. She'd been drinking for a few *weeks* before that weekend bender. I never said anything at the time because I was so bitterly disappointed, and I wanted uni to be an escape from it all. I didn't want to be talking about my messy mother again. So I said nothing. Jess,' she says, squeezing my hand and fixing me with her gaze, 'you are not to blame.'

I struggle to process this.

'Are you sure?' I whisper, voice cracking. 'You're not just saying that? Because, Stell, I hate so much that that happened. I've been so mad with myself . . .'

Stella's demeanour has gone from sheer mirth to one of concern and sympathy.

'Oh Jess,' she says. 'I can't believe you've been carrying this around this whole time. Why didn't you say anything?'

'I was scared I'd lose you.' I sniff. 'I know I should have been honest. I've thought about it a lot and I guess I was just a kid, so I was still learning maybe? Not that that is *any* excuse. But I'd only met you two the year before and I'd never had such brilliant friends before. I was *terrified* of messing it up. And then when I did get the clarity to understand that I should have said something, it felt like too long ago, and your mum was clean again, and I didn't want to drag up bad memories for you. I should have spoken about it ages ago but I've been too much of a chicken and I am so sorry, Stella.'

Em swipes a tear from her eye and takes another swig of champagne.

'Oh love,' Stella says. 'It can't have helped that I literally never spoke about my mum's problems, can it? No wonder you didn't want to say anything. But listen, even if your money had led to her falling off the wagon again – and it didn't – it still wouldn't be your fault. You are not accountable for anyone else's decisions, let alone my mum's. Okay?'

I nod, feeling so grateful for her generosity in this moment.

Stella chuckles when she's satisfied that I've absorbed her words.

'Jeez, talk about dramatic.'

Em nods. 'Carrying guilt around is literally so bad for the chakras, babes.' She frowns, eyeing me up. 'Well done, you, for getting it all out there. I can already see your aura changing.'

'Not that again.' I smile.

'Much lighter. So what caused the big reveal? Unless, wait.' Em pauses, looking thrilled. 'It's totally your Saturn Return, Jessie. You're taking stock and re-evaluating life. These moments of clarity are so powerful for your transformation, babes.'

'My app did say I should "turn my face to the truth" today,' I concede.

Stella yawns. 'Good for you. But the only thing I want to turn my face to is a large bowl of pasta.'

We head back in our suite and, fresh from the shower, I take charge of the room service menu feeling a hundred per cent lighter.

'Good news, Stell,' I call through to her bedroom. 'There's an entire pasta section! And this one sounds amazing. Listen, pasta alla ruoto; piping hot linguine served inside a cheese wheel, which is then scraped to coat the pasta in cheese.'

'Hell yes,' Stella replies. 'And garlic bread? And olives? Shall we just have an Italian feast and have done with it?'

'And maybe a green salad, just for a bit of health?' I offer, which weirdly no one responds to.

There's a knock on the door five minutes after I call the order through.

'Can't be food already, can it?' I mutter, quickly ditching my post-shower robe and pulling on joggers and a jumper because I already know that the others aren't going to be answering the door.

I pad through to the hallway and sling the door open ready to embrace the food.

'Jess!' says Luke, a big smile breaking out on his face when he sees me.

'Hey,' I squeak, suddenly regretting the fact that I just

moisturised the crap out of my face and must be shinier than a sequin right now.

Luke's giant physique takes up the entire doorframe.

'Just the person I was hoping to see,' he says.

'Me?'

'You.'

'Erm, why?'

'Can I come in?'

Em emerges from her room and bounds over, delighted by the arrival of Luke.

'Come in, come in!' she says, bustling him towards the sofas. 'Jessie, where are your manners? We've just ordered room service. Will you stay and eat with us, Luke?'

On the one hand, this sounds amazing. On the other hand, my shiny face.

Luke runs a hand through his hair and says: 'I would love to, but sadly I'm needed down at the gym tonight. That's actually why I popped by.' He turns to look at me. 'Apparently my tennis classes are getting booked up pretty quickly and I just wanted to check in to see if you wanted to come along to one?'

He looks almost bashful. Em appears to be watching a tennis game of her own, head turning from Luke to me and back again.

Suddenly Luke seems to remember that Em is also in the room. 'Either of you, I mean,' he adds. 'All three of you, obviously.'

'Sure,' says Em, narrowing her eyes. '"All three of us",' she repeats in a ridiculous over-the-top voice, actually adding finger quotes.

I very briefly scowl at her and she beams back at me. I'm glad someone is loving this! Although wait, I should be too. Luke has just come to my suite to personally offer me a tennis lesson – something Croissants would die for, I bet.

'So, just let me know if you fancy it,' Luke says, catching my eye for the quickest moment. 'Because I'd be more than happy to add you into the class, even if it says it's fully booked.'

'Oh, erm—' I manage, a true wordsmith of our time.

'That's very thoughtful of you, Luke,' chips in Em. 'I'm sure Jess would love that. I'm actually really great at tennis already so I'll pass. Leave you two to it.'

Oh my god. Emerald is about as subtle as a loudspeaker.

Stella finally emerges from her room, slaps her little brother on the back and announces that she fancies a game of cards while we wait for food.

'Fancy losing at Uno, little bro?' she asks.

'No, but I'm happy to make sure you lose,' he says, following her over to the dining table.

'As if.' She shakes her head. 'You guys in?'

I gratefully accept, pleased to have something to do that isn't, you know, being gormless around Luke. I grab a seat and resolutely ignore Em, who sits opposite batting her eyelashes at me like a lunatic. When Luke takes the seat next to me and sits with his body angled in my direction, I swear I hear her whisper a laddish 'oi oi'.

Uno should be a family-friendly classic but Stella and Luke are so competitive that swear words are soon flying across the table as they try to outdo each other. When I play the plus four card on Luke, he shoots me this adorably sad look.

'Jess, how could you?' He grins, clutching at his heart.

'Don't hate the player, Luke,' I shoot back.

Emerald does some eyebrow pumping at this and I glare at her. When the direction of play changes and Stella plays a plus four card on Luke, he says: 'Sis, what the hell?'

'What happened to "Jess, how could you?"' Stella mocks.

'You're my sister, you can handle it,' he says, before announcing that he's about to win.

'Jammy bastard,' says Stella as Luke plays his final card and wins the game. 'You always do this.'

'I guess I'm just better at cards than you.' He shrugs, a glint in his eye.

'Please!' Stella tuts. 'This is a kids' game anyway. Next time we're playing poker. For money.'

'You don't even know how to play poker!' Luke replies.

'Guess what, I'll learn. And then I will take all of your money.'

'Okay, Stell, good luck with that.' He laughs, checking his watch. 'I'd better go.'

'Oh this is unfair. You're leaving us with Stella while she quietly seethes about losing a game of Uno to her little brother?' I tease. 'Have some humanity, Luke!'

He looks me straight in the eye and then holds out his hand to me. 'You're very welcome to come to the gym with me.' He's still light in his tone, but his eyes are saying something else. I think. I'm sure. No, I'm not. Oh no.

I swallow. I look at Stella and thankfully she's too engrossed in shuffling the deck of cards to have noticed. I deliberately don't look at Em. And then, just as I think I am about to take his hand, Stella says, 'Gym or pasta? Tough choice! We're not all weirdos like you, little bro. And we're having a girls' night in.' And then she stands up and bustles him out of the door.

Half an hour later and we're sat cross-legged on a picnic blanket in the living room enjoying the most delicious spread. Never mind pasta bowls, we each have our own wheel of cheese with a hole in the middle filled with pasta. It's so rich, and so good, that every time I think I've had enough I end up going back for another forkful. I'm halfway through one when my phone lights up with a call from Bryan, my editor at the *Carpston Courier*. Startled, I hit ignore and push my phone across the floor so I can't see it.

'Don't think I didn't see that.' Stella looks right at me.

'What?' I ask.

'Jessie, that's the second work call I've seen you ignore already this trip. Is everything okay? And why is bloody Bryan ringing you on a Sunday night?'

'Probably can't figure out how to turn his computer on again,' I say vaguely.

125

Stella snorts. 'Come on then, what's the latest on the buffoons in your office? Is Arjun back after he had to "take the week" when his mum's hamster was allegedly ill?'

I giggle at this. Arjun joined the digital team (so – me) a year ago because Bryan decided that the paper needed someone Very Young and who understands youth culture. I was thrilled to have someone to line-manage but it swiftly became clear that Arjun spends approx. zero time content-creating, preferring instead to swipe endless dating apps. So for the past twelve months I've been doing my job *and* Arjun's *and* trying to encourage some journalistic nous in the actual teenager I share a desk with. It's been a lot.

'You'll be thrilled to know that Tinkerbell the hamster is absolutely fine now.' I grin, kicking my legs out in front of me. 'I did actually think I'd have a juicy story to sink my teeth into a few weeks ago. Bryan came into conference and announced there'd been a drugs raid in Carpston which reminded him of his—'

'Time at *The Sun*,' Stella and Em chime in unison.

'Exactly.' I chuckle. Bryan loves to bang on about this 'time at *The Sun*' but when I looked into it, I discovered that he spent a week there on work experience before being told to go home because he messed up the assistant editor's sandwich order. So I did feel a bit dubious about how many drugs raids he actually managed to 'cover' during this inauspicious week.

'Tell me more,' Em says. 'Is there a secret cartel in Carpston?! Because that would be exciting for you!'

'I know! My ears totally pricked up and straight away I was thinking, what are we talking about here? Cocaine? Ketamine? Heroin? Who'd have thought sleepy old Carpston might well be the new Medellin. Is there a Pablo Escobar in our midst? I'd ruled out Mary, who runs the coffee mornings for retired people, because although she always has a glint in her eye, on balance, she seemed an unlikely candidate. But Percy and Sue, the pub landlords? My money was on them.'

'The Crown!' Stella gasps. 'We've been for drinks there a few times. I remember that landlady. Sue loves a showy jewel, there's always something sparkling on her when she's pulling pints.'

'Precisely. Drugs money.' I smile. 'Only, it turned out that Bryan's "trusted source" on the drugs raid intel was, in fact, his wife. And she'd been offered some "cannabis oil" at one of her weigh-ins at the church hall.'

'Oh boy.'

'All that fuss for—'

'CBD oil at the local slimming club.' I can't help but laugh.

The girls are chuckling too, until Em turns suddenly serious.

'You're too good for that place,' she says.

'What kind of journalist confuses CBD oil with a drugs raid?' Stella points out.

'Anyway, enough about my ridiculous job. It sounds like things at the charity have been super busy, Stell. Is everything okay?'

'Chaotic, but good,' she says. 'I've spent the past six months or so working with a potential new celebrity patron for the charity. She's the perfect face for us, you know, single-parent upbringing, council estate kid, massive success story in spite of all the extra hurdles she's had to jump to get there. Even now there's still this stigma attached to people from low-income, single-parent families, which is fucking ridiculous, but that's why we set the charity up in the first place. So, anyway, it took a lot of persuading to get her to come on board, lots of hectic meetings with her agent et cetera, but it's been so worth it. She signed up with us last week.'

'Ah, Stell! Congratulations.'

'Thank you,' she says, then yawns. 'God, I'm still catching up. Think I'm going to get an early night. See you guys in the morning.'

As soon as Stella's shut her bedroom door, Em scooches closer to me with a look on her face. I know very well what's coming.

'It was nice to see Luke earlier,' she says suggestively.

'He's so pretty,' I say, biting down on my index finger.

'He's so into you.'

'Oh sure.' I chuckle.

'Babes, did you not see the bit where he completely forgot I was in the room and asked you out?'

I roll my eyes. 'He did not ask me out. He asked all of us to his tennis class, Em. There's a bit of a difference there. Besides, everybody fancies him and I'm on a man cleanse now. The end.'

'A man cleanse?' Em clutches at her stomach as she laughs. 'Oh Jessie! I love you, but you are barking up the wrong tree, my friend. You don't need to ditch men full stop, you just need to pick a good one.'

'Like it's that easy,' I say.

'You just need to stop waiting for Sensible Simons to ask you out, and find someone who makes you feel actual things, and go for it,' Em replies, like this is the simplest concept in the world.

'Funnily enough, my new best friend Dita Ortiz said something similar earlier. "Yessica, you should not cleanse passion from your life,"' I say, rolling onto my back to mull it over, now so full of pasta that my tummy feels like it takes a minute to catch up with the rest of me.

'But the thing is, Em, I've never really "felt things" before,' I confess. 'Maybe the occasional butterfly but never anything ground-breaking. Otis took so long to get over our break-up, we'd talk for hours about his heartache, and how crippling it was for him, and he just assumed that I felt the same. But the truth is, I only felt a bit sad when we split up and mostly relieved, I think. Does that make me a monster?'

Em comes to lie down right next to me like we're sardines in a tin.

'No, it does not,' she says firmly. 'And it's precisely why you needed to split up with him in the first place. But I think you're lying to yourself.'

I push up on my arms.

'Why?'

'You have felt things before, it's happening right now. With Luke!'

'Well, sure, but I'm just one of many admirers. He's not going to pick me when he's got hot influencers on his tail, is he? Have you seen Croissants?'

'Oh Jessie, you sweet, adorable fool.'

'What?!' I say, feeling a bit dejected. 'We're hardly sympatico, are we?'

'First of all, who actually uses the word "sympatico" in a sentence, babes? Like, out loud? And secondly, if your Saturn Return doesn't involve banging Luke then I will eat my diamond tiara. And it sounds like Dita Actual Ortiz agrees with me. You swapped numbers with her, right?'

I nod.

'So message her now, find out what she's doing! If she's free, I think we should meet Dita for a nightcap.'

'What!' I squark.

'Oh come on, it'll be fun! Stella's passed out already and it's not even 9pm.'

Thirty minutes later and the three of us are in Dita's 'room', which is actually a series of rooms taking up the entire top floor of the original building. She has her own music room with a grand piano, and a plunge pool up here. It's even more luxe than our spa suite. As Dita bustled us inside she explained that she'd done her drinking for the day, so a nightcap was off the cards, but would Emerald and I like to join her for 'sleep preparation' instead?

I did not know what to expect.

And now all three of us are covered in mud.

'I do the mud as often as I can,' Dita explains, lying prone on a massage table in her own private treatment room. 'So excellent for the skin. And then we breathe the lavender to help with a good rest. So vital for good health when you are my age.'

Em and I sniff dutifully from the comfort of our own massage tables, which were speedily set up for us by a discreet member of staff when we arrived.

'Totally,' says Em. 'Thank you for inviting us along!'

'There was more than enough mud,' Dita says. 'And I do enjoy the conversation.'

'How long do we keep the mud on for?' I ask. My face feels like it's been plastered in concrete and every time I smile, it cracks.

'Another half an hour should do the trick. How are things with your lover, Yessica?'

'Omg, he's very much not my lover.'

'Yet,' chirps Emerald. 'Those two are written in the stars, Dita, I can just tell.'

'So tell me, what's his star sign?' Dita asks.

'Oh my god, *great* question! I can't believe I haven't asked that myself yet,' says Em.

'Erm, I don't know? I think he's relatively close to Stella's birthday and she's a September baby.'

'Yes, that's right. You know when Stella and Fran went out to America to see him a couple of years ago? Didn't they go for his birthday?'

'Oh yeah, I think so.'

'And that was mid-October. I remember because I'd got tickets for us to go to some new Christmas market thingy and Stella couldn't make it, and she was horrified that Christmas markets even existed in October. She said that she doesn't even think about Christmas until after Luke's birthday. Remember?'

'I mean, not really . . . '

'Well, I do! He's definitely mid-October which makes him a . . . ' Em twists her head from side to side to look at Dita and me, lying next to her.

I try to shrug but my shoulders have also been cemented into place.

'LIBRA!' they both cheer in unison.

'Great,' I say, trying to muster some enthusiasm to match. It *is* very cute that Em has found a fellow cosmic enthusiast in Dita.

'So, erm, a set of scales?' That's literally all I've got.

Dita purrs like a cat. 'A Libran. How divine for you, Yessica. The most attentive boyfriend in the zodiac, did you know that?'

'Yes.' Em claps. 'So true. Level-headed, check. Mild-mannered, check.'

'Sí sí. And people will flirt shamelessly with a Libra.'

'Well, that's definitely true,' I huff, thinking of Croissants. 'And also not exactly great from where I stand.'

'The Libra takes this with a pinch of salt,' says Dita.

'Totally.' Em nods wisely. 'The very good-looking ones are also very well adjusted so they just shrug it off. It won't go to his head. Wait!' she shrieks. 'Dita, you'll never guess what sign Jessie is.'

'I will guess.' She sits up then, her face caked in mud, and looks closely at me. 'Sagittarius,' she announces.

'How did you know?' I gasp.

'Dita is exceptional at this game.' Dita shrugs.

'And you know what that means, right?' Emerald is on the edge of her own table now, legs swung off the side, practically giddy.

'What?' I ask warily.

'Sagittarians and Libras are the perfect match!' She claps again.

'It's true.' Dita nods. 'You share kindness and loyalty. You will have a strong and deep emotional connection.'

'Deep connection, huh?' I roll the words over in my mouth. 'You know, Zodiac Girlie was talking about depth yesterday morning. Water gives way to emotional depth. And Dita, I haven't told you yet but I actually nearly died in the sea yesterday, with Luke.'

Em gives Dita a *she-didn't-really* shake of the head.

'And then we kind of both told each other stuff we hadn't really spoken about before,' I say, before pulling myself up. 'I'm getting carried away.'

'There's nothing wrong with getting carried away,' says Dita firmly. 'Especially when the stars have found you a perfect match.'

The perfect match. Surely that's not possible. Is it?

Chapter 11

Monday dawns a little cooler, a little cloudier, and a lot more baffling if Zodiac Girlie is to be trusted. I roll over to face Em, who, despite having her own bouncy hotel bed complete with pillow menu in her *own* bedroom, passed out in mine last night.

'Morning!' I say, seeing that she's awake and thrusting my phone in her face. 'Em? What's Zodiac Girlie banging on about today?'

She reads the Stars in Brief.

Don't set fire to yourself to keep warm.

'Admit it,' says Em, yawning. 'You're getting a little bit into this now, right?'

'Well . . . ' I hedge. The whole star sign match with me and Luke is quite exciting, I must say.

'I know this isn't your thing, but I can see that you're trying for my sake and I love you for it.' Em beams. 'So, okay, I think this means that you don't always need to put other people first which is definitely a *you* trait, Jessie. It's saying that you should spend some time looking after number one, do what feels right for you rather than prioritising everyone else.'

We both muse over this for a bit before Em adds: 'Although, you know, don't ditch Zodiac Girlie because she is so wise.'

'So you're saying I should do what feels right for me . . . with caveats?' I point out.

'Precisely.' She laughs.

'Does that mean I can spend all day in the library?'

'Erm, I guess.' Em looks underwhelmed by this plan. 'Or, given that we're only here for a week and the facilities are amazing, you could let me book you in for something this morning?'

She's scrolling through the treatment menu on her phone when her eyes light up.

'You're right,' I admit, stretching out my whole body under the covers. 'It's not every day we get to wake up in a place like this and I can take a book with me to the spa, anyway. But Em, you look like you're plotting something.'

'Who, me?' Em grins, pure mischief across her face as she taps away on her phone. 'Don't you worry your pretty little head about it. All you need to do is meet me in the spa at 10am.'

'Well, in the spirit of putting myself first I would like to say that I'm not doing anything dramatic,' I say sternly. 'No more cardio and ice bath combos.'

'I mean, you didn't even do that one so—'

'And absolutely no colonics.'

'They do colonics?' Em asks, scrolling through her treatment menu with intrigue. 'Sign me up.'

'You're so weird.' I yawn. 'And to be clear, I won't do that.'

'Okay, Meatloaf.' She nods solemnly. 'Listen, I get it. The only thing you want inside you is Luke's massive penis.'

'Emerald! For heaven's sake,' I almost yell, my eyes widening. And then I say, 'Exactly how do we know it's massive?'

'Have you seen the height of him? The size of those trainers?'

And she starts laughing which makes me grin and then I'm laughing too, not about the size of Luke's trainers or his, you know . . . other stuff, but because only Em would say something like that about a man that she's also called my perfect match. And when I'm laughing, it sets her off even more and she looks delighted.

'You are going to have a lot of fun,' Em says, taking hold of my shoulders and looking me in the eyes. 'Jessie, please try to have fun with that gorgeous man who is *very* tall with *very* large feet. You have noticed that, haven't you?'

She's smirking even though she's trying to be serious and I am smirking although I am also feeling quite flustered by the way our conversation has panned out. I decide I need to change tack.

'Please pick something nice for me?' I say, nudging her phone, still open on the spa's treatment list. 'After all, today is my day for not, erm, setting fire to myself. Shall I just book it myself?'

'Will you let me do something for you, please?' Em says, quite firm. 'And calm down. All I'm doing is booking us in for treatments.'

'You've got a glint in your eye.'

'It's the sea air, babes,' she replies dismissively, although I can't help but feel like something is up. 'Now, I'm off for an early morning forest bathe. See you later.'

At the spa, a central glass atrium welcomes guests with jugs of herb-sprigged water and an overwhelming sense of calm. From here, you can potter off to the stunning indoor pool, flanked with loungers, each one with its own perfectly rolled towel ready for you. Or follow the timber-clad corridor through to the treatment zone, where countless rooms offer all types of indulgence.

I wonder what Em's arranged for us this morning. Maybe a neck massage? I read an article about our generation being blighted by 'tech neck' because we're forever staring at our phones. Apparently a wrinkly and chronically sore neck is my destiny.

At least I have beautifully pedicured toes, I think, watching them catch the light as I pad through the spa in sliders, finding the girls in a sunken seating area in various stages of undress. Stella, in cycling shorts and matching bralet, has cucumber slices on her eyes and Em's lounging around in a bikini with her hotel robe thrown over the top.

'Don't mind me,' Stella says, motioning towards her face. 'I explained to my masseuse that I'd been burning the candle and she suggested sliced cucumbers on my eyes before we begin my facial.'

'Facial sounds good,' I coo. 'Is that what we're all having?'

Em looks triumphant, like she's up to something, and with Stella blinded by cucumbers she's not even bothering to hide it.

I feel a rising sense of panic.

'Actually, Jessie, you and I are trying the new couples massage,' she announces, with a huge grin.

'Oh! Well that sounds totally fine. Really fun, actually,' I reply, relieved, until I notice that Em still looks like the cat that got the cream.

I narrow my eyes at her and she beams back, like butter wouldn't melt.

Warily, I pour myself a water, deciding that hydration will be the best way to get through whatever it is she's up to.

'Stella?' calls a masseuse in a linen tunic. 'Whenever you're ready.'

Stella peels the veggies from her face and leaps up.

'Enjoy your couples massage, kids.' She grins. 'See you back at ours?'

As our friend disappears off into a low-lit room, I round on Emerald.

'What are you up to?'

'Shh, Jess, we're meant to keep our voices down in the chill-out room.'

'There's literally no one else in here.'

'I sense that you're on edge.'

'Because you're up to no good, it's written all over your face!'

Em pretends to look affronted. 'I always have your best interests at heart, Jessica Jones.' Then she looks over my shoulder and smiles. 'Oh look, it's Luke. Hi, Luke!'

I turn to see all six feet five inches of Luke walking in and my heart crashes against my chest.

'Hey,' he says. 'Everything okay? Your message sounded kind of urgent.'

I scowl at my best friend. *What message?*

'Thank you so much for coming.' She presses her hands together. 'Jess and I are meant to be having a couples massage together soon but I've just found out that a really important work call has been moved forward. This musician I'm working with is having a crisis about her world tour costumes. Apparently, Tina's stylist has ordered some stuff and she's worried it won't work with the jewels we've been working on together.' I narrow my eyes. This is a lot of information, some may say *too much* information. 'And Tina waits for no man. So sorry, Jess, such terrible timing.'

Oh please. I fold my arms across my body as Em pulls various *can-you-believe-it* faces. *Obviously* Luke isn't going to believe this cock-and-bull story.

'I hate to leave poor Jessie stranded because she's been so looking forward to this massage! And, I did check, the spa have no other massages available all day for her to take instead. So it really is now or never and I wondered, Luke, if you'd mind filling in my spot?'

My mouth drops open. I mean, I knew where she was going with this but somehow, the actual saying of it makes me even more gobsmacked.

Time slows right down as every tiny part of me cringes hard. Because obviously in a dream world where Luke isn't Stella's little brother and also definitely likes me, a couples massage would be ideal. But I live in the real world and therefore must insist that Luke doesn't have to do this. All I need to do is find the words.

'Honestly—' I begin.

Right when Luke says, as cool as you like: 'Sure, I'd love to.'

'Are you sure?' I ask, and it must come out a bit harsh because he looks taken aback.

'If you're okay with that, of course,' Luke backtracks. 'I wouldn't want to impose. I'm sure they'll let you do the massage alone.'

'They won't,' Em says firmly. 'I checked.'

'You've been doing a lot of checking,' I say suspiciously.

'It pays to be thorough,' says the most haphazard person I know and then Em takes my hand and squeezes it. 'There needs to be two bodies so you can practise techniques on each other.'

Oh my god, *what?!*

My eyes widen and I feel myself squeezing her hand really hard. She does not stop smiling at me.

'Erm . . . ' I manage.

'And goodness knows you need this, Jessie. Those nodules.' She shakes her head, as if she can see that my nodules are in a state. 'And actually, Luke, with all the exercise you're doing, this would no doubt be great for you too. Am I right?'

Luke shoots me a look, one eyebrow raised, like a challenge.

'I, erm . . . Sure,' I say eventually. 'Unless you're busy, Luke? You're probably busy, right? I wouldn't want to get you in trouble so early on in the new job.'

'I'm free as a bird.' Luke grins.

'Perfect!' Em pulls her hand from mine and claps, looking at us like we are little chicks about to fly the nest. 'Right, well, I think I'm going to get myself an iced latte . . . '

'I thought you had a meeting,' I say.

'Yes, yes, of course. I'd better go to my meeting!' And she actually winks at me.

'Our friendship is over,' I whisper as she walks past.

'You can thank me later,' she whispers back, eyes sparkling.

Two massage beds are set up next to each other in the treatment room, with sheets folded down on top of them. Soft music plays and the lights are turned down low. It's warm but not too hot, and there's the intoxicating smell of essential oils in the air.

'Hey, thanks,' says Luke, walking alongside me as we're shown

137

in. The size difference between us is ridiculous. 'For letting me join, I mean. Em's right, my muscles are in bits and I haven't tried out the treatments here yet.'

'No problem,' I waver, still on edge. 'Thanks for coming to the rescue. You're making a bit of a habit of that.'

Luke looks puzzled.

'When you saved me from certain drowning?'

He laughs softly. 'Ah, okay. It was me who put you in danger in the first place so I'm not sure that counts. I guess this is the least I could do.'

'Welcome,' says one of the masseuses as he hands us both PAPER UNDERWEAR to put on. 'My name is Ric and this is Enya, we'll be your massage guides today,' he adds, gesturing to his colleague.

I stare dumbly at the paper undies in my hand.

'We'll give you both space to get changed and be back shortly. Please arrange yourselves on the beds when you're ready,' Enya says as the pair of them leave.

Dear god. I take a deep breath and tell myself to be cool. It's fine. Just an almost-naked massage with Luke.

'I think they're assuming we're a couple.' Luke glances at me once we're alone, a shy smile across his face.

'I don't know.' I grin. 'I'm always getting naked and putting on paper pants with my mates.'

Luke laughs, runs a hand through his hair.

'Lucky mates,' he says.

I was not expecting that and my stomach flips.

'Looks like there's a bathroom through there,' I say, pointing, my voice a bit wobbly. Oh no, I have to get a grip. Nothing has even happened yet. We're still in our clothes!

'Do you wanna . . . ' Luke nods towards the bathroom. 'Or I can? I mean, I assume you don't want to get changed in here, unless—'

'I'll go!' I say hurriedly, scurrying inside with the paper pants in hand. They rustle as I put them on and I wonder why they have to be quite so unattractive. How can a spa this luxe offer pants this basic? I bet Dita wouldn't wear these. She'd probably insist on the finest silk underwear for her treatments, right? Especially if her treatment involved being barely dressed around an utter hunk.

I keep a towelling robe wrapped tightly around me when I emerge to find Luke in nothing but his paper pants looking like the inspiration behind Michelangelo's *David*. It's just a case of inhaling and exhaling, I remind myself when I realise I've stopped breathing.

'Well, this isn't awkward,' I say.

Luke takes one of the sheets from the massage beds and holds it up.

'Here, I can hold this in place between us while you get on the bed if you'd like? Promise I won't look,' he adds, biting a beautifully full lip.

''Kay, thanks,' I say, dragging my eyes away from his lips.

It is going to be difficult getting a grip while I'm in this small room with him. Do I need to get a grip? Why do I need to get a grip? Oh, Stella, yes. Younger brother. Stella. Pact. Best friend. I exhale a very long breath, walk over to my table and untie my robe with him holding up the sheet between us. I chance a glance at Luke and note that, as promised, he's looking determinedly away. So now I'm naked but for paper pants with an unwanted robe in my hand, which I need to dispose of while not straying far from the sheet and thus flashing Luke. Hmm. There's a chair in the corner and, now basically naked, I bundle the robe into a ball and turn to fling it onto the chair.

Only, as I turn, I stumble over Luke's foot and the next thing I know I'm falling *towards him*. His reaction is instant, reaching his arms around me just like when I nearly drowned that time. I'm folded into Luke's arms, wrapped up in the sheet he'd still been holding when he went to catch me. My face is pressed against his chest. I can smell citrus on his skin. Hear his breath quickening.

The air around us grows heavy.

I track my gaze up to meet his and his eyes flash.

'You okay?' he asks gruffly, the beginnings of a smile playing at his lips.

Unable to catch myself in time, I say: 'We must stop meeting like this.'

Am I flirting with him?!

'I, for one, think that would be a great shame,' he replies.

Wait, is he flirting with *me*?!

'Why's that?'

'Beautiful woman falls directly into my arms?' His eyebrow has arched, grey eyes pinning me to the spot. 'I don't hate it.'

Somewhere, in the back of my mind, I wonder quite what is happening here. But in the moment, I step back, away from the sheet, to take a better look at him. To try and get a read on him.

I only remember that I'm mostly naked once I've completed the step.

Luke swallows, hard.

'So!' I say, briskly stepping forward once more. 'Don't mind me, just heading right back into your arms. Can't be getting in trouble for being a flasher.'

'I'm very much not complaining, either way.' He looks down at me, eyes smouldering. 'Jess, I—'

'Oh, sorry, are we interrupting?' asks Ric as he and Enya glide back in. 'It happens sometimes. It's an intimate setting and—'

'No, no!' I insist, fleetingly glancing back at Luke.

'Well . . . ' he says, cocking his head to one side.

I scramble onto the bed, covering myself in the sheet and plunge my face directly into the hole so no one can see quite how flustered I am right now.

Chapter 12

Okay, this is better. Much safer territory. Now there are two other people in the room there's much less opportunity to share confusing moments with my best friend's little brother. And I have to say the massage is amazing. Enya started with my legs, smoothing and gently pummelling, and she's now moved up to my back.

'We're using a blend of essential oils today,' explains Ric. 'Rose, for arousal, and bergamot, a mood booster.'

Not sure I need much help with either of those. Or is it all the essential oils' fault?

I hear Luke sigh happily and I can't help it, I turn my head to the side and open my eyes to look at him.

He's already watching me.

'That good, huh?' I ask in one giant exhale as Enya works on my shoulder blades.

'Pretty good,' he says, Ric's hands gliding across his glistening back. 'I'm used to sports massages which usually just hurt like hell.'

'Do you get them a lot?'

'Used to, when I was playing. There'd always be some knots to work out after a game, or some twinge to ease. I hated them at the time but I kind of miss them now.'

141

'Do you ever wish you could go back?' I ask. 'Wait, sorry, you don't mind talking about this? Because we can change the subject.'

'No, it's cool.'

'I meant, do you wish you could change your path somehow? Not pick up that injury that put a stop to your tennis career?'

'No,' Luke says in a heartbeat. 'I'm not saying it wasn't tough, it really was. But if life had turned out differently then I wouldn't be here right now. With you.'

'I *am* pretty great.' I grin, presumably so relaxed by this massage that I'm suddenly bigging myself up.

'Agreed. You've been a great friend to Stella so, in a way, you've been a huge support to me too.'

'I, erm . . . '

'Don't know how to deal with compliments?' he offers, eyes bright.

'Exactly. It's not very British to accept compliments, Luke. You've spent way too long in America.'

He laughs at this. 'I called a tap a faucet the other day and Stella looked like she was going to punch me.'

It's my turn to laugh, now. 'You should be careful, no one wants to face the wrath of Stella.'

Including me, I think. What would she say if she knew I'd been flirting with her sibling while half naked in a couples massage orchestrated by Emerald? I can only imagine.

'Speaking of siblings, you've got a brother, right?'

'James, yes, certified disaster zone.'

'How so?'

'Oof, well, it's a long story but basically he had this huge falling-out with my mum and dad back when I was at uni. Pretty much cut all ties with them. There were things said on both sides that shouldn't have been said, the whole situation was horrible, but I think James has always had this entitled streak in him. Like, he thinks people owe him a favour. And when Mum and Dad wouldn't help him out with a new business venture, he just upped and left.'

'Wow.'

'Yeah. Mum was devastated. Dad was furious. They're such good, kind people.' I shake my head. 'So when I finished uni, I went back to my hometown. I'd planned to stay in Manchester – I'd been working part time in a bookshop to fund uni and they had a permanent job coming up. But when it all kicked off with James I just felt this need to go back home. Does that make sense?'

Luke nods. 'You wanted to support your family.'

'Yes. So I went home and a job came up at the local paper and, well, here we are.' I pause, once again finding myself sharing personal stuff with Luke.

'Do you still speak to James?'

'Mm hm,' I say. 'Things were tricky for a while but we're still in touch, and his relationship with my folks has turned a corner now. But we've never been super close like you and Stell.'

'Family dynamics, hey?'

'Right.' I smile, as we're both instructed to turn onto our backs.

This is only the second massage I've ever had, and so far I have a hundred per cent strike rate of falling asleep in them. Not today, my friend. Every single part of my body is alert to Luke's presence. The room is thick with the smells of rose and citrus, the air warm and cocooning. It's heavenly.

'The other benefit of no longer being pro is that I can eat what I like,' Luke's saying. 'And I developed a serious thing for plant burgers in the States.'

By now I'm lying on my back, nothing but a towel covering my boobs as Enya sets to work on my arms. It feels so nice that I let out a groan of delight.

'You really like plant burgers, huh?' says Luke.

'Oh my god.' I laugh. 'That was for the massage, not the plant burgers. Although they do sound good. Are you vegetarian?'

'Vegan,' Luke says.

'No way!'

'You sound surprised.'

'You're just so . . . big.'

No. I did not just say that?

I look over to see Luke pretending to look hurt. 'Vegans can be strong too, you know.'

'Clearly.' I chuckle. 'I've been vegetarian since I was a teen. Mum was horrified when I made the big announcement.'

Luke laughs. 'You know what I've missed most about the UK? Chip shop chips.'

'Oh come on! First you expect me to believe you're vegan and now you're claiming you love chips? It's all lies, surely.'

'Says the girl who claims never to have fallen in love.'

'Why's *that* so unbelievable?'

Luke looks at me like I'm from another planet.

'Just look at you, Jessica Jones.' He shakes his head. There's something about the way my full name sounds on his lips that is as hot as hell.

So much so that I have forgotten all my words again, other than to let out a gasp as the masseuse moves on to knead my thighs.

'You're just . . . I don't know. You're a catch, is all I'm saying. Beautiful, funny, kind . . . And so small, too.' He's grinning now. 'I could carry you around in my pocket.'

I can't help but laugh at this. 'Where would we go? The chip shop?'

'I can think of some other places.'

Jeez. Heat pools around my body and my heart starts racing at this.

I clear my throat. 'Jess and Luke's Pocket Adventures. Maybe I could write a book on it. I'd have us going to Cappadocia in Turkey, where we'd take a hot air balloon ride over the famous cone-shaped caves.'

Luke shoots me a look. 'That's on my bucket list.'

'No! Same. It looks fascinating. I might be a bit nervous in a hot air balloon though, I'm not great with heights.'

'Ah but you'd be in my pocket so you'd be very safe and cosy. I could just let you know when to come out and look at the best bits.'

I giggle, delighted by this idea.

'Speaking of caves, we could also go to—'

'Petra,' we both say at the exact same time.

'Stop it,' I say. 'Don't tell me that's on your list too?'

'A city carved out of rock? For a man who's quite into architecture? Of course it's on my bucket list!'

I love this about Luke.

'You know you can take a camel ride down into Petra itself?' I say, getting carried away with our imaginary escapades.

'Woah, not sure about that,' wavers Luke. 'Maybe I'll have to go in your pocket if we're going down that route.'

'I'm going to need to get some bigger pockets,' I say. 'What's up with camels?'

'They look kind of weird?'

'Rude.' I laugh. 'Poor camels.'

Luke grins. 'I apologise to all camels. You know, all this sightseeing is very cultured of us. I think the Pocket Adventures could probably do with some beach time, too.'

'Totally.' I nod in agreement. 'You could also take me to the Maldives in the pocket of your boardshorts. I could climb out onto your lap once we hit the sand.'

Luke turns to look straight at me, a huge and very sexy smile on his face.

'Jess,' he says, voice low, 'this was all extremely wholesome until you mentioned climbing onto my lap and now my mind has gone somewhere very different.'

My heart is pounding by now, and I'm pretty sure I can't blame the rose essential oils, but somehow I manage to say: 'Has it gone to the bookshop to buy *Jess and Luke's Pocket Adventures*?'

Luke laughs softly at this. 'Let's go with yes, for decency's sake. Do you mind me asking you a personal question?'

'Shoot,' I say, feeling both super relaxed and very alert.

'I just . . . uh . . . I got the impression at the garden party the other day that you might, I don't know, be into somebody else?'

I cast my mind back, remember that Em and I came up with my fake crush on some footballer to throw poor Stella off the scent of my real crush. The look on Luke's face when he saw Stella pointing out my red herring romance. It's mad enough to think that he might like me now, let alone on Saturday just a day after we'd met.

'Ah. You're talking about Terry Carver, the footballer?'

'Pretty sure it's *Perry* Carver, world famous midfielder.'

I smile. 'I mean, I think the fact that I still don't know his name tells you all you need to know about that.' There's no way I'm going to explain the embarrassing fact that Em and I had to come up with a decoy crush so Stella wouldn't figure out just how much I fancy her little brother right now. For a moment Ric is standing between Luke and me, but when he moves, we're both still looking at each other. I say, 'I'm not into anybody else.'

Luke's eyes twinkle with what looks like relief and he gives me that full wattage smile. I get the impression that he's about to say something more, but our massage has stopped and Enya asks: 'Would you like to try some moves on each other?'

Luke's eyebrow is arched as he looks at me for an answer.

My heartrate is through the roof, my fingers already imagining what his skin would feel like under them.

'You know, Jess, my shoulders could still use some TLC,' he says, swinging his legs off the side of his table and smiling mischievously at me.

And I can't help it. I *know* I shouldn't even be here in the first place, let alone entertaining the thought of rubbing arousing oils into Luke's mostly naked body. But apparently I have fully lost all forms of self-restraint here in this massage room.

'Fine,' I say, rolling my eyes as if this is a massive inconvenience when we all know I cannot wait to get my hands on him. 'Enya, could you pass me my robe please?'

I stand in the corner, with my back to the room and slip the robe back on, very aware that Luke is right behind me as I dropped the sheet to the floor. But then I swallow and turn to see Luke looking really quite pleased with himself. He rolls back onto his front as Ric pours a few drops of essential oils into my hands and encourages me to warm it in my palms and breathe in the heady scent.

The next thing I know, my hands are on Luke's strong, solid back and I'm making gliding motions from the base of his spine up to his shoulders. I'm trying very hard to follow Ric's instructions, using my thumbs to work deep into Luke's taut muscles, alternating the pressure of my touch, but it's not that easy now that I've developed a one-track mind. Luke lets out a low moan so I repeat that move again. Temptation to fling off the towel covering his lower body: high. Temptation to bend down and trail kisses down his back: off the charts.

'God, you're good,' Luke says, stretching up into a low cobra as I finish up. 'If you'd have been my sports masseuse I'd never have quit. May I return the favour?'

'I think we're out of time,' I say, nodding towards a discreet clock in one corner of the room.

'Oh man,' says Luke, flashing me a look. 'In that case, I definitely owe you one.'

'Here,' I say, handing him a robe as Enya and Ric leave the room.

'Thanks,' he says, wrapping it around himself. 'Time just melted back there.'

'Must be my magic hands.'

'I think it was.' He smiles. 'Devastatingly, I have to get back to work.'

'That's cool, I've got a very busy schedule of swanning around the spa to crack on with.'

'Okay.' He grins, stepping towards me and leaning down to brush the side of my cheek with a kiss goodbye. My senses are struck at once with the warmth of his body and the smell of his

147

skin.

'Hopefully see you again very soon, Jess,' he says.

Em is loitering outside the treatment room when we emerge, eyes darting between the two of us, her face lighting up in a smile.

'You have got to get a grip,' I hiss as we walk off together.

'I take it that went well,' she says.

'I need a cold drink.'

'To the bar, then,' Em says.

So apparently, daytime drinking is my new thing. We're sitting at the spa bar – not the one in the restaurant, this hotel has myriad options for throwing back alcohol – and Em has ordered us both iced cocktails.

I sip mine shakily, grateful for the shot of booze.

'You look like you need to calm your nerves.' She grins.

'Stop looking at me like that.'

'Not until you tell me how the massage went.'

I sigh. 'You're like a dog with a bone.'

'Give me the tea.'

'Right, well, this is going to sound a bit mad, but I think Luke was flirting with me.'

'When you say *you think* . . . '

So I explain the 'beautiful' comment, and the fact that he asked about Perry Carver. 'I'm making it up, right? They used rose essential oils for "arousal", and obviously I nearly died when they told us that, but I reckon that's got to my head?'

'WRONG!' Em spins a cocktail stirrer around excitedly. 'OMG, JESSIE! He was definitely flirting with you. You just can't tell because it's been so bloody long for you, you poor thing.'

'Hey!' I say. 'Well, actually, you're right I guess. So long.'

'So very long.'

'You really think he was flirting?'

'Oh my god, yes!'

'It definitely felt that way, I think. Or, at least, my heart was beating way too fast and my stomach felt like it was swirling around and I swear my pupils were massive, like they just wanted to allow as much of Luke as possible into my brain. Does that sound normal?'

'Yes, babes. That's exactly how I felt with Henry.'

'Which one?' I couldn't help it.

Em ignores this. 'That's how it should feel! I'm so pleased for you, Jessie.'

I take another sip of cocktail.

'And the whole pact thing . . . ' I hedge.

'We've already established that it's not even a thing.'

'But I did say to myself that it was,' I reason. 'Only now, after this, I feel a bit more determined to not worry about it? I don't know, Em. I really like him.'

'That pact was so long ago.' Em's on the edge of her bar stool. 'We were just kids.'

I nod. 'So I'm wondering if maybe it is okay to feel like this, about Luke. And that even though it seems crazy to think that he might feel the same—'

'Not crazy.'

'That, I think, if he carries on flirting with me like this then I'll properly reciprocate. Because oof, Em. The way he makes me feel!'

'Praise be!' Em beams, holding her hand out for a high-five. 'I am thrilled for you, my friend. Ooh, to be a fly on the wall the next time you two hang out.'

Chapter 13

One of my greatest achievements in life is being able to wrap a towel around my wet hair in a perfect twist. I step out of my shower – I went for mood: romantic – and fold my hair up to let it dry. I slip my hotel robe and slippers on, deciding that a coffee is needed before we head down to lunch.

I can't believe it's Monday lunchtime already. It feels like so much has happened in the space of a few days. Sadly I have not yet mastered the coffee machine. So many little buttons to press, I think, stabbing at them and achieving nothing other than knocking it off its little plinth, so it's now slightly wonky.

A knock at the front door interrupts me and, with the girls still getting ready in their rooms, I abandon hopes of a beverage and pad over to open it.

Luke leans against the doorframe.

'Well,' he says, steel-grey eyes taking me in. 'Today is my lucky day.'

'Hey.' I smile, delighted to see him. 'How so?'

'You answered the door.'

'So I did,' I reply, remembering my memo to self about flirting. 'Funny that, given that it's my door you're knocking on.'

'So it is,' he says, eyes twinkling. 'I could have been stuck with my sister though. And yet here you stand, all adorable in your towelling robe.'

'I'm catching you up,' I say, patting the towel twisted high on my head. 'See? I'm almost as tall as you now.'

Luke steps in through the doorway, closing the gap between us. He towers over me, so close I can smell him.

'Absolutely. Just a few more feet to go,' he teases.

'I'm not *that* small!' I laugh.

'The perfect size, I'd say.' He's practically smouldering now, that deep Northern accent of his driving me slightly crazy.

'You arrived just in time,' I tell him.

'I did?'

'I was just giving the coffee machine a piece of my mind.'

His lips twitch. 'Oh dear. You want some help?'

'Yes, please,' I reply, my heart pounding as he follows me over to the desk where the kettle and mini fridge are. I watch as he grabs a couple of coffee pods from a selection box next to the machine.

'Mind if I make one for both of us?' he asks.

'Please do. Though I'm pretty sure it's broken.'

'Are you always a coffee person?' Luke asks.

'Always! Coffee in the morning is basically the law.'

'Well, we wouldn't want to break any laws then, would we?'

The way he's looking at me right now.

'Absolutely not.' I shake my head. 'I'm definitely not much of a rule breaker.'

'That's what Stella said, too.'

'Wait, you spoke to Stella about me?'

'Of course.' He shrugs, like this is no big deal. 'She said you were the one keeping her and Em in line at uni. Which is odd,' he says, turning to give me his whole attention, 'because you look like you could be trouble to me.'

'That's funny,' I say, my insides flipping, 'because I have had exactly the same thought about you.'

151

'I'm actually pretty well behaved.' He's smouldering at me now. 'Years of tennis training mean I'm very good at doing what I'm told. I mean, here I am, rescuing you from a day without caffeine, for a start.'

'Well, let's not get too big for our boots,' I counter. 'You haven't actually fixed the coffee machine yet and like I said, I'm pretty sure it's faulty.'

Luke takes one look at the machine and then turns back to me, taking another step closer.

I hold my breath. Is he going to kiss me right here in the living room?

What madness is this?

Luke reaches past me, brushing ever so lightly against my body as he does so. I hear a switch flick.

'I think I've figured it out.' He grins. 'Sometimes these things do need turning on.'

Now he looks quite pleased with himself and I am more turned on than the coffee machine will ever be.

'Ah.' I bite my lip.

'So,' he says, dropping his voice a notch, 'shall I get on with these drinks or is there any chance of us breaking a few rules?'

'Sounds like Stella's already told you I'm not one for rule-breaking.'

'Okay,' Luke concedes with a grin. 'And for reference, next time you just need to turn the machine on.'

I'm trying very hard to look affronted but it's not working. There's a huge smile on my face and my cheeks are flushed.

'All right, genius. I'm still so relaxed from that massage, so sue me.'

'Building a case against you already.' Luke hands me an espresso and makes a tiny cup for himself. With his massive build the cup seems almost non-existent.

'What, you're taking me to court now?' I laugh.

'Crimes against coffee machines,' he says solemnly.

'Well, good luck with that,' I retort. 'Juries love me.'

Luke laughs hard at this.

'Knew you were trouble,' he says. 'Which actually works perfectly for what I have in mind for us later.'

Us? Later? I'm basically breathless.

He scratches his head, then, suddenly looking both hopeful and shy at the same time. 'I was wondering if you fancied spending some time together, just me and you?'

Scream!

'I'd like that,' I say, trying to keep my smile from giving away quite how much I'd like that. Don't want to seem over-keen; after all, aren't there rules about that? I realise I have zero clue how to handle this situation. 'But, you know, given how much trouble you think I am, you'll probably have your hands full.'

Luke shoots up both eyebrows at this. Clears his throat.

'Lucky me,' he manages. His eyes seek out mine again. Looks at me like he's hungry.

'So, what did you have in mind?'

'Midnight swim?' he suggests. 'At the outdoor pool. We're not strictly meant to use the pool out of hours but I am kind of in charge around here so . . . '

I take a sip of my drink, giddy at the thought of this. Then I smile back at him. 'I'll see you there.'

'All right, dickhead, you're here early,' Stella says, walking out of her bedroom in running clothes to find us in the living room. I spin around and fidget with the coffee machine, which is no doubt extremely suspicious.

'Thought I'd get some stretching done first,' Luke says to his sister. 'But when I got here Jess was having some trouble with the coffee machine.' He flashes me the briefest smile.

'Oh Jess,' Stella says sympathetically. 'Did you forget to turn it on?'

'All turned on now,' I puff, and although I'm looking at the machine, I hear Luke's delighted laugh.

To say that Stella and Luke are competitive would be an understatement. They're off for a run together but since Luke announced that he was going to do some stretching, Stella decided that she was too. And now there's a sense of one-upmanship running through their stretching routine.

Luke's doing lunges and YES, you can imagine how great that is for my eyeballs and me.

But now Stella's doing them too.

'Little bro, can't you go deeper than that? Look at this,' she says, flinging herself into a lunge.

'I struggle with my quads,' Luke says, looking actually quite put-out that Stella's better than him at something. 'It's a tennis thing.'

'Oops, touched a nerve. How about we do planks?'

'Easy,' says Luke, dropping into a plank that I would like to lie on top of. I've settled myself onto the sofa to watch because, why not. The siblings don't seem to mind.

Stella arranges herself into a forearm plank next to him. 'Jess, time us!' she says. 'See who can last the longest.'

'Does it really matter?' I suggest. 'It's the taking part that—'

'YES,' they both shout.

So I time them. Stella's brows are furrowed in concentration, a bead of sweat trickling down her face. Luke's arm muscles are flexing hard and I cannot wait to get into the pool with him later. A midnight swim sounds unbelievably sexy. To think just a few days ago I was fantasising about getting in the pool with him and now it's actually going to happen. Me and Hot Swimmer, I think, drifting off into my own private fantasy.

'Jess?'

'Earth to Jess!' Stella shouts, interrupting my daydream. 'Did you time us or what?'

'Huh?' I blink.

'The plank off, Jessica.' Stella tuts, like it's the most important thing in the world right now. Oops. I turn to look at the

154

timer, which is still running even though Stella and Luke are now standing in front of me, hands on hips, very much no longer planking.

'Erm, sorry guys,' I begin. 'I got distracted.'

'You're weird today,' Stella says. 'We'll just have to go again. This time, Jess, we'll need you to focus.'

'We don't need to go again, I clearly won that last one,' argues Luke.

'No you did not. You got up before me.'

'You'd lost your form! Your hips had dropped. That's not a plank. I won.'

'Did not!'

'Yes, I did,' insists Luke.

'Did not.'

Luke sighs. 'Fine, we'll go again. Prepare to lose twice.'

Eventually, they stop squabbling and make to head out, which I'm thrilled about because it's been exhausting just watching them. Boundless energy is clearly another genetic similarity.

'Sure you don't want to come?' Stella asks.

'Christ no! I mean, thanks, but no.'

'Last one out buys the next round,' she shouts at Luke, running towards the door. He scrambles after her, the two of them still bickering as they set off on the run.

'Well, well, well.' Em jumps out from her bedroom as soon as the front door slams shut. 'A midnight swim, hey? That escalated quickly.'

'What?' I squawk. 'Were you listening the whole time?'

'Yup.' Em shrugs, like that is perfectly normal behaviour. 'Took a front row seat to your first day of full-on flirting and I must say, Jessie, I'm impressed. This is a whole new side to you!'

'Well, obviously I'm very cross at you for eavesdropping but also, thanks, I guess?'

'You're welcome. So, you know what I'm thinking, don't you?'

'Is it something to do with auras? Or are you currently in communicado with the crystals?'

'In communicado,' snorts Em. 'Honestly, Jess. Naturally I am thinking about what you're going to wear on this sexy date of yours.'

'I figured my swimming costume might be best? Given that it's, you know, happening in the pool?'

Em tuts at me. 'No, no, no. That dreary old black thing will not do. You and I, my friend, are going to the hotel shop. Come on!'

For a start, I did not know that the hotel has a shop, but it does make sense given that Stella has been wearing a never-before-seen outfit every single night to dinner. It's so pretty in here. Beautiful fabrics and stunning summery clothes line the rails. A whole wall filled with swimwear options and those large brimmed hats that must be a nightmare to pack.

'Oh yes, babes,' coos Emerald, holding out a couple of pieces of string.

'Absolutely not.' I shake my head.

Then she pulls out a sheer triangle bikini.

'I might as well just be naked!' I squeal.

'Exactly.' She beams. 'Luke will have a heart attack.'

'I'm not sure that's quite what I want to happen?'

'Okay, leave it to me,' she says, shoving me into a changing room. 'You strip, I'll feed options through. You do not have the power to veto.'

'But—'

'No power to veto,' she barks.

Soon there's a pile of swimmers hanging in my cubicle and I'm dutifully working my way through them. I can't say I've given swimwear much thought before. Otis never wanted to travel abroad because of 'the heat' and, of course, the sand, and my journalist's salary hasn't exactly afforded me many opportunities to prance around pools, anyway. There's not much call for sexy

156

swimwear at the municipal pool in Carpston where I go to get some lengths in – I arrive wearing a supportive supermarket costume and leave with the threat of verrucas.

'How are we doing?' Em asks in a tone which means *Can you hurry up and put something on?* I pull back the curtain in a very skimpy red number which I'm pretty sure I haven't tied up right.

'It's giving *Baywatch*,' Em says approvingly. 'But I think we could do better on the colour. Your dark hair and green eyes are crying out for something green, or maybe a rich blue, or . . . Oh, try this!'

'Are you going to exit my cubicle before I do?'

'Such a prude.' She tuts. 'Bodies are just bodies, babes.'

I pointedly draw the curtain and then slip into the cornflower blue bikini she just handed me. It definitely feels like my boobs are supported which is a good start. I slide back the curtain.

'Ladies and gents, we have a winner!' Em cheers. 'Sweet mother of mercy, your boobs look incredible. And that waist! Oh boy. Can I come along tonight? Hide in the bushes? I'm dying to see Luke's reaction to you looking so beautiful, so sexy in this.'

'Absolutely not! Stop being a weirdo, Em.'

Em sighs. 'Fine. But when you get back later, I want every detail.'

'Promise,' I say, heading back in to get dressed. Only then do I look at the price tag. Only then do I have a small heart attack re the cost of these few pieces of blue fabric. Surely I can't . . . I mean, financially it does not make sense. I should be putting every spare penny into my house fund, right? Because that's the plan.

Only, now that I think about it, the plan kind of changed before I even got here. To the point where I don't seem to have much of a plan anymore. I take one last look in the mirror, and for the first time in a long time I like what I see. I look happy. And my boobs do look pretty good!

I buy the bikini.

Midnight can't come soon enough and infuriatingly, midnight is still so very far away. The seconds plod by and I spend the rest of the day in a state of sexy turmoil. I half-heartedly nibble my way through lunch. I do a yoga class with the girls and try very hard to empty my mind as instructed but I cannot shake Luke from my thoughts.

'Jessica Jones, what is wrong with you?' Stella eventually asks over dinner. Still four hours to go. 'You've been weird all day. Is everything okay?'

Startled, I shoot Em a look over the dinner table. We're back in the restaurant, making our way through the menu.

'I'm fine!' I squeak. 'Just a little, erm, distracted.'

'Come on, Stell, Jessie's always been a *bit* of an odd-bod,' Em chips in helpfully.

Stella gives her a look that acknowledges this as fact. I try not to pout.

'Yes, but you've been ignoring calls again today,' Stella points out.

This is true. Bryan's been calling me non-stop and I've been taking the very immature approach of not picking up. I know I'll have to face up to work soon, but I just don't want to. Although, as I look at Stella's concerned face now, I realise this could be the perfect time to offload some of that stuff *and* deflect from the fact that I'm counting down the minutes to go swimming with my best friend's hot little brother later, which is an entire other can of worms.

'Is something up with work?' Stella presses, dog plus bone. 'Because I've actually been seriously impressed that you haven't been taking calls on this trip, Jess. Can't remember the last time we hung out when you weren't checking the website, or scrolling emails at the weekend. I'm literally the worst for this so I can't really pass judgement, but I do think it's important to take a break from work. This is your holiday, after all, and you don't take many of them. So, well done, you, for ignoring bloody Bryan.'

'Yes!' Em says. 'He sounds so useless. Surely there's someone else in the office who can put up with his crap while you're on holiday.'

Right, well, here goes!

'I'm actually *not* on holiday,' I say tentatively.

Stella and Em exchange looks.

'Okaaaaaaay,' says Stella cautiously, like she's trying to communicate with a wild animal. 'So where do you think you are, Jessie?'

'Oh babes,' sighs Em. 'Did you spend too long in downward dog earlier? That shit can really go to your head after a while.'

'Guys,' I giggle, 'I'm fine, I promise. I mean that I'm not *technically* on holiday because, well, I quit my job!'

'WTF?' Em shouts.

'WHAT THE—'

'Yup!' I beam. 'I am currently unemployed or, as the cool kids call it, funemployed.'

'The cool kids do not call it that,' Em butts in. 'Continue.'

'Right, so I totally quit my job, like a crazy maniac, literally the day before we came to Gurnard Cove.'

And suddenly it all comes tumbling out, like a pressure valve finally released, and it feels so good to talk about this with the women I trust most in the world.

'You know how super annoying Arjun was, right?' I'm saying. 'I tried so hard to encourage him and he literally did no work. Well, I went on this training course for digital editors recently, which meant I was out of the office for a few days, and when I got back, Arjun and Bryan had suddenly become best mates. Like, Arjun was calling him Big Bry and everything.'

'Ew,' says Em.

I nod. 'I *never* reached nickname levels with my boss and I'd been working on that paper for years. It turned out that while I was away, Arjun had secured himself a promotion and a pay rise, and that *he* was now *my* boss. I'd only been gone for a few days and suddenly that hamster-loving slacker was going to be head of content?'

159

I pause, take a breath. Probs shouldn't be so rude about Arjun, really.

My friends are agog.

'You deserved that job title,' Stella says.

'That's what I thought! But I'd been leapfrogged by a teenager who'd been working at the paper for less than a year. It didn't seem fair, or right, and I was so stunned, not to mention really upset, and do you know how I found out? Bryan emailed me. He didn't even have the decency to tell me face to face, so he cc-d me into a formal email confirming Arjun's promotion.'

'NO!' gasps Em.

'That was also my reaction!' I say. 'This is going to sound silly, but that wasn't even the final straw. After all my hard work for that paper, basically carrying the entire news team and doing all the digital work on my own, and now this, and I still didn't consider leaving the job.'

'So . . . what happened?' Em probes.

'Arjun replied to the email, asking Bryan to confirm that he would also have a new wardrobe budget because he'd be doing a lot more on camera for the *Courier*'s TikTok going forward. And Bryan said yes! It was like the straw that broke the camel's back. A promotion and a wardrobe budget? I was so cross, so sick of being undervalued, so completely exhausted with it all.'

I pause to look at my best friends. They're holding hands above the table, their faces lit up like the Eiffel Tower.

'We're going to need more wine,' Stella tells a passing waiter.

'Yes, Jessica. YES!'

'May I just say that I love the fact that it was the wardrobe budget that tipped you over the edge,' guffaws Stella. 'Classic. I'd have been the same, Jess.'

'So what did you do next?' Em asks.

'Firstly, I went and had a meltdown in the conference room. Shut the door, closed all the blinds and screamed.'

'This is so dramatic,' whispers Em.

'I know! I've never been so cross. I kicked an old fax machine and everything, but then I felt so bad and tried to fix it, which I obviously couldn't because—'

'You're useless with machinery?' offers Stella. Em nudges her with an elbow.

'Because I've never used a fax machine,' I say. 'And then, once the red-hot rage had cooled down a little, I straightened myself up and walked back into the newsroom, with literally everyone watching, and into Bryan's office.'

'And?' Stella's gripped.

'And I told him what I thought of him,' I say, wincing slightly at the memory. 'I did not hold back. I told him I'd been undervalued and treated with no respect. The more I talked, the more his three chins wobbled with the shock of it all. He was so surprised he couldn't speak. Once I'd finished, I told him that I was leaving my role with immediate effect, marched back to my desk, packed up my stuff and left.'

'Holy shit,' says Em.

'Jesus, Jess.'

'Did you get one of those sturdy brown boxes to put your pot plant in like you see in the movies?'

'Sadly not. I stuffed everything into a couple of sad-looking bags for life,' I reply, watching my friends' shocked reactions. 'Oh god. Do you think I did the wrong thing?'

'What? No way, mate! You finally did the right thing! Those gobshites did not deserve you and your talent. I just . . . I can't believe it.'

'Me neither,' marvels Em. 'This is some serious main character energy, babes. I absolutely love it. You totally did the right thing.'

'Yep, you're a legend, Jess,' says Stella.

'Thanks, guys,' I say, wavering slightly. 'It's just that all this no-longer-being-employed is a bit fiscally terrifying. Especially if I keep spending unmentionable amounts of money on sexy swimwear for tonight.'

Wait. Oops. Oh no!

Em gives me a startled look.

'What's happening tonight?' Stella asks.

'She's confused, poor thing,' says Em quickly, holding a hand up to my forehead like I might be about to faint. 'There's a lot going on and her energy is all over the place. Would you guys like me to explain about chakras, because—'

'No, thank you,' Stella says firmly. 'Let's focus on Jess right now. Look, I get that it's scary leaving the safety of a full-time job, but this is going to open up so many doors for you. And you have savings, right?'

I nod. 'I was hoping to put down a deposit on a flat in Carpston but, I don't know . . . With my parents gone and my relationship with Otis over, and now my job at the *Courier* jacked in, I'm not all that sure that there's much to keep me there anymore.'

Em whistles. 'Big changes for our Jessie.'

'Bit scary,' I say. 'I think that's why I haven't said anything until now. I felt like voicing it all made it more real, somehow.'

'We're here for you,' Stella says. 'Come and stay with me and Fran while you figure it all out, if you'd like?'

'Erm, no, Jessie will be coming to stay with me,' Em says. 'We'll be out every night. Actually, I'm organising a sex party—'

'You already mentioned that and it's a firm no,' Stella butts in.

I laugh. 'Thanks, guys. I feel very loved.'

'I'm just so pleased you told Bryan to stick it. But, wait, why's he calling you?' Em asks.

'No clue,' I admit. 'I don't yet feel brave enough to talk to him on the phone. Pretty sure the last thing I said to him was "eff you".'

'Sounds pretty tame given the circs, babes.'

'I'd have called him Bollock Face because he does look like a giant ball sack,' says Stella. 'Have you thought about what you might do next?'

'Yes, endlessly,' I admit. 'But I can't seem to settle on anything. It's almost like I'm so worried about what I'm going to do next that I can't make a decision.'

'I hear you,' Stella says, grabbing my hand. 'It can be hugely overwhelming. This is one of those times where you need a little time and space so you can really listen to your heart.'

'Stella!' Em gasps, impressed. 'That is so true, babes. I feel like you read that on Zodiac Girlie, am I right? I knew that she'd rub off on you eventually.'

She claps her hands together like a proud parent and Stella chooses to ignore her completely.

'Jess,' she says. 'What are your options?'

I nod. 'As it stands, I plan to carry on volunteering at the local charity bookshop as soon as I get back from this holiday, but after that I'm in two minds. Do I look for other digital editor jobs? Or do I try to work out how I can actually work with books and earn money for it?'

Stella looks thoughtful as she processes this.

'I think, if you've got some cushion with your savings, then volunteering is a great idea in the short term while you apply for other jobs. Maybe you could try both – bookshop gigs and journalism jobs? It would keep all options open to you, and maybe doing some different job interviews would help you to figure out where you really want to be.'

'That sounds sensible,' I say.

'I mean, sure, although you should clearly be working in a bookshop, babes,' says Em. 'I'd focus on that if I were you. And also just enjoy this time, embrace it as a chance to try something new.'

'So, mixed advice then.' I grin.

'We're here for you, Jess,' Stella says.

'Thanks, guys.' Finally sharing this with my friends feels like a weight has been lifted. The future's not that scary, right? Well, maybe still quite scary, but I can't help but feel excited about it all too.

Chapter 14

The clock has been ticking so slowly that I've literally shouted at time twice but finally, thank all the deities, it is now five minutes to midnight. After much deliberation with Emerald, I'm wearing a sundress over the cornflower blue bikini, my hair piled up in a topknot and just a bit of waterproof mascara on my lashes. Plus three thousand pounds worth of diamond necklace, which Emerald insisted was actually quite a low-key amount of diamonds for a swim.

She tied it round my neck and it shimmered in the light and I did not argue.

Stella's already asleep in her room when Em, now in soft pyjamas and fluffy slippers, basically slaps me on the butt as I go to leave.

'Go get some!' she cheers, waving me off.

I'm too flustered to respond.

Heart racing, I walk in the moonlight across the lawn and down the steps to the pool. I can hear the roar of the ocean beyond the cliffs.

And I can see Luke.

He is sitting on the pool's edge with his feet dangling in the water. My heart goes crazy, my brain not quite able to process that this is happening. It's dark, but wall lights illuminate the pool and I can see a bottle of champagne with two flutes set down next to Luke.

He must hear me coming because he turns, his face lighting up in the moonlight when he sees me walking towards me.

'Hey,' I say softly, nerves kicking in as I sit down next to him.

'Hey yourself.' He smiles. 'It's good to see you.'

'You too. You picked a decent spot.'

He grins. 'Beautiful, isn't it?'

'Is this where you bring all the girls?' I ask. I'm aiming for playful but not sure I hit quite the right note.

A brief frown flashes across his forehead before he looks at me in earnest, shaking his head. 'There are no other girls. The only person I'm interested in is you, Jess.'

It seems so strange to me that this could be true, and yet I also believe him. This beautiful man with all these options open to him. Why me? I wonder. But one thing's for sure, I'm not going to waste this night asking questions.

Our shoulders are touching as we sit side by side. The water glows blue in the evening, illuminated by pool lights.

'So,' I say after a long pause. 'Wanna race?'

Luke raises an eyebrow as he side-glances at me. 'I mean, I never turn down the chance to be competitive but, just to warn you, I am quite fast.'

Should I tell him, I wonder, or save it 'til later?

I go for the latter.

'I'll do my best to keep up.' I grin.

'Sure?' he asks.

'I'm pretty sure,' I reply, standing up and pulling my dress off over my head. I swear I hear him gasp as I throw it onto a lounger.

'Jesus,' he says. 'You are beautiful, Jess.'

I don't know how to reply to this so I just carry on talking.

'We should establish some rules of the race.'

'Oh?' A smile twitches at his mouth, his eyes still on me.

'Mmm.' I nod solemnly. 'No sabotage, obviously.'

'You think I'm going to cheat?' he asks, pulling off his T-shirt and dropping it onto the same lounger as my dress. Our clothes are tangled together in the moonlight.

'Hard to tell.' I cock my head to one side.

'Hmm,' he says, 'you just focus on trying your best, and I'll see you at the finish line.'

'Hoh.' I laugh.

'Any more rules, or shall we race?'

'We haven't established a prize for the winner yet,' I say. I'm about to walk over to the pool steps when Luke catches my hand. He spins me back towards him until my body is pressed up against his, and I'm breathless. Engulfed by him. He lets go of my hand, slowly circles his arms around my waist, and tips his head down so that his mouth is just centimetres away from my ear.

'Winner takes all?' he whispers.

'Agreed,' I manage, very *very* aware that if I just tipped my head up his lips would be on mine. Every part of me screaming to do exactly that. But now that I know what's happening, now that I'm certain he likes me too, I want to wait. I want to make him wait. I want to stretch this moment out because lord knows stuff like this does not happen to me and I want to make the most of every last drop.

So I take the smallest step back, unable to tear my eyes off Luke. And he keeps his eyes on me as I ease myself into the water.

'Ready?' I challenge.

Luke smiles at this, dive-bombing into the pool and sending so much splash up into the air that my face is wet.

'Oh my god.' I laugh as he emerges.

'Couldn't resist.' He wrinkles his nose. 'It's actually quite cold in here.'

'I know,' I say, shivering. 'Didn't you say the pool was heated? You basically lured me here under false pretences.'

'Guilty, your honour.' He laughs. 'No, I promise it is heated, it's just that we're outdoor swimming in May, in Northumberland, at midnight, so—'

'Do you need a moment to acclimatise?' I tease. 'You know, before you lose?'

'That won't happen. Unless you *want* me to throw the race?'

'So cocky.' I chuckle. 'You just try your hardest, Luke. I'll see you at the other end.'

He watches as I line up, ready to swim. He gets into position next to me, and I can see how confident he is.

'On three?'

'One, two, three, go!'

I push off, my arms getting into the familiar rhythm they know so well. I strike through the water, faster and faster. I can see that he's not that far behind me, so I drive harder, enjoying the feeling of gliding through the cool water. I reach the other side in no time, turning to see Luke hit the wall seconds later, a look of surprise written across his face.

'Not bad.' I grin. 'A good effort. God loves a tryer.'

'Okay.' He laughs, pushing his hair out of his face as he struggles to catch his breath. 'Okay, okay. You're fast. You're really fast. I feel like there's something you're not telling me?'

I bite my lip.

'Might have omitted a few key facts,' I say, although I am now seriously distracted by the fact that his hands are around my waist in the water, tracing the line of my bikini. It feels almost too good, like I might just melt into water myself if he carries on for much longer.

'Oh really?' he murmurs. 'And what facts are those?'

I hitch a leg up around him, pulling his body closer to mine. Luke sighs and I'm almost undone.

'I used to swim for my county,' I half-whisper into his ear.

Luke looks impressed, amused and stone-cold focused all at the same time. 'Hmm,' he says with a shake of the head. 'Withholding information. I'll have to add that to my dossier on you.'

167

Then he cups his hands under my ass and hoists me out of the pool so that I'm perching on the side.

'Ah yes, the court case,' I reply as his broad torso steps between my thighs. His hands trace down my sides, his thumbs circling just below my ribcage, and I'm not sure how much longer I can withstand this.

'The court case,' he confirms. 'It's basically watertight, now.'

'Are you making water puns because we're in the pool?'

'Well, that would be very shallow of me.' He grins as I wrap my legs around him again, tracing flecks of water with my fingers as they trickle down his chest. He pauses, watches my fingers and tracks his gaze back to mine, holding me with his steel-grey eyes.

I cannot wait any longer.

'Luke,' I say. 'Water you waiting for?'

A low rumble of laughter and then he's scooped me up from the side of the pool and brought me back into the water. My back is pressed against the side of the pool. He's directly in front of me.

'Jess,' he mutters, something flashing across his eyes as he closes the space between us.

The feeling of his lips grazing mine sends my whole body into overdrive, every sensation heightened in that moment. The gentle lapping of the water between us. The feel of his hands on mine, holding me tight.

'Luke.'

And then his phone rings.

His phone rings.

'Fuck's sake,' he mutters, pressing his forehead against mine in frustration. 'That's my work phone. I'm so sorry but I have to take that, just in case. Please,' he says, inching back the tiniest amount even though everything inside me is screaming for him not to do that, 'hold that thought.'

All I can do is nod.

He pulls himself up and out of the pool, every part of me wishing he would hurry up back over here because this is without a DOUBT the sexiest thing that has ever happened to me in my entire life, by about a thousand per cent. The water. The moonlight. The sheer Luke-ness of Luke.

I hear him pick up the phone, I hear him ask what's wrong, and I see his face fall. And I know, in that instant, that he's not getting back in. When he hangs up he pads back over to me, crouches down so he's closer.

'Jess.' He shakes his head again, only this time he looks quite cross. 'You would not believe how sorry I am to say this, but I've got to go. One of the cleaners has got locked into the fitness centre and until the grounds manager starts next week, I'm the only one with a set of keys. I . . . I can't believe how bad this timing is.' He gives me a look of pure regret and I feel it too.

'The fitness centre's only ten minutes away, and it shouldn't take me long to sort out, but this water's not that warm and it could be thirty minutes before I get back.' Luke rubs the back of his head with one hand. 'God, I want to ask you to wait but I know that's not the right thing to do.'

I'm basically ready to shout 'I'll wait' but he's right, the water is pretty cool. I consider reaching my body up, kissing him anyway, but I don't want to rush this just because he's got to go. I want more of that magic we shared. More more more, to be honest. So I rethink.

'Hey, don't worry about it,' I say, getting out of the pool. 'We can . . . reschedule.'

Luke looks agitated as I towel off.

'Jess, you're killing me,' he says. 'Tempted to quit my job right now and stay right here with you.'

I laugh at this. 'We don't need two unemployed people in this situation,' I say. And I see he looks confused so I add: 'I quit my job before I came here. Listen, there's always another night, right?'

'Yes, please,' he murmurs, handing me my dress. 'I really am sorry.'

Chapter 15

Luke haunts my dreams in an incredibly hot way and I wake up desperate, literally, to see him again. My fingers reach for my phone, my subconscious telling me that I need to message him immediately to arrange another meet-up. Maybe now, I wonder, though when I check the time I realise that I've slept in and he's probably already at work.

Plus, we haven't actually swapped numbers yet. It's Tuesday morning and I don't have Luke's number and I was in such a sexy slumber last night that I slept in.

What's even going on anymore?

My phone does remind me that Zodiac Girlie isn't going anywhere any time soon.

Today's advice?

Eat the cake.

'Easy,' I say to myself, dropping back onto my pillow with an oof. Luke is my black forest gateau and I will demolish him whole plus cherry on top.

Maybe a cold shower first?

'Babes, we're going tree hugging,' announces Emerald over break-fast. By now we have a favourite table in the restaurant, with views out over the grounds. Close enough to the buffet for repeated pastry dashes, secluded enough to cackle together over old jokes without being overheard and/or judged by the other guests. Pretty sure Dita Ortiz would not want to hear about the time we all got mumps and could eat nothing but ice cream for an entire weekend. Mumps don't scream Hollywood to me.

'Nope.' Stella shakes her head as she slathers a piece of sour-dough with jam.

'Yes.'

'Nope.'

'Yes,' Em says it more forcefully this time. 'It will be good for you. Tree hugging releases oxytocin, the hormone of love and trust.' Then she winks at me and I know exactly what's on her mind.

'I know what oxytocin is.' Stella rolls her eyes, mouth full of toast. 'I just don't need to release it via hugging a tree, Emerald.'

'Well, this one's non-negotiable,' Em says. 'I had to book ahead.'

'You're a liability.' Stella tuts.

Half an hour later and we're standing in the middle of beautiful woodland with our guide, named Birch. True story. I step into a stream of sunlight and shade my eyes, wondering if hugging a tree might actually help me out right now. Let's just say I've got a one-track mind and Luke is the track.

Stella stands next to me, hands on hips, frown on face.

'This is bat shit,' she says.

'Possibly,' I agree. 'Or it could be a super cute idea? If Em's right and we release some oxytocin, maybe that will help with you and Fran?'

Stella scowls at me. 'I'll pretend you didn't just suggest that hugging a tree will solve my relationship problems, Jessie. At least one of my friends needs to be sane, okay? And that one friend is clearly you.'

We both look over at Em, currently running her fingers through a patch of soil and then breathing in the earthy smell. I nod solemnly. 'Say no more.'

'All right, everybody,' says Birch. 'First of all, we're going to work on our breathing. Inhale. Exhale. Inhale. Exhale.'

'Good job he's here,' mutters Stella, to my right. 'I've wanted a refresher course on how to breathe for some time now.'

I chortle, poking her in the ribcage. 'Shh!'

Em is breathing loudly to my left.

'Good. Now, let's choose our tree. Then, once you've found one that feels right for you, go ahead and embrace the wood.'

Em takes this and literally runs with it, turning to wave goodbye to us before skipping off into the woodland, bounding from tree to tree. Meanwhile, Stella and I move off together.

'Are you okay, Stell?' I ask.

She exhales loudly. 'Yes, I definitely am,' she says. 'Just got a lot on my mind, you know? The Fran thing.'

'The Fran thing,' I repeat, wanting to give Stella space to talk.

'Suddenly loads of our friends seem to be having kids, right?'

I nod. It definitely feels like there's been a fair few baby announcements in our wider friendship group recently.

'And in a way I feel sort of jealous of them, which sounds awful, I know,' she says.

I grab her hand. 'It doesn't at all, Stell.'

'I just don't understand how they've made that decision. Not just made it but also cracked on with it! It feels like my social media feeds are one long line of baby announcements or births and I just . . . I just don't know if I even want that.'

'It's okay to feel that way.' I squeeze her hand. 'It's a massive decision. One that I really can't advise on from any point of authority, obvs, but I have heard a lot of people say that there's never a "perfect" time for having kids. Aren't you supposed to sort of fit them in around what you're doing?'

'So I hear,' Stella muses. 'But I give so much to work and I

172

don't know if I'd have anything left . . . '

'Have you spoken to Fran yet?'

Stella winces. 'I was going to the other day but I've basically been putting it off.' She pulls her phone out of the back pocket of her yoga leggings and brings up her messages with Fran. The latest message is a link to a house for sale.

'Are you guys moving?' I ask, surprised.

'Not as far as I'm concerned. But Fran thinks we should get into catchment for the "really good primary schools".' Stella sighs.

'I feel for you Stell. It must be hard when she seems so committed to this that she's already thinking about schooling and you're—'

'Nowhere near that, just yet,' Stella fills in.

'Exactly.'

'Fran really likes this house because it's a three bed so there would be plenty of space for "the kids". Kids, Jess, plural!'

'Oh no no no,' Birch interrupts, suddenly leaping into our line of vision and shaking his head. 'Mobile phones are very much not allowed during our tree hugging morning.'

'Actually, my friend's going through some—' I begin to protest.

'It's okay.' Stella smiles at me. 'Thanks, mate, for listening.'

'Always,' I say, while Birch proceeds to hold his hand out expectantly and Stella hands over her phone. 'Often,' he says, 'you will find the trees have all the answers you need.'

Stella tries to look like she's taking this comment seriously which makes me chuckle. Birch rounds on me.

'Now scatter,' he says, flinging his arms wide. 'Out into the woodland. I want you alone, free, at one with nature.'

I give Stella one last fleeting glance before we spread out, walking deeper into the woods. I find myself alone and eyeing up a tree, feeling slightly foolish. There's nothing but the sound of birds singing to one another and the gentle crunch of what I assume are cute woodland creatures padding over leaves on their morning commute.

Should I ask for consent? Seems polite.

'I'm coming in for a snuggle, is that okay?' I whisper to one tree. Pause.

No response. Can't say I'm surprised because, you know, I'm talking to a lump of wood.

'Well, here goes.' I step forward and wrap my arms around the trunk of a large tree, my face alarmingly close to its bark. No doubt there are thousands of tiny bugs roaming around on here, a thought I don't dwell on for too long.

I feel nothing. Other than some unacceptable thoughts about Luke and wood which I will not repeat for decency's sake. Alas, my mind is in the gutter.

But then, as I wrap my arms tighter around the trunk, I'm flooded with a feeling of lightness. I feel calmer. My heartrate seems to be less spiky and, without wanting to sound like a total Emerald, I feel grounded. And grateful. I'm doing okay, right? I've totally got this. So what if I've quit my job and now have no clue what I'm doing with my life? It's all right to take a pause, to re-evaluate what I want and to blooming well have some fun. I take a moment to appreciate how incredibly lucky I am to be having this experience.

I breathe in and sigh happily.

'Thanks, tree, you're the best.'

What sounds like a man clearing his throat startles me out of my reverie. But since Birch's tree hugging class spread out and I'm on my own, it must just be some weird squirrel noise I haven't heard before. The woodland really is full of mystery, I marvel, cuddling tighter around the trunk.

'Jess?'

All right, squirrels don't speak.

Or know my name.

I spin around to find Luke standing behind me, an amused look on his face.

Naturally my calm state jacks up to one of sexy frenzy *and* embarrassment, which is a combo I haven't experienced before. I don't love it.

'Sorry to disturb,' he says, as if this is a normal, if not *expected* thing to find me doing. 'I was just out for a run and, well, you look so cute there. I couldn't jog past without saying hello.'

On closer inspection, Luke is indeed wearing his running kit. I notice the way his tight T-shirt wraps around his biceps as he stands with hands on hips, ever so slightly folding forward to catch his breath. He's stopped in a shard of light which highlights his skin, glistening from the effort of his run.

Gulp.

'You caught me.' I smile sheepishly, trying to engage my brain and also stop hugging the tree. I unwrap my arms and give the trunk a pat. 'Trying this for the first time. I thought it would be lame but it's super nice. I love wood, it's my favourite.'

Oh god no. Where did *that* come from?

What happened to being sexy and flirty, Jess?

Luke arches an eyebrow and then comes the disarming smile, all for me.

'Lucky tree,' he says. 'I'm actually quite jealous.'

My heartrate notches up another gear.

'You're a big boy.' I grin. 'You can handle it.'

Honestly sometimes, the *things* that come out of my mouth. This is all the oxytocin's fault.

Luke's still watching me, looking decidedly like he can't handle it.

'Did you get everything sorted last night?' I ask.

'Eventually, yes, though it took ages. Thanks for asking and sorry, again—'

'Luke,' I say. 'You don't have to apologise.'

He runs a hand through his hair. 'I'm going to need to see you again. Quite soon, if you'll let me?'

My heart flutters. 'I'd like that.'

'I'm meant to be taking a table tennis class this afternoon, but no one's booked onto it. If you're free, we could have a one on one?'

175

Oof.

'Table tennis.' I pretend to mull this over even though we all know I am definitely going to show up for this 'one on one'. 'Pretty sure you'll beat me at that, Luke.'

'Only fair after you annihilated me at swimming.'

I smile. 'Okay, since it's in the interests of fairness, I will be there.'

Luke's face lights up. 'Great! I'd better get on but, also, we're having a staff party tomorrow to celebrate our first week at the hotel. It's not strictly for guests but I'm pretty sure I can make an exception for you, if you'd like to come?'

I blink. Sort of blindsided and therefore, apparently, speechless.

'You absolutely don't have to. Stella and Em are invited too, if that helps?' he asks, misreading my silence for uncertainty. The reality is I'm surprised by the invite. So far we've kept whatever this is between the two of us (well, and Emerald) but now he's inviting me to a big party? It all seems like so much more than I'd ever expected and my brain is struggling to process it.

'Will Perry Carver be there?' I tease.

'He is very much not invited.'

'Shame. Still, I guess I could pop along.'

'Please do.' Luke grins.

'Seriously,' I add, 'thanks for inviting me.'

'I'm really pleased you can come,' he says. That honesty of his so disarming. 'We're doing a barbecue in the woods . . . your favourite,' he adds, basically smirking now. I die a small death. 'I'm only sorry that it will be after your crushing defeat at table tennis.'

'There's literally no denying that will happen.' I laugh.

Luke fixes me with his gaze, and my insides melt like candlewax.

'Don't forget, winner takes all,' he says, before running off.

I lean against the tree and tip my head back, flustered.

'I love wood, it's my favourite?' Emerald honks as we pedal our way through a spin class, side by side. 'Jessie, you didn't?!'

'It's your fault!' I wail, already out of breath. 'Turns out hugging trees plays havoc with your hormones. Things were going so well, I felt like I was actually being quite flirty for once, and then I hugged the bloody tree and all sorts of crap started pouring out of my mouth.'

'Now now.' Em looks at me as sympathetically as possible as she struggles to get a hold on her mirth. 'Let's not get cross. What I think you're trying to say is "thank you, Emerald".'

'Pretty sure I'm not,' I puff.

We've only been in here for ten minutes but already the sociopath leading the class has us pedalling so fast I can no longer feel my legs. Em's been dying to get me on my own all day for a debrief on the midnight swim and now Stella's off having an archery lesson. As a side note, the thought of my forthright best friend learning how to shoot things is alarming, I must say.

Emerald bites her lip. 'Tell me more about the swim and the flirting.'

I look around the class, conscious that I don't want to say too much when there's a high chance we could be overheard.

'The swim was *amazing*,' I exhale.

'Did you sm—'

'No!' I squeak, flustered. 'It was very sexy until we had to cut it short. I *think* I was even doing a decent job at flirting, but then today I got hot and bothered and started talking about wood. Oh, and I also called him a big boy. I blame the trees.'

'Are we sure it's the tree's fault, Jessie?' Em looks thoughtful. 'Or is your big fat crush getting the better of you?'

I groan, reaching for the towel slung over my bike and mopping my brow.

'Let's practise your flirting techniques,' Em says. 'Pretend I'm Luke.'

'Em, I'm hot enough already. If I start picturing Luke in spin class I might need medical assistance.'

'Oh boy, you have got it bad. Look, the hard part is over, right?

177

You already know he likes you, he's made that crystal clear. So all you need to do now is be open, honest, engaging. Maybe don't call him big boy until you're actually smashing, by which point, you can totally go in for that,' she snorts.

'It's too soon to laugh about that,' I huff. Man, crushes are so confusing! No wonder I've avoided them like the plague all my life.

'Oh,' I add, suddenly remembering. 'Luke said there's a staff party tomorrow night and we three are invited.'

'Now that is exciting!' Em cheers.

'I'm just worried that I've made a fool of myself with all the unmentionable chat about wood and now he's gone off me.'

'Wait, did he invite you to the staff thing before or after you said those things?' Em asks.

'Erm, after.'

'So, he's definitely not gone off you then,' she says as if this is obvious. 'Why would he? You're adorable, Jessie!'

'Really?' I puff.

'Saints alive.' She rolls her eyes. 'You really are quite obtuse sometimes, sweet Jessie. But don't worry, Em's here to look after you. And I think that this night out is just what we need.'

'Em, we're at a luxury spa. Every single need is being catered for at all times. Someone literally took our dirty laundry and returned it cleaned, ironed and folded. Underwear and all! I've never had my knickers ironed before. What more could you want?'

'A chance to let our hair down! Blow off some steam! I know this place is amazing and all that but you have to admit, an old-fashioned night out would be so good right now. I mean, we've never looked better, for a start. All this pampering. And you don't have a cold for the first time in your adult life.'

'Hey!'

'Come on, you're usually so snotty, Jess.'

I stick my bottom lip out. Being called obtuse and snotty in a short space of time feels like a new low.

'And besides, we haven't been out, the three of us, in ages.

When we get together it's brunches or dinners these days. Aren't you tired of being so grown up all the time? I mean, we're not even thirty yet and we haven't been *out* out in ages.'

'I don't think it's going to be a mad night out or anything,' I say. 'Luke said something about a barbecue in the woods.'

'I'm going to be wearing sequins whatever the weather.'

'Good for you.' I smile, her enthusiasm infectious. 'He also invited me to table tennis later.'

Em is so thrilled she takes her hands off the bike and claps. The teacher takes this as a sign of her enthusiasm for spin and woops back.

'Yes.' She grins. 'This is perfect. I can already picture Luke standing behind you, helping you with your serve. Only obviously he's using it as an excuse to get close to you and the next thing you know you can feel him pressed up against you and his massive—'

'EMERALD! Seriously, stop it. I already can't think straight.'

She's properly laughing now, the swine, so I pedal harder and faster in a bid to take my mind off everything.

In hindsight, spending an hour before a hot table tennis date doing spin class was not my finest decision. As a non-regular spinner, my legs are now killing me. Who does this regularly? Only monsters, I decide as I hobble back towards the gym.

Still, not even aching muscles can kill the excitement I feel for finally seeing Luke again. It's been hours. And I've spent every waking moment getting flashbacks from last night in the pool. The way his hands felt on me. The way his lips grazed mine before he had to go.

He must have seen me coming because he jogs out of the gym, calling my name.

'Hey,' he says, looking concerned. 'Are you okay?'

'I'm fine,' I breeze. 'For some reason decided to do a spin class earlier.'

'Ouch,' winces Luke. 'Do you want to sit table tennis out?'

'No,' I reply hastily. 'I'm definitely good.'

He tentatively grabs my hand and leads me towards a room in the gym where two tables are set up, and pours me a glass of iced water. When he hands it to me, our fingers brush and my gaze tracks up to meet his. He's looking at me so intently I wonder whether it would be okay to throw all of my clothes on the floor right here, right now. Clothes borrowed from Em, btw. A cute tennis skirt and polo shirt which she said give me 'Wimbledon vibes'.

'So,' he says, 'shall we?'

I nod, and we take our places at either end of the table.

'Are you going to be a secret table tennis champion as well?' he asks, as I somehow manage to serve and land the ball on my first shot.

'Very much not.' I laugh. 'That was beginner's luck.'

'You're doing well,' he says as we play, but then I fire a shot off at a crazy angle and Luke ends up leaping to catch the stray ball, affording me a glimpse of his torso under his T-shirt as he jumps.

'Is there any sport you're not good at?' I ask as he sends it back over the table.

'Well, I was desperate to be a cricketer when I was a kid,' he says, serving hard.

'I have terrible memories of cricket growing up,' I say. 'My brother James loved it too, and he was good, so we spent a lot of time ferrying him to matches. I never did understand why cricket matches took so long. My parents ploughed a lot of time and energy into him and for a while, it looked like he might make it professionally, but pro sport is brutal, as you know,' I say, glancing over at Luke. 'In the end he just wasn't quite good enough.'

'That's tough,' says Luke.

'Yeah, he didn't take it too well. Kind of went off the rails for a while.'

'I meant tough for you,' Luke says. 'Dedicating all that time to him.'

'I hadn't really thought about it like that,' I say. 'I guess sometimes I did feel a bit resentful, but you don't question things when you're young, do you? I could see how proud my parents were of him, and that made me happy.'

I pause to think on this.

'How do you do that?' I ask.

'Do what?'

'Crack me open like that. Here I am just sharing personal stuff with you again,' I say.

'Funny, I was thinking the same thing about you.'

'Ah, well, that's because I put a spell on you.' I smile.

'I knew it.' He grins.

We're still playing, on and off, when Luke hits the ball over to my side and I reach across for it even though I am quite clearly never going to return his serve. But as I do so, I feel my leg spasm and I gasp in pain.

Luke is by my side in seconds.

'I think it's just cramp, I'm fine,' I say, grimacing but not wanting to seem like a total dweeb.

'You are not fine,' he says, leading me over to a chair and sitting me down. 'Did you ice, after spin class?'

I shake my head.

'I'll be right back,' he says.

Luke returns with an ice pack wrapped in a hotel towel. He walks straight over to where I'm sitting, kneels down in front of me and asks permission to ice my leg. Then he presses the pack against my thigh and holds it there.

'I'll never win anything at this rate,' he says, which makes me laugh.

'Did it on purpose.' I grin.

'Didn't I say you'd be trouble?'

I bite my lip. The ice is making my thigh feel infinitely better

181

already, or is it the knowledge that his fingers are so close to my skin? The ice pack pushes against the hem of my skirt. I look up, catch his gaze, watch him swallow.

'Luke,' I whisper.

And that's all it takes. His thumb inches off the ice pack and onto my thigh. The feel of it makes me inhale sharply and Luke's eyes darken at the sound.

'ARE THEY IN THERE?' shouts Stella.

Shit! I push my chair back, a kneejerk reaction, panicking that we're about to be busted. The door bursts open and Stella is standing, hands on hips, in front of us.

'Why didn't you tell me?' she demands.

Oh my god, she knows. And she does not look happy. I open my mouth, no words coming out. Luke is still kneeling, some distance away from me now, ice pack in hand, looking as shifty as I feel.

'You know I love table tennis!' Stella is giving Luke a cross look. 'Why didn't you tell me you were playing?' she repeats. 'And what's happened to you?' Stella frowns at me.

'I, oh god, so . . . ' I gabble.

'Did you do this?' Stella asks Luke.

'What do you mean?' I ask, about to try and explain that whatever is going on between me and Luke is very much mutual. Because right now Stella appears to be accusing Luke of instigating it?

'Let me guess, you got way too competitive and now poor Jessie's injured because of it,' Stella grumbles.

Luke and I share a look of realisation. She's not talking about *us*. She's just grumpy not to have been invited to play and she's being protective of me.

Phew. That's a relief, I think, although I feel distinctly guilty for sneaking around like this. And also incredibly miffed that the moment between me and Luke has gone. With a glance of crushing disappointment, Luke stands up.

182

'I hurt my leg in spin earlier so I managed about five minutes of this table tennis class before needing a sit down,' I explain.

'Spin is the devil's work.' Stella tuts. 'Ah well, little bro, looks like you're taking me on instead.'

She grabs a paddle, marches over to the table and so begins an extremely intense match in which every point is contested as the siblings bicker for top spot. Thwarted, again, I sit with the ice pack melting against my leg and kick my trainers up on the edge of my seat.

Honestly. If I have to wait much longer I might literally burst. So much for eating the cake, I think grumpily. I can't even get my hands on a ruddy slice without being rudely interrupted.

Chapter 16

I am a strong, powerful woman and I will not spend another day in a state of perpetual mooning over Luke, I decide when I wake up on Wednesday and my thoughts immediately fly to tonight's party. To seeing him again. To finally, finally, *finally* getting close to him. To doing things I've probably never done before because I have definitely never felt like this before.

All to say: if I don't take action now, I will spend the day getting so worked up that I'll probably end up saying more ridiculous things to him tonight. And nobody wants that.

So today, I am a woman of action.

Plus, it turns out Zodiac Girlie totally agrees. My Stars in Brief this morning are literally bang on the money.

It's time for big moves.

Eek! I check the hotel's list of today's scheduled activities on WhatsApp and settle on coasteering. Sounds terrifying. Sounds like the exact thing I would never normally do in real life. The perfect distraction before I make big moves!

The rest of the girls still aren't up because it's *checks time* 6am and there are four hours until we go coasteering. Four hours to not think about Luke. I can totally do that! I'll go for an invigorating early morning swim, I decide. But when I peek out of my bedroom window, I see that it's absolutely lashing it down. My weather app predicts rain and cloud for the next few hours, which is a more standard British May, I guess, even though there has been the recent spate of blissful warm days. Usually, I'd be mildly disappointed by this forecast. There's nothing worse than walking to work in the rain, trusty rain trousers clinging to my legs, cagoule zipped up so tight I look like Kenny from *South Park*. So much so that Arjun used to sing R.E.M.'s 'What's the Frequency, Kenneth?' to me when I arrived at work, which is a lyrical reference I did not expect him in all his youth to get.

Thankfully, I will never have to deal with Arjun again. I feel slightly sheepish that I've been ignoring Bryan's calls all week, and now that I've activated Action Woman mode, I vow to call him later and find out what on earth he wants.

Quietly, I pull on my swimming costume with leggings and a jumper over the top, and pad out of the house. Our spa suite has a selection of umbrellas in the hallway so I grab one and dash across to the indoor pool, which looks almost more inviting against the backdrop of rain and low-lying clouds outside. I ease my body into the deliciously warm water, a couple of other swimmers already getting their lengths in, and start to swim. There's something so soothing about the gentle exercise and as I stretch out, my mind wanders.

To Luke. What else is there? Goddammit! I just can't get my head around the fact that he likes me. The man who makes me out of breath without even taking a step actually *likes me*. My stomach swoops and dives every single time this thought pops into my mind, which is all the time, so right now I'm existing in a state of perpetual excitement and disbelief. And as if my physical reaction to him wasn't enough, there's the whole emotional connection too. I think about how he manages to be kind and thoughtful while making it quite clear that he likes me. Our shared thing for architecture. The fact that he too loves a library. How just being together opens up this channel of communication between us and we find ourselves sharing things with each other that we don't normally talk about.

It's mad, really. I'm trying very hard not to get my hopes up too much, to put a lid on this excitement before it boils over. Because the fact is, Stella could well be seriously grossed out by the whole thing. And I'd get that. I think back to Emerald and her mega crush on James when we first met. Whenever he called – which wasn't very often because James is nothing if not succinct when it comes to his approach to brotherly love – she'd paw at my hand like a hungry cat, hoping to catch snippets of his voice. Once, when he came to stay, she tried to cast a love spell on the sofa where he'd be sleeping for the weekend. She spent hours cooking up this horrific smelling potion in the kitchen, which had in it strawberries, dried roses and, inexplicably, vodka. The flat smelt like a decaying bunch of flowers in a long-closed pub by the time she announced it was ready, and then spritzed it all over the sofa. Needless to say James did not fall in love with Em after a night on the rancid sofa, neither did he notice her much at all, to be honest. At the time, I remember feeling a bit relieved about this, but now, looking back, I am shocked and appalled on Em's behalf. She is such a beautiful person, inside and out, and I can't think of many men who haven't fallen at her feet over the years.

That's my weird older brother for you.

'Yessica, you are laughing while you are swimming. I adore this for you.'

I *am* snorting with laughter, it turns out, as I tread water to find Dita Ortiz in a designer swimsuit with ruffled straps, enormous diamonds hanging from her ears and an expertly coiffed up-do, draped across the edge of the pool.

'Hello, Dita!' I swim over to the edge. 'Didn't see you there. Are you coming in?'

'Of course.' She eases herself into the pool. 'What is amusing you today?'

'Oh, just remembering the time my best friend made a love potion to try and woo my older brother.'

'Which of the girls is this? Let me guess, my astrological partner in crime, Emerald?'

'You're so right.' I beam. 'Stella, our other friend, is not a making love potions kind of gal.'

'Sí, sí. And did she succeed?'

'Only in making our landlord very cross. We had to pay for our sofa to be professionally cleaned because the potion stained it red.'

Dita titters at this. 'My friends were always mooning over my brothers when we were growing up.'

'Really? Did you mind?'

'Not at all,' she says as we swim together. 'I saw it as a compliment, and it made me feel proud, too.'

'How would you have felt if your friends dated your brothers?'

'Plenty of them did.' She chuckles. 'I did not mind one bit, as long as everyone was treating everyone with respect and kindness.'

'That's very emotionally intelligent of you,' I say. 'My friends and I made a pact not to date each other's siblings when we were at uni. At the time I thought it would be so weird but now, well, to be totally honest, I'm massively regretting it.'

'Ah yes, the Sagittarius and the Libra. Our perfect match.'

'I'm worried about what Stella will think.'

Dita considers this. 'You have been friends for a long time, no? Then she will already love you with all her heart, just as she loves her brother. I think she will be very happy, and lucky, to hear of this.'

'I hope so. I've never felt this way about anyone before.'

'I have seen this Luke around. He looks delicious, like churros, the kind you can't take one bite of, you have to eat the whole thing until you are covered in sugar and you have liquid chocolate running down your fingers.' She pauses to give me a delighted look. 'Yessica, he will be excellent for you.'

'You don't think—' I begin, and then I don't know how to end my question.

'What is it?' Dita asks.

'I just don't really understand it, Dita. I think he likes me but why? As you've just said, he is delicious to look at. And extremely kind, and funny. And delicious.'

'You said that one already.'

'So why does he like me?'

'Yessica, you are more stupid than you look.'

'Excuse me?'

'Poor, stupid Yessica. You have no idea how lovely you are, I see that now. You deserve to find the right kind of love, with the right kind of man. And yet you have spent more time worrying about your friend's feelings than you have talking to me about how that delicious man might taste between your lips.'

I splutter, accidentally swallowing pool water.

'Dita only speaks the truth. You deserve good things, Yessica. You have a kind soul. Have faith in yourself, as my good friend Nicole always says.'

'Nicole sounds wise.'

'Very wise. We starred together in a film many years ago and have been close ever since.'

'When you say Nicole . . . '

'Kidman,' Dita fills in.

'Sure.' I nod. Why wouldn't it be?!

'It's a miracle, really, to have found such a close friendship from that film. The director, Bryan, was awful, the most ungenerous man I have ever met.'

'I know a Bryan like that,' I say.

'Oh.' Dita's eyes light up. 'You go first.'

After I've filled her in on the rudimentary awfulness of my former editor, Dita is horrified on my behalf.

'Thank god you quit!' she says. 'I vowed never to work with Bryan the director again.'

'Yes, Dita! We should totally stand up for ourselves in the face of awful Bryans.'

'Quite.' Dita smiles, before announcing that she's finished her swim. I get out too, thinking about how Nicole Kidman vicariously thinks I should have faith in myself. It's not the first time I have heard that – if from wildly less A-list sources in the past – I think after I've said my goodbyes to Dita and am drying myself off. And I guess there'll be no hiding things from Stella later once the party starts, which means it's time to come clean to her.

'Where's Stell?' I ask, finding Em at the gym waiting for me on her own.

'Sends her apologies,' Em says. 'She's taken your hot lover off for a cookery class.'

'He's not actually my hot lover just yet,' I protest, and I must look disappointed because Em asks: 'What's up?'

'I think I need to have a chat with Stella about Luke.' I wince.

'Makes sense.'

'I just want to make sure she's okay with it before things go any further between us.'

Em starts clapping. 'Are you planning to smash him at the party tonight?'

'Not *at* the party, no!' I laugh.

'After?'

'Well, I don't know! I mean, obviously I would love that. But I just have this doubt in the back of my mind, this feeling that I definitely need to check in with Stella first before anything major happens. I think it's only right, don't you?'

'Sounds sensible,' Em says. 'Maybe you could talk to her tonight when we get to the barbecue? I'll totally leave you guys to it, you can get a drink together and just talk it out.'

'Yes, that sounds good, if a little terrifying.'

'You'll be fine, Jessie. She's going to be cool about it, I can sense it.'

189

I chew my lip in thought. 'I hope so. Also, did you say cookery class?'

Em nods. 'Stella said something about wanting Luke to learn some basic life skills now that he's back in the UK.'

'I'm pretty sure Luke has lots of life skills already.'

'I bet you are.' She grins. 'But Stella said, and I quote, "he can't cook for shit", and she's worried that he won't survive the harsh British winters without learning how to make some things.'

'That's very sweet.'

'I know, right? They're such cute siblings. Like, so competitive and always arguing, but it's obvious how much they love each other. Jess? Jess! You've got that long-lost dreamy look on your face again.'

I try to arrange my features into something less dreamy.

'Shall we, erm, coast?' I suggest. 'I need distractions.'

'Talk me through this one again?'

'Coasteering is where you move from one part of the coast to another using only your body, no boats or rafts or anything. So there'll be some climbing, some swimming, probably some crawling through holes . . .'

'Sounds very much not your thing,' Em points out.

'I know, right!' I say cheerily. 'Just trying to take my mind off—'

'The horn?'

'Exactly,' I whimper.

'Speaking of the horn,' says Em, giving an appreciative whistle. 'Who is this?'

I turn to see what she's looking at.

'Hi!' says a tall blond in a wetsuit. 'I'm Ryan, your coasteering guide for the day.'

'Hello,' purrs Em. 'Aren't you a long drink on a hot day! And let me tell you, Ryan, I am quite thirsty.'

Oh dear, I think, poor Ryan doesn't stand a chance.

Emerald pulls off the wetsuit look with aplomb, she could easily be off to compete in some glamorous Australian surfing competition.

We're at another part of the coast where Ryan is explaining how to signal for help if we get stuck down a pothole or find ourselves being dragged out to sea.

'This all sounds absolutely terrifying, Ryan,' I squawk, suddenly regretting my rash decision to take part in this.

'Don't worry, I've got a super easy route for us today as this is your first time coasteering, I just have to go through the safety procedures first. And if you love it, we can come back and do some bigger stuff another time. Like scaling that.' He points to a vertical cliff and I gulp. 'For today, we'll stick to this section of the coast. If we make our way around this part of the headland, we'll get back to Gurnard Cove and the beach hut.'

To my absolute relief, he demonstrates towards a much less terrifying part of the beach where the sea butts against some average height rocks, rock pools forming on top.

'Okay.' I exhale. 'I mean, I'm still terrified but—'

'Let's get started!' Em cheers, butting in.

Thirty minutes later and we're both a salty, wet mess. We've swam a bit, climbed a bit and batted away an angry seagull.

'Why are those guys so aggro?' I ask as we cling to a rocky outcrop like limpets.

'No idea, babes. One stole my chips once. I was so cross.'

'I saw one pecking at a pile of puke at Newcastle train station the other day.'

Em scrunches her face up. 'Maybe that's why they're so cross? Because they make bad choices.'

'You're doing really well,' Ryan encourages from his position on a rock further ahead while Em mutters something to me about how he would not be a bad choice for her. 'If you clamber up to join me, there's a stretch where we can walk and dry off for a bit.'

Em and I drag ourselves out of the water and follow, drying off in the sunshine since the rainclouds have cleared and chatting happily together, in between the moments where Em is making her feelings for Ryan crystal clear.

'Are you sure about Ryan?' I whisper as he gestures towards a swirling pool of doom in the middle of the vast ocean and suggests we willingly jump into it. 'He's clearly a lunatic.'

'Pretty sure he's just doing his job,' Em says, flashing him her most dazzling smile.

'Are you ready to jump?' he asks.

I look down and conclude that he is, indeed, a maniac. To make matters worse, Emerald is very keen to make the jump. In fact, Ryan has barely finished explaining our next move before she's thrown herself off this mighty rock and into the swirling unknown below.

I scramble to the edge and peer over, certain that she has been lost forever, dashed into the rocks and buried at sea.

'Emerald!' I shout down into the abyss.

Nothing. The waves continue to crash into the rocks. The sun beats down on us.

'EMERALD!' I yell, panicking now.

Suddenly a fan of blonde hair bobs up to the surface, followed by the rest of her. Em's smiling face breaks through the water.

'OHHHH MYYYYY GOOOODDDDDD,' she shouts up to us. 'That was incredible! Come on, Jess!'

I mean, she can't be serious. It must be at least a twenty-foot drop from here to the water. I turn to Ryan.

'How far is it?'

'About five feet,' he says, as if this is a reassuring amount of feet.

'That's almost as tall as me!'

'Exactly, not far at all. The sea is completely calm,' he adds, 'so you'll be grand.'

Barf.

'No, I won't! I can't do it, Ryan. I'm too scared.'

'We could go together if you like, on the count of three?'

I take another tentative look over. On second viewing, it isn't quite as far as I'd previously thought. Em's swimming happily in the sea, bobbing up and down in the gentle waves which, actually, aren't crashing against the rocks. More, sort of, puttering against them. It's actually quite a tranquil scene.

But still.

My stomach is in knots. I'm sweating into my wetsuit. I feel paralysed by fear even though I'd love to join Em in the water. I look around the headland and see the hotel's beach bar is in sight now, so close after our morning of scrambling over rocks to get here. But I know, deep down, that I'm not confident enough to make the jump.

'I can't do it,' I whisper as the wind whips up. 'I just can't.'

'That's totally okay,' Ryan says in a reassuring tone.

'But how will we make it back to the beach now?' I ask, deflated. So much for my day of action.

Ryan smiles. 'Ah, well, I always like to have a back-up option up my sleeve,' he says, walking over to another part of the rock. 'Behold, some steps down to the beach.'

'Really?' I ask, relieved. 'Thank god! I thought I'd have to scramble all the way back again.'

Ryan shakes his head. 'You'll be enjoying a drink at the beach bar in no time. Want to head over now?'

'I think I'll stay and watch Em for a bit,' I say, lying down on my belly with my head jutting out over the rock. I wave down at her as she ducks and dives in the possibly freezing water like a mermaid.

'You okay?' she calls up.

'Just a big chicken,' I say. 'Thankfully there are steps to the beach, too.'

'Omg, Ryan!' Em shouts. 'You didn't tell me about the steps!'

He grins broadly. 'I thought you might enjoy the jump.'

At this point, Em winks at our guide and then gives me a look which confirms to me that Ryan won't escape our spa break without being seduced. Ah well, I think to myself, at least she's branching out in the names department.

Chapter 17

I'm a woman on the edge. On a countdown yet again to seeing Luke and I'm not too sure how much more I can take of this. So I've found solace in the library, burying my head in books since Em and I got back from coasteering.

'There you are.' Stella flings herself into the room, causing the pages on my open book to flap about. 'We've been searching for you all day!'

'Well,' Em counters, floating in behind her. 'More like the ten minutes since we finished our red wine bath, Stell.'

Stella grimaces. 'I would never have agreed to that if I knew that I was going to be bathing *in* red wine. I thought you meant have a bath with a nice glass of rioja. My spa robe looks like a bloody crime scene.'

'Look at your skin and thank me later,' Em says. 'Besides, if it was good enough for Cleopatra . . . '

'I thought she bathed in milk?' I ask.

'Wine too,' Em explains.

'What didn't that woman bathe in?' Stella asks. 'The point is, I'm in need of a drink, so can we get going? Staff party starts soon!'

'Hold your horses! We've only just found Jess and obviously we need to get dressed first,' Em points out.

'Do we?' Stella asks, looking down at her leggings and yoga top.

Emerald is horrified. 'Guys, as if we're going out in *athleisure*. Getting dressed up first is literally the most fun part of a night out!'

'That does sound fun,' I say, bubbles of excitement popping in my belly. 'I might wear that black dress I wore to dinner last night?'

'Sweet Jessie,' – Em smiles sympathetically – 'you are getting some extra help tonight.'

'Am I?'

'Yes, babe. Just a little helping hand in the wardrobe department, that's all.'

I shoot Stella a help-me look. 'Soz, Jess, but Em's right and if I have to see that LBD one more time I will scream. Let's get you in something more colourful.'

'Yes, EXACTLY!' Em high-fives Stella.

I pout.

'Come on,' they say in unison, dragging me out of my sweet reading nook.

I'm marched back to the hotel's shop where clearly Stella's become a regular customer because the woman behind the till knows her by name.

'I'm thinking colour drenching for you tonight,' she tells me as I'm hustled inside a changing room and told to strip.

'Ooh yes,' agrees Em.

I hear the sound of clothes hangers scraping along rails as my best friends and the woman from the shop discuss me as if I'm not actually here.

'She's got a great rack.'

'And she never gets those bangers out! Seriously, if I had such marvellous breasts they would be on show twenty-four/seven.' That was Stella.

'Hundred per cent.'

'She's only little so big prints will dwarf her.'

'How about this?'

'Ooh!'

'OOH.'

Someone says 'knock knock' and then the changing room curtain is yanked to one side and there stand Stella and Em, looking delighted.

'We've found the one.'

'The *ones*,' Stella corrects.

Em shoves a pair of red trousers towards me while Stella dangles a couple of straps of matching red string in front of my face.

'What on earth is that?' I ask.

'Just look how cute this little top is,' she replies.

'That's not a top! It's barely even a shoelace.'

Stella tuts and holds it in front of my body. Turns out it's one of those bandeau tops with spaghetti straps. As if I'll ever fit into it.

'It's red,' I whisper. 'I'm a pasty brunette!'

'You'll be surprised,' says the sales assistant. 'Red can look stunning with your skin tone.'

'Agreed. So before you argue,' Em says, handing me a teensy weensy bralet, 'get your boobs into this first. Then try it all on.'

I open my mouth to, well, argue, but they've all bustled out again before I get the chance.

These two.

So I strip down to my knickers and do as I'm told.

There's a rustling of the curtain seconds later. 'Come on! Let's see!'

I take a deep breath and step out.

'Oh *shit*!' shouts Stella.

'Even better than I'd thought!' Em claps.

'You look lovely.' The sales assistant smiles, but then it's her job to tell people that, isn't it?

Stella turns me so I can look in the full-length mirror and I take in my reflection. The cigarette pants are super cute, I must admit. And the top is really nice too, but it's cropped so you can see an awful lot of waist, which I am v much not used to.

'Where have you been hiding?' Em grabs me by the shoulders and beams at me in the mirror.

'Is it a bit . . . much?' I ask.

Everyone vehemently shakes their head.

'You look banging. Look at that tiny waist! My little pint-sized beauty.'

'Do you think?' I ask, fidgeting with the straps of the top. It's all a far cry from my usual look.

'Luke is going to have a heart attack,' Em whispers while Stella is distracted by the shop assistant handing her a pair of shiny pink shoes.

'OMG don't,' I giggle, fanning myself.

Emerald shakes her head at me. 'I can guarantee that he won't be able to take his eyes off you.' Then she calls over to the assistant and says: 'She'll take it!'

So, once again I've been strong-armed into buying things in the hotel shop before actually looking at the price tag. I'm going to make a wild guess that this combo will be a smidge more than my usual Zara haul. I peak at the label on the trousers. Sweet mother of Mary. Wincing, I take another look at my reflection. I do feel pretty good in this. Maybe even really good? The cut! The fit! And I'll definitely get some wear out of the trousers, I decide. The tiny top? Maybe not so much. But I so rarely treat myself to stuff like this, and even though I can hear my savings account sobbing quietly at the hit, I decide to go for it.

The whole lot comes to the price of the sofa I'd been eyeing up for the new flat I'm probably not going to buy anymore and I have to steady myself against the counter as I hand over my card.

'I've got the perfect accessories to go with this.' Em beams at me as I'm handed an expensive-looking bag filled with my purchases. 'And those.' She nods towards Stella, who has just spent her own small fortune on the shiny shoes.

'I just love nice things.' She shrugs as I grin at her.

Back in our suite, we're all showered (mood: excited), in various states of undress and surrounded by everyone's make-up. Em's got the treasure trunk out again and Stella and I migrate towards the case like magpies, oohing and ahhing at all the shiny things. There's no denying that Emerald has a serious talent for jewellery design. Her pieces are stunning.

'Jessie, I'm thinking this for you,' she says, dropping a huge amount of gems into my hand. I'm so confused by the contraption that I try looping it around my neck, at which point Emerald tells me it's a diamond pavé link belly chain.

I don't even know what those words mean.

'A diamond pavé link belly chain?' I repeat incredulously, holding it up to the light.

'Yes and it's going to sit beautifully above the waist of those new trousers. Those baby diamonds will catch the light every time you move.' Em loops the chain around my waist and gently fastens it.

I swallow hard. 'Em, this is very kind of you but there must be hundreds of diamonds on this thing. What if I lose it? How much does it cost? I'm not sure I can handle the pressure!'

'Jessie! Relax! These babies are insured whereever I go so don't worry your pretty little head about it. Now all you need are these diamond drops to go with,' she says, handing me some earrings with a massive stone hanging at the end of each one. 'Right, let's get dressed!'

When Em said she was wearing sequins whatever the weather, she was not lying. She steps out of her room ten minutes later wearing a gold one-shoulder jumpsuit literally covered in sparkles. It would be an outrageously OTT look, but naturally Em makes it scream easy breezy cool, with her blonde hair styled in jagged waves down to her shoulders and nothing but a slick of red lipstick on her face. She looks *amazing*. Like one of those street style photos from Copenhagen Fashion Week.

'You look beautiful,' I gasp as she adjusts her second crown of the week.

'Son of Jupiter, *you* look beautiful,' Em counters, kicking my bedroom door open.

'Is this tiny top a step too far?' I waver. 'I could bung on a classic white tee instead? I mean, we are just going for a barbecue at a campfire and I feel like we're dressed for some kind of mad, high fashion disco?'

'Yes.' Em nods solemnly. 'Mad high fashion disco is exactly my vibe.'

I snuggle her tighter. 'I am so lucky to dance in your disco,' I say fondly.

'Oh, the feeling is mutual.' She grins back. 'Only your vibe is less of a disco, more of a cosy reading nook?'

'That's exactly my vibe!' I beam, thrilled. 'Which is why I'm going to pop a T-shirt on.'

'You'll do no such thing. That diamond belly chain is from my new collection, Jessica. It hasn't even launched yet so you're the first person in the entire world to get to wear it. If you stick a T-shirt over it, I will be personally offended, as will the diamonds.'

I look down at my sparkling midriff.

'Oh, well, in that case.'

'COME ON, LADS, I NEED A DRINK.'

We rush out of my room to find Stella, resplendent in a buttercup yellow dress with enormous sleeves, pacing impatiently.

'Stella, you look divine,' I say, suddenly feeling overcome. 'My best friends are so beautiful! I love you so much!'

'Has she been drinking?' Stella asks Em.

'It's just so nice to be together,' I sniff.

'You big softie,' Stella says, slipping into her exceptionally high new shoes which make her at least three times as tall as me. 'Now, quite clearly I cannot walk anywhere in these. I'd call reception for a golf buggy but I figure most of the staff will be at the party tonight. Do you think we can get an Uber?'

'From one part of the hotel to another? I doubt it.'

Em chuckles. 'There's no need, I have sorted us a ride. Is everyone ready? Follow me.'

'Emerald Bay, you didn't?' Stella asks, impressed, as we all stare at the golf buggy parked (quite badly) by the entrance to our spa suite.

'I very much did.' She pulls a set of stolen ignition keys out of her sequinned clutch bag and jingles them at us.

'Did you steal that?' I squawk. The hotel has a number of these buggies zooming around the grounds at any given moment, ferrying guests from one place to another. But they are always driven by a member of uniformed staff and definitely not by light-fingered guests.

'I prefer the term "borrowed". I'll take it back tomorrow.'

'Em! How did you even do that?'

My best friend shrugs. 'And to think my teachers said I didn't learn anything at boarding school. While everyone else was in maths, I'd be out borrowing things.'

In spite of the fact that we find ourselves in a grey area, legally, I can't help but laugh.

'Does that mean you're in, Jessie?' Em asks.

'As long as you promise to take it back tomorrow,' I say sternly. 'First thing.'

'Good, because you're driving.' She chucks me the keys.

'What?' I ask, stepping back as if she's thrown a piece of hot coal at me. 'I can't drive it! That's definitely very illegal. What if I get arrested? I can't afford points on my licence, guys. Think of the insurance! What if I crash? What if we fall off the edge of the cliff and I kill us all?'

Em has folded her arms.

Stella is examining her nails.

'Babes, we're on private land. I'm pretty sure you won't get arrested. Stella can't drive because there's no space for all of her legs behind the wheel, so she'll have to stretch out in the back.

And I can't drive it because we all know I am a terrible driver.'

'Yeah, you really shouldn't have a licence,' Stella says. 'Remember when you drove us round the roundabout the wrong way because there was no traffic and you said you "couldn't be arsed" to go around it properly?'

'Roundabouts are so tedious.' Em tuts. 'But Stella has a point. I probably would drive us all off a cliff whereas you, Jessie, will guide us safely to the woods with your usual care and attention.'

'*Illegal* care and attention,' I mutter, accepting the keys. 'Come on, then, but for heaven's sake put your seatbelts on, everyone.'

Stella, as instructed, spreads out across the backseat while a whooping Em hops in next to me in the front.

'I brought tunes,' Stella says, cranking her phone up to full volume and playing a carefully curated Spotify playlist which, she says, features all of our favourite uni bangers. It soon transpires that this mostly comprises Drake's 'Hotline Bling' on repeat plus a smattering of Mark Ronson.

So, tonight is a night of firsts and we haven't even left the grounds of our spa suite yet. The first time I've worn a diamond belly chain that costs more than my annual salary. The first time I've driven a golf buggy in heels and cigarette pants. The first time I've been invited to a barbecue by the hottest human on the planet. My stomach somersaults in anticipation.

'I think we can afford to go a bit faster than this?' Em suggests gently as I pootle along the gravel lanes.

'Yeah, mate, we're being overtaken by snails. And I wouldn't mind getting there *before* midnight?' Stella calls over.

'There's no need to be rude.' I laugh, slamming my foot down on the accelerator until we're practically blazing through the grounds of the hotel. Well, sort of. The golf cart has a max speed of twelve miles per hour. 'Woo,' I hoot. 'This is exhilarating!'

'That's the spirit!' Stella calls.

'Yaaaaasssss,' Em cheers. 'Oh btw, it's a full moon tonight, guys.' She pumps her eyebrows at me. Alarmed, I try to turn my thoughts back to the ten and two o'clock position of my hands on the steering wheel.

'Go on then,' Stella says indulgently, leaning forward. 'What does that mean?'

'Well.' Em rubs her hands together. 'A full moon is kind of dynamic. The end of one phase and the start of another. It's the perfect time to take a minute and reflect on what's going on in our lives. Maybe get a little fresh perspective on things.'

'I'm looking forward to getting a fresh perspective on a bottle of beer and a hot dog,' Stella says above the tinny din of Ellie Goulding warbling about love.

'You never know, Stell. Maybe you'll wake up tomorrow with your energy levels recharged.'

'Maybe. Or maybe I'll wake up tomorrow with a hangover, hugging a kebab like it's freshers' week all over again?'

Em rolls her eyes. 'Did everyone plant their seeds of intention when I texted you about the new moon a few weeks back?'

Out of the corner of my eye, I see Stella shaking her head.

'Um, sort of,' I say, eyes on the road. Before we all signed up to Zodiac Girlie, Em would send us regular astrological notes of her own. The last one landed around the time I vowed to be firmer with a lingering Organic Otis. 'I promised myself that I would be clear with Otis and then I did tell him to move out – albeit once you guys got me drunk and forced me to ring him the other night.'

'Good.' Em nods approvingly. 'Tonight those seeds will be at their fullest potential. It's the perfect time for manifesting our goals.'

'What are your goals, Em?' I ask.

'I'm spending time consulting my emotional landscape,' she announces. I daren't look at Stella in the rear-view mirror. 'So really, I'm open to anything. Which is good, because with tonight's full moon, *anything* could happen.'

And then she winks at me and my stomach flips like a pancake.

Thankfully we make it to the barbecue in one piece, physically. Mentally? Not so much. My personal emotional landscape takes a battering the minute we tumble out of the golf cart and into the woodland clearing because I immediately spot Luke and my heartrate notches up a thousand gears.

Surely other people must be able to hear it beating?

He's standing with some friends, a bottle of beer in his hand, wearing an olive green linen shirt which looks so good against his dark skin. I can see that he's twisting his left wrist, his fingers skittering, that continual energy of his always looking for an outlet. And my instinct is to rush straight over and take that hand in mine but I do need to at least try to be cool.

Just behave normally, please, Jess.

'Let's get some drinks.' Stella takes the lead, wending her way over to the bar with Em and me in hot pursuit. I take a minute to look around. We're not far from where I came to the old tree hugging incident about which I will forever cringe. When Luke said there'd be a barbecue, I'd pictured a few cast-iron grills with some plastic chairs dotted around. Once again, I underestimated just how ridiculous this place is. Along one side of the clearing is a garden kitchen, complete with outdoor sink, storage, an integrated fridge, pizza oven and built-in barbecue. One of the women I've seen teaching gym classes at the spa has an apron tied around her waist and is currently turning burgers on the grill.

In front of the kitchen is a sunken area filled with outdoor cushions and beanbags. Then there are two massive picnic tables with long benches, where some people are already sat tucking into bowls filled with salads, nuts and crisps. My stomach rumbles. Usually, a table full of food would be my first port of call but tonight, all I can think about is Luke. I glance back at him as we arrive at the makeshift bar, a trestle table filled with beers and wines, plus a couple of kegs and a few members of staff pouring pints.

He's sharing a laugh about something or other. I love to see him laugh, the way his whole face lights up with it. He senses that he's being watched in that way that you do sometimes, and turns to seek me out.

He holds my gaze and electricity fizzes in the space between us.

He starts walking towards us and he has determined, powerful strides which gives me butterflies. And he's smiling. And I can feel the grin stretch across my face as he gets closer.

Em pokes me in the ribcage excitedly.

But before he reaches us he is stopped, near the speakers, by someone else calling his name.

It's Croissants. Dressed in spray-on, high-shine leather leggings and a matching bandeau top.

I watch in horror as she corners him. And I have never thought badly of a pastry before but so help me god, right now I could swear off croissants for life.

Chapter 18

'Jesus H, what the hell does she want?' mutters Stella, and I assume that she too is witnessing the influencer flirting with her brother. *Again.* Bloody Croissants. Em and I are standing, wide-eyed, watching as Croissants paws all over Luke. I know I should be pulling Stella aside for The Conversation but I've been blindsided by the current scene, and now I'm staring helplessly at Croissant's hair. It's loose today, fanning out around her sculptured shoulders, and I can see a croissant-shaped necklace hanging around her neck. She toys with it while she talks to Luke, which seems to involve her having one hand on his bicep. He looks both uncomfortable and like he's trying to be polite so as not to upset a hotel guest.

'You going to go and give her what for again, Stell?' asks Emerald.

But Stella, I realise, is glaring at her phone.

'Huh?' She looks up, brow furrowed, before returning to her phone. 'Sorry, guys, terrible timing but my assistant has sent classified information to the wrong person and cc-d me on the email. Shit. I need to sort this asap.' She waves her phone around as if hunting for signal. 'I'm going to have to go deal with this.'

'Oh no, wait, I was hoping we could, erm, have a chat?' I say.

Stella frowns. 'Everything okay, Jess? Because I love you and I'm here for you and I would love to chat, but unless you're facing imminent danger then I really do need to go and deal with this work cock-up.'

She glances back at her phone and her frown gets deeper.

'Oh Christ, there's a pile-on. The emails are flying in now. Fucking hell, handling this mess is going to take all night. Sorry, Jess, what was it you wanted to say?'

There's no way Stella will appreciate me keeping her away from work drama just because I want to hook up with her little brother. I'll have to find another time and another place.

'I'm fine, Stell, it can totally wait,' I insist. 'Can we help in any way?'

'Thanks, but I don't think so. I'm going to head back to ours now,' she says.

'Babes,' Em says, pulling a sad face, 'we'll miss you.'

'Have fun for me. Late night! Maybe a kebab!' she calls as she hurries off with her phone glued to her ear.

'Shit,' I mutter. 'I really wanted to talk to Stell.'

'Hate to say it, Jessie, but right now you've got bigger problems,' Em points out, nodding back towards Croissants, who's hand has now migrated to Luke's shoulder.

'She looks like Sandy from *Grease* in the best possible way,' I sigh, taking in all that skin-tight leather and ultra-high sandals. 'How can she walk through the woods in those heels?'

Em clicks her fingers impatiently. 'Never mind how she looks,' she says, 'what about the fact that she's all over Luke? Again.'

'I don't love it,' I say darkly. 'And do you know what? Zodiac Girlie told me that today it's time for "big moves". So I'm going to big move my way right over there and deal with this immediately.'

'Yes, Jessie! Get it, girl.' Em is delighted. And then, when it becomes clear that I have not moved from my spot, she adds: 'What are we going to do? I'm assuming I'm helping? I could fake an emergency, tell her the police are looking for her, something like that?'

'Could be a bit extreme?' I say. 'I want to get rid of her, not make her feel like she's about to be arrested.'

'You never know, maybe she totally deserves it.' Em sniffs. 'Perhaps she's the head of a criminal underworld. Just look at her hair, it's very suspicious.'

'So shiny,' I concur. 'What's she even doing here, Em? It's meant to be a staff party.'

'Perhaps I can help,' says the dude behind the bar, pouring pints.

'I'm sorry, but we weren't talking to you,' Em says, quite dismissively, when she realises some random man has been tuning in to our conversation.

But something about this person gets my attention. I turn to look at him, eyes narrowing.

'You can help?' I say.

'Yes,' he replies with a big grin and a noticeably Spanish slash German accent.

'Oh my god,' I whisper, mouth wide open. 'Dita? Is that you?'

'Hello, Yessica,' says the person behind the bar, a big and very Hollywood smile now lighting up their face. 'I came in disguise. It is very good, no?'

'Dita Ortiz?' Em practically shouts while we both try to shush her.

'It is I.' Dita extends a beautifully manicured hand with a flourish. Other than the perfectly lacquered nails, her disguise is first class. Those famous dark curls have been hidden under a choppy wig, her face now framed with glasses and a pretend beard. She's also wearing a baggy T-shirt and jeans, which make her look like approximately half the other people at this barbecue. 'Although tonight, my name is Derek.'

'Derek?' I splutter.

'Is very British, no?'

'So tell me, Derek, what are you doing?' I ask.

'I wanted to be with the normal people and come to the party,

207

but I did not want to make a fuss,' she says. 'And sometimes it is so fun being incognito for the night.'

'This is amazing,' whispers Em.

'I wanted to pull the pints for an evening. I take notes for my next role, perhaps.'

'You'll be working in a bar for your next role?' asks Em.

'It is unlikely.' She sighs. 'Producers, they tell me I am too glamorous for bar work. It is outrageous, I think. But always, I take notes, just in case.'

An idea is forming at the back of my mind. I chance another look at Luke, who catches my eye and pulls an apologetic face at me as Croissants continues to hog his company.

'Dita, sorry, Derek, I really think you can help. Luke's been commandeered by a hot influencer and I need to get her away from him, asap, because tonight is meant to be our night and honestly, if I don't get some time with Luke soon I'm going to pop like a helium balloon. Pop, I tell you!'

Em puts a calming hand on my shoulder and grimaces at Dita.

'Poor thing. She's got it bad,' she explains.

Dita nods sympathetically.

'And there's one thing I know Croissants will prioritise over flirting with hot dudes,' I say once I've taken a breath.

'I know exactly where you're going with this. Genius.' Em grins, before sipping from the pint of mostly froth Dita hands her and spluttering.

'What is it?' Dita asks.

'Selfies with celebrities,' I say. 'Have you seen her socials? Any chance she has of posting a picture with someone "of note" and she's all over it.'

'Yes, she has been trying to talk to me all week.' Dita scrunches up her nose. 'So far I run away, or send Viktor to distract her.'

'Who's Viktor?' I ask, feeling like I'm missing something.

Dita nods towards the man standing next to her, dressed in an identical outfit except for the pair of reflective aviator sunglasses on his face. 'My bodyguard. He comes everywhere with me.'

'No, sure.' I nod. 'Of course.' Actually, come to think of it, there is always someone loitering a short distance away from Dita every time I see her. When we first met in the library, I'd assumed another hotel guest had come in at the same time as Dita, but now I realise it was her bodyguard.

He tips his head at me once in acknowledgement, arms folded across his chest.

'Cute,' Em says, eyeing up Viktor. 'You remind me of Wills' bodyguard.'

'Sorry, who's Will?' I ask.

'You know Wills, married to Kate?'

'Are you talking about Prince actual William?'

Em shrugs. 'We've only hung out a couple of times, don't get excited. Tell me, Viktor, how often do you work out?'

Viktor remains unmoving, his stare fixed on the middle distance, but I swear I see his mouth twitch the tiniest bit at this blatant display of flirting from Em.

'Em, could we focus please?'

'Of course,' she demurs. 'So we already know that Croissants is desperate to get a picture with Dita, right?'

'Yes, and that Dita's here in the best disguise ever.'

Dita nods. 'Derek Orb,' she says.

'Do we really think Orb is an actual surname?' ponders Em.

'That's not important right now!' I say, starting to get a smidge exasperated.

'Wow, someone's getting antsy.'

'Point is,' I plough on, 'no one here will have any clue who Derek really is. All we need to do is let Croissants know that Dita Ortiz has been spotted somewhere else in the hotel – anywhere but here – and she'll be off in a flash. Don't you think?'

'Hmm, she has seen me in the hotel already,' Dita says. 'Maybe you could tell her that I wish to speak to her? I think that will work.'

'Yes!' Em beams. 'Love this. She'll go off on a fruitless mission to find Dita leaving you clear to bone Luke.'

Viktor clears his throat politely.

Dita produces another pint of froth and hands it to me. 'And who will tell this influencer of my fake location?'

'Ooh, can I? I would love nothing more than to dispatch that pastry-based bell-end,' says Em.

'Actually, I think I'd like to do it if that's okay?' I say.

'Mate, of course. Bit of Dutch courage first?'

She nods towards Dita's pint with a smirk, and I take a regretful sip. So frothy. But still, I feel fortified as I roll my shoulders back and stride over to rescue Luke.

'Jess, hi.' Luke looks incredibly relieved when I join the group. 'God, you look—'

'Oh sorry, we're having a private chat,' Croissants interrupts, looking me up and down dismissively.

I stand my ground.

'I'm actually a big fan,' I tell her truthfully. Or at least I used to be until she repeatedly had her hands all over the man I like.

'Oh, so sweet,' she says, and I can see the façade slip over her face as she goes into professional influencer mood. 'Would you like a selfie, honey?'

'Erm, thank you,' I hedge, as she pulls a small knitted croissant out of her bag and hands it to me.

I wince at Luke. I'd forgotten that she takes this prop with her everywhere, handing it to anyone she's photographed with.

Reluctantly, I take the croissant while she grabs my phone and starts titling her head to the left to get her angles just right, while I'm stood here, holding a knitted croissant like a total loser. But with reason, I remind myself.

'I'm doing so well for selfies with famous people tonight,' I fib, feeling a bit bad for lying.

'Really?' Croissants casts around hopefully.

'Mm hm. I met Dita Ortiz back at the hotel bar on my way over here. She was very friendly when I asked her for a picture. Oh, that reminds me, she said she was hoping to see you tonight, so I said I'd keep an eye out for you, and let you know if I saw you.'

'Really?' Croissants eyes have widened.

'Yep. She said she'd be at the bar all evening, I think she's reading scripts. She had her laptop with her.'

'Maybe she wants a selfie too,' Croissants suggests, already hitching her bag up over her shoulder. 'Even Hollywood megastars can't get enough of me these days. Mind you, is it any surprise when you look this good?'

And just like that I'm feeling less bad about fibbing to Croissants.

She hastily hands my phone back. 'Feel free to post that, honey, and don't forget to hashtag croissants! And like and subscribe to my channels! Buh-bye, nice to meet you.'

And she's gone.

YES! SUCCESS! See ya later, Croissants.

'Jessica Jones.' Luke looks impressed. 'Did you just make that up? To get rid of her?'

'What makes you think I was lying?' I challenge.

'You had this look on your face I hadn't seen before.'

'What look?'

'Kind of mischievous. And you were blinking a lot.'

'Probably hay fever.'

He folds his arms with a smile.

'Fine, I may have been telling a small fib,' I concede.

'My knight in shining armour,' he says, pressing a hand against his chest. 'I needed rescuing, persistent croissants are my least favourite.'

I chuckle. 'How do you feel about persistent pains au chocolat?'

'Oh same.' He laughs. 'The only thing that's persistent round here is my desire to spend more time with you. I was going to say beautiful, by the way.'

'You've lost me.'

'When you turned up. I was going to say that you look beautiful. The prettiest knight I ever saw.'

I can feel my cheeks flush at this.

'Look, I even brought my own chainmail,' I say, thumbing the diamond chain around my waist.

'I noticed,' he says in that deep voice of his, running his finger along the chain, which makes me gasp. 'You've been distracting me since you got here and now, I would very much like to finally buy you a drink, if you'll let me?'

Luke orders two drinks while Emerald makes a beeline for Ryan and I grab a couple of free deckchairs.

'Nice guy, that Derek,' Luke says, handing me a glass of wine and setting his own bottle of beer down on the ground between us. He sits down next to me, his legs spread wide. 'Weird accent though.'

I turn to see Dita/Derek giving me an exuberant thumbs-up and bite my lip.

'Absolutely terrible at pulling pints, too.'

'Mm, I already learned that the hard way. It's like a mini festival, here,' I say. Everyone's gone all out with what they're wearing. I spot Julian, the man who first showed us round and introduced me to the weird and wonderful world of mood showers, in a skin-tight animal print onesie plus headdress. I definitely did not need to feel worried about being overdressed.

'It's the first night we've had to let loose since we started so everyone's gone big. I'm so glad you came, Jess,' he says, not looking at the crowd at all, eyes trained instead on me.

I feel like I melt under his gaze.

Luke pops the cap off his beer – v sexy move – and I say: 'I wasn't going to miss this.'

'Are you feeling better, after that spin class?' he asks, eyes briefly flickering down to the thigh he iced.

212

'Much,' I swallow. 'Thank you. And I went coasteering today which really helped.'

'It did?'

'Yes, basically everything hurts now instead of just my legs.'

'Good strategy.' He laughs softly. 'Just spread the pain out.' Then he holds his drink up and says: 'Cheers. To being here, together.'

'I'll cheers to that,' I say, holding my drink up.

'You have to maintain eye contact,' he says. 'Otherwise it's seven years of bad sex.'

I splutter, very much not expecting this, and now all I can think about is smashing Luke, as Emerald would say, and it's got me so giddy that I can't think straight. Luke and I are still holding each other's gaze, his eyebrow arched, the beginning of a smile playing at his lips, when I finally remember I should actually clink his beer bottle.

'To being here together,' I say.

'Mate!' A couple of the guys I saw Luke with earlier bound over. 'There you are. Want to get some food?'

Only then does Luke break eye contact, by which point I feel like we actually were having sex with our eyes alone. He begins to say no to his mates, explains that he's kind of busy here, but my stomach is rumbling and we do have all night.

'I am actually pretty hungry,' I confess.

'Yes, Luke's friend! I'm Liam, by the way. Let's go.'

Luke hooks his fingers into mine as we follow them over to the outdoor kitchen.

'Just so you know, I'm going to kill Liam for interrupting us,' he says quietly.

I turn and give his arm a playful tug.

'Come on, it'll be fun. Besides, the night is young.'

'I'm going to hold you to that, Jess,' he growls.

A group of us grab plates and pile them high with salads, breads and various grilled things. And when someone finds a spot on

213

the long picnic table for us all, Luke makes a beeline for me, taking the spot next to mine. The heat from his body drives me quietly insane.

'Here you go, man,' says Liam, dishing out some grilled mushrooms onto Luke's plate. 'Has he bored you about being a vegan yet, Jess?'

'Mate,' Luke groans, as if he's not thrilled with being the subject of the conversation.

I laugh. 'I wouldn't say that he's *bored* me about it,' I counter.

'So he has.' Liam grins. 'Did he tell you that he did a ton of research into it back when he was playing tennis competitively? How he realised that there were loads of reasons why going plant-based could help his performance?'

I try not to focus too hard on Luke's 'performance' and instead bump shoulders with Luke, who is looking slightly mutinous now.

'Honestly, I'm interested. I've been thinking about going vegan for a while now.'

Luke looks at me, says: 'I didn't know that.'

'I keep watching programmes on Netflix about how it's meant to be really good for longevity,' I confess sheepishly.

'Me too!' Luke says. 'There's been a lot of really interesting research in that field recently.'

I'm nodding along.

'Oh man, you should propose immediately,' says Liam, watching us. 'You two are made for each other.'

'All right, all right,' says Luke, and he gives me this bashful look, and honestly, I do not know what to do with myself now.

'We're not actually, erm, together,' I say.

'Oh shit, sorry. You really look like you are,' Liam says.

'Yeah, well, I'm working on it,' Luke says.

I turn to look at him, his eyes burning right into my soul.

Liam whistles.

And I don't really have the vocabulary to deal with this, so instead I ask Luke how his cookery class with Stella went.

214

'She's convinced that I can't cook, for some reason.' He rubs his head. 'I don't know why, I've survived this long cooking for myself.'

'What's your go-to meal, then?' I ask.

'I do a mean avocado on toast.'

'Is there much cooking involved in that? Or is it more just toasting breading and then putting things on top of it.'

'Ouch!' He laughs. 'I also do nachos with grilled vegan cheese.'

'Again,' I say. 'That's just putting things on top of things and applying heat.'

Luke leans back, folds his arms across his chest. 'All right then, what culinary delights do you have on offer?'

'I like to cook. Risottos, ramens, and I do a great veggie chilli.'

He considers this.

'It's a date, then,' he says.

I give him a quizzical look.

'You make the chilli, I'll bring the nachos.'

'Okay.' I grin, heart soaring at the thought of a proper date, just the two of us. 'And maybe while we're there you can teach me how to put things on toast.'

Luke shakes his head at me with a smile.

'You should be,' butts in Liam, who I'd entirely forgotten was across the table from us.

'Sorry?' I ask.

'Together, I mean,' he says, looking at Luke and me. 'Just saying.'

I spot the bonfire on my way back from the loo. It's just been lit, crackling slowly in a clearing away from the rest of the party. It's not yet dark and everyone else is still eating and drinking over by the outdoor kitchen area. A few others have started dancing near the speakers, and I see Emerald in quite a compromising position with Ryan en route to the toilet. She gives me a thumbs-up as I walk past.

On my way back to Luke, I decide to text Stella. She's still not back and it's been ages.

Everything okay? X

Fine, only just sorted work drama out.

Yikes. Want me to come and get you?

I think I might bail

What? No! It's so fun here!

We miss you

I know, I know

Fran's just messaged – really think it's time we had a proper chat

Just want to clear the air tbh

Going to call her shortly x

I get that

Love you Stell, hope it goes okay

Clearly, my own heart to heart with Stella is going to have to wait, I realise as I sit back down next to Luke. But that doesn't mean my entire night has to be put on hold, does it? I reason that we've waited long enough, that we deserve some time together.

'Will you come with me?' I ask.

'Anywhere,' he says. I hold out my hand and he takes it and we leave his group of mates behind, and I swear I hear Liam saying 'go on, son' as we move off. I lead the way back to the bonfire, and we stand alone there together, watching the flames, his fingers twined through mine.

'You must stop rescuing me like this,' Luke says.

And it's now. I can sense it.

I look up to read his expression, a soft smile playing on his lips as he watches the flames crackle in front of us. He turns to look at me too, the fire reflected in his eyes. And the smile on his face turns into something else entirely. Pure desire. I let go of his hand, step myself closer in towards him, tip my head up like an invitation.

He takes it.

This is no gentle, inquisitive kiss. After the longest wait, he kisses me like he's hungry, teeth grazing my lip. My whole body responds and I sigh, which seems to send Luke into a whole other gear. He lifts me up, carries me around to the other side of the bonfire so that no one can see us now, and my lips don't leave his. My hands run though his hair, breathless with wanting him. Finally he sets me down, sitting himself down on the grassy clearing beside the bonfire and pulling me lightly towards him. I'm laughing as I sit in his lap. And I pause, fireworks exploding all over me, wanting to take him in. He's so beautiful, I feel like I need to pinch myself in this moment.

'Luke,' I whisper, breathless.

He leans back, hands in the grass behind him.

'I've wanted to kiss you for so long,' he says, finding my lips again. It's intoxicating, this sensation, and we stay like this for a long while, taking short breaks every now and then to look at each other, to smile, to appreciate what is finally happening between us. 'I have not been waiting patiently,' he adds.

This makes me laugh.

'Me neither. It's felt like the longest, what, six days?'

'Agreed,' he murmurs, hands down my back. 'But I also can't believe it's only that long. I feel like I know you, Jess.'

And he's right. It's been such a short time, and we're only just getting to know each other, but I also feel like there is a bond

217

between us. Maybe it's because I already knew him through Stella, because he's my best friend's family? In many ways I feel like Luke has been a part of my life way longer than this past week at the hotel. I can't quite put my finger on it, but when Luke says he knows me, the feeling is mutual. And I've got so many questions, like where do we go from here? What's next, for us, if there is going to be an us. But now is not the time for questions. The bonfire roars nearby and Luke's mouth is on my throat, my chest. Instinctively I move my hands up inside his shirt and gasp at the feel of him. He closes his eyes for a moment, and when he opens them to look at me his pupils are dilated.

'Jess,' he says, pinning me to the spot with that steel-grey gaze. 'Will you come back to mine now, please?'

'You cannot imagine how much I want to do that,' I say. 'It's a lot, by the way. A *lot*. I just . . . I really need to talk to Stella first.'

He pushes his hair back, puffs his cheeks out while he exhales. 'I get that,' he says, shaking his head. 'I mean, I wish we didn't have that to deal with, more than I've wished anything. Ever.' His eyes trail over me like I'm dinner. I climb off him then, because this position is not helping either of us focus.

He lets out a low groan and I sit down next to him, biting my lip.

'Me too,' I say, barely able to look at him without wanting to pounce. The invitation back to his is right there, so tantalisingly close. I could just go. It will be, without a shadow of a doubt, the best night of my life. If kissing here by the bonfire is the starter then I can't even begin to imagine what the main course will feel like. I swallow, hard. 'But it's only right that we make sure she's okay with this before it gets any—'

'Hotter,' Luke suggests, giving me a wistful look.

'I was going to say further' – I grin – 'but yes. Definitely that.'

He leans forward now, rests those long arms of his on his legs.

'You're right,' he says, looking off into the distance. 'You're a good friend, Jess. We could do it together, maybe tomorrow?'

'Yeah.' I nod, very much distracted by the way he's still breathing that little bit quicker than normal. Meanwhile, my heart is still pounding.

'So, do you want to head back to the party?' he asks, flashing me that look again.

'We could just stay here?' I suggest. 'Do some more of . . . this. It's not the worst way to spend an eve—'

Luke does not argue and I do not get to finish my sentence. I don't know how long we stay here like this for, but sometime later fellow partiers start migrating to the bonfire. Someone hands us drinks. There's laughter and more music and here comes Em, reeling me towards her with some exuberant dance moves. My cheeks hurt from laughing as we swirl together, safe in the knowledge that Luke is never far away. My own personal beacon of happiness.

Chapter 19

I wake up with a huge smile on my face, feeling pretty incredible after last night. Every time I close my eyes I can have flashbacks to Luke's touch – the way his fingers grazed that belly chain, the sensation of his lips on mine. I've got goosebumps just thinking about it. So Mission Tell Stell begins first thing for two equally pressing reasons. One, after last night I cannot physically last much longer without racing over to Luke's bedroom and locking us both in there for the foreseeable. And two, she's my best friend. Telling her the truth is absolutely the right thing to do and I'm starting to feel increasingly uneasy about the fact that she still doesn't know.

The question of how she reacts to that information remains to be seen. Will she hate me? No, surely not, I know Stella well enough to know that our bond is too strong for that. But she would be well within her rights to put a stop to this thing between us before it becomes something *more*.

The thought of that makes me feel queasy. The more time I spend with Luke, the more I want to be around him. I find myself storing up little things to say to him, like a squirrel, until I see him next. I imagine his reaction when I hear something I know would make him laugh. The look on his face. The kindness behind those eyes.

All told, I've simply got to get on with it.

Quick check of Zodiac Girlie.

The only way out is through.

Hmm. I guess that means no short-cuts, right? I need to go and get on with it! The girls have messaged to say they're already at breakfast so I pull on some jeans and make my way out of the door to join them, a mix of nervous energy and anticipation, when my phone rings. I realise with a sinking feeling that it's my old editor, Bryan. I've been ignoring him for almost a week now, and in the spirit of getting stuff done, I finally decide to answer.

'Hello, Bryan,' I say warily.

'Jessica, finally,' he says, and I can picture his wobbling chins and his three-day-old shirt as he speaks. 'How are you?'

'I'm fine, thank you. Currently on holiday. So, how can I help?' I ask, hoping to dispatch him quickly.

'Ah yes, your jaunt to Northumberland. I've been trying to get hold of you all week.'

'Yes, well, I no longer work at the *Courier* so I didn't feel the need to take your constant calls.'

Ooh, she's ballsy today!

'About that,' begins Bryan. 'When do you think this little protest might be over, Jessica? Because we really could do with you back in the office asap.'

'Little protest?' I repeat.

'All the quitting business. Have you got it out of your system, now?'

Anger rises deep inside me. It's an unfamiliar feeling and as I press my spare hand against the front door of our suite to steady myself, I notice that my fingers are shaking. How dare he? I'd almost forgotten quite how infuriating and belittling my old boss could be.

'Quitting business?' I repeat, slowly. 'I did actually quit, Bryan. I do not want to work at the *Courier* anymore. You constantly thwarted my goals and then you promoted Arjun over me while I was away on a conference. It wasn't exactly the ideal working environment,' I point out as I push through the front door and make my way towards breakfast.

'Ah yes, Arjun. I may have been a little hasty there.'

Curiosity gets the better of me. 'How so?'

'Now, Jessica, I may have been a tad quick to promote him. But sometimes you have to go with your gut as a leader and that's what I did. You'll understand one day when you're more senior. But really I am willing to admit that perhaps I should have consulted you.'

'You're telling me,' I mutter uncharitably as I march through the tranquil gardens towards the main hotel.

'And perhaps, well . . . he may not be quite as effective a journalist as I had imagined.'

The penny has dropped! Just a casual few months too late, but oh well.

'Bryan, we had literal conversations about this at work,' I reply, exasperated. 'I told you countless times that Arjun was never going to cut it as a journalist, but you insisted that it was my management technique that needed work. You told me I was the problem, not him. So I spent weeks, months even, working tirelessly to train him up as well as covering all the work he was supposed to be doing, and my own. It was exhausting, Bryan. And I got nothing back. No, actually, what I did get in return was a complete lack of acknowledgement from my own manager. You! You were my manager and you ignored me. And then instead, you promoted him above me.'

'Yes, precisely. And there's no need to hash through all that again, Jessica, but I would like to know when you intend to return.'

I've reached the breakfast room now, spotted Em and Stella at our table. Em's cradling a vat of coffee, head in hands after what turned out to be a super late night at the staff party last night. My whole mood lifts when I see my best friends.

'Bryan, you aren't listening. I do not plan to return.'

'All right fine.' He sighs, as if this entire conversation is frustrating for *him*. 'How about a promotion, Jessica? You were angling after deputy editor, correct?'

'Well,' I splutter, blindsided. 'Yes I was. And you told me that I didn't have enough experience.'

'We can make that work,' he says.

I stop walking. And I try to process what is happening as I hover next to a selection of fruit juices by the breakfast buffet. I've finally been offered the promotion I've spent the past eight years angling for. Deputy editor of the *Carpston Courier*. I *deserve* that job title. I've worked so hard for that paper, being constantly overlooked by a senior team of middle-aged men who sit around in badly ironed suits and talk about the good old days on the news desk.

'I've had books editor okayed for you, as well,' Bryan adds after a long silence.

'Books editor,' I repeat, turning the words over in my mouth. The amount of times I pressed to review books for the newspaper and was thoroughly rejected. Only now that I've finally had the guts to quit the paper are they coming back to me with this, what I thought would be my dream job title.

'Sounds good, doesn't it?' asks Bryan. 'Jessica Jones: deputy editor, *Carpston Courier*. Plus books. Hmm, we'll have to work on the title I suppose. Deputy and books editor? I tell you what, leave it to me, I'll have a think on how to phrase it before we get your new business cards printed up. And a pay rise of course. Did I already say that? Commensurate with the title, so that will be another seven thousand.'

I put my hand on the table next to me. Wow. This is big. The title and a pay rise that will make a proper difference to my take home pay every month. I could afford to save a bit and go on breaks like these more often. I suddenly see Em and Stella and me on a beach in a hot climate.

'So, see you on Monday?' Bryan asks.

And for the briefest moment, I waver. I see a flat and I see me hosting Christmas there and Mum and Dad back from their travels and maybe having a spare bedroom where they could stay and then I shake my head and think no. No. I cannot actually consider going back to this quite frankly awful working environment. It's like I've got Stockholm syndrome and now that the option to go back has been presented to me, I find myself oddly open to it. It's what I thought I've wanted for so long, after all. But I don't need it.

Because I look over at Em, tearing a croissant in half and laughing maniacally at me, and realise that I truly have changed. I don't want to go back. I know life isn't going to always be swanning around spas with my best friends, flitting from pedicure to massage like a total lush, but it also isn't going to be trudging back to the journalism job I very much no longer want. Where my days are grey. Not because of the weather but because there is no joy in any of them. I want adventure. I want excitement. I want to go and grab life by the balls just like my parents currently are. And with them gone from my hometown, there really is nothing keeping me there anymore.

So I take a deep breath, and then I speak as slowly and clearly as my ragged nerves will allow.

'I'm going to say this once more, for the cheap seats at the back. I quit, Bryan. I will not be coming back. I wish you and the paper all the best, going forward, but I will not be a part of it. Thank you and goodnight.'

I've reached our table now and with that, I hang up.

Em raises an eyebrow. 'Are you feeling all right, love? You just wished someone, I'm guessing Bryan the bastard, goodnight and it's not even 10am.'

'Seemed dramatic?' I ask.

224

'Did you just quit again?' she asks, a little confused.

I collapse down into a spare seat and gratefully accept my own vat of caffeine from Stella. 'I think so?' I puff. 'He offered me deputy editor.'

'What?'

'And books editor.'

'And you said . . . '

There are a few beats of silence. I look from one to the other before I announce, 'No! I said no! I basically had an out-of-body experience over by the fruit juices and decided there and then that I definitely do not want to go back to Carpston.'

Em's eyes are wide. 'Jessie, your Saturn Return is bigger than even I could have predicted and I am totally at one with the stars.'

'You totally are.' I exhale.

'I'm proud of you,' she says.

'Yeah, fuck Bryan,' adds Stella, reaching out to grab my hand.

'Yes, exactly! Eff Bryan!' I say shakily, squeezing Stella's right back.

'Are you okay?' Stella asks.

'Think so. I feel like a weight has been lifted.'

'I'm so proud of you.' Stella smiles at me fondly. 'So proud. In fact, you sit there, I'm going to fetch you some breakfast treats while you recline and soak up this moment for a while longer. The usual?'

'Oh, yes please.' I grin as Stella heads towards the buffet.

'Did you see what I did to the croissant?' Em says, chuckling at her own gag. 'Real Croissants is over there by the way. Weird that she didn't manage to find Dita last night.'

I glance over at the influencer, resplendent in pink gingham this morning.

'Oh man, I still feel a bit bad about that,' I say.

'I literally can't wait to hear about your night,' says Em before Stella gets back to the table a veggie full English for me. 'So, what does Zodiac Girlie have to say to you two today?'

225

I repeat my only-way-out-is-through mantra, looking nervously at Stella as I realise that now is the time to have this chat.

'Mine simply said "major turmoil time",' says Stella. 'Which even I, a cosmic refusenik, can understand.'

Em sucks in her breath like a plumber assessing a leaking pipe.

'Ouch, that's a tough one. Sometimes the stars can be a cruel mistress. Today might be a bit dicey for you, Stell.'

Yikes. I fidget nervously with my napkin. Is my Luke revelation going to cause my best friend major turmoil? Argh. I don't want to do that to her! My stomach flips in anticipation, although Stella seems less concerned by the prediction.

'Major turmoil time.' She chuckles, demolishing a cinnamon bun. 'It sounds like a retro sitcom about the war.'

'Hmm.' Em looks genuinely worried. 'Did it say anything else?'

'Nope.'

'Let's make an extra promise to all be there for each other today, you guys. Major turmoil time could mean—'

'That the enemy is invading and we all need to hide in bunkers?' Stella suggests.

Em sighs. 'No. It could mean—'

'That we should roll up our sleeves and chip in with the war effort?'

'Oh for heaven's sake, Stella!' Em huffs. 'I'm trying to help.'

Stella looks suitably chastised at this.

'Sorry, Em,' she says, sticking out her bottom lip. 'I know you are. I love you for it. And I promise that if I come across any moments of turbulence today, I will try to stay calm and then immediately come and find you.'

Em nods, placated.

'But now, I've got to love you and leave you.'

'You're going?' I ask. She can't! We need to talk! Major turmoil time is now!

'Me and Luke are hanging out this morning. The kid messaged to say he's got some spare time. We're meeting in ten.'

'But—' I stutter. Oh man. Is Luke going to chat to Stella first? Should I be there for that? Or maybe they are just spending some sibling time together. We really should have discussed this last night but I got way too carried away with all the kissing. Damn it.

'You okay?' asks Stella.

'Can we talk?' I say. 'Once you and Luke have finished hanging out?'

'Wait, you wanted to chat last night before I had to go deal with work, right? Is everything all right?' Stella frowns, concerned.

'Yes, fine,' I insist. 'Just, you know, fancy a chat.'

'I can cancel Luke?'

'No, don't do that, you need some bro time.'

'Okay, shall I call you when I'm free?'

'Yes please.'

And with that, Stella leaves us to it while Emerald pumps her eyebrows at me.

'Let me guess,' Em says. 'It's time to talk to Stella about how much you like her hot little bro?'

I squirm. 'Pretty much.'

'So you had a good night last night? Because from what I saw, you two were creating more heat than the bonfire.'

'Oh my days,' I squeak, giddy and relieved to be able to talk about it at last. 'Yes we did, Em, yes we did. Although you and Ryan didn't exactly keep it PG either.'

'I know,' says Em, clapping. 'But this is standard me behaviour. This is not standard you behaviour. Tell me more.'

'Things . . . *happened* last night, Em,' I whisper, unable to keep the huge smile from my face.

'OHMYGOD. SEXY THINGS?' she shouts back, causing fellow diners to turn their heads.

'Shh! No! I meant *emotionally*. God, it was the best night, Em. Connections galore. And the kissing! Luke asked me back to his and it took every inch of restraint not to go.'

Em looks suddenly furious. 'What the hell, Jessie? Why would

227

you not go? This is the stupidest thing you have ever done and it's already a crowded field, my friend.'

'Hey!'

'What did I tell you about the importance of pleasure, babes? Do you not listen?!'

'Okay, jeez, take a breath, Emerald. I know all of that, and of course I listen to you. I've been actively engaging with Zodiac Girlie, right? I just can't let things between us get any deeper until I've been honest with Stella.'

'You and your moral code!' She tuts. 'I'd almost forgotten that you want to get the green light from Stella before you spend the rest of the holiday smashing Luke.'

I cover my eyes. It's way too bright and I'm way too tired to be processing such thoughts right now.

'Babes, your aura.' She giggles. 'If anyone ever needed some good sex to cleanse and purify, it is you.'

I groan. 'And now they've gone to hang out, and I don't know if Luke's going to say something, and I really want to just get this off my chest because I'm feeling bad about it. And I still don't have Luke's number.'

'I'm sorry, why don't you have his number?'

'Maybe because we keep getting thwarted when we spend time together? And then last night I was way too busy snogging his face off to think about practicalities. And we're in a luxury spa, Em! I don't even have to remember my own name, here, because everything is catered for without me having to *think*. So I didn't think to ask for his number and now I can't get in touch and I don't even know where they've gone so I can't—'

'Oh my god.' Em seems exasperated. 'Calm yourself down, Jessie. Stella said that she was meeting him in the maze first. You could catch up with them there?'

I consider this. 'Two things. One: there's a maze here?'

Em shrugs. 'I hadn't seen it either. Past the herb garden, apparently. But I haven't seen that either. Who's hanging out in a herb garden when there's pools and massages and a free bar to be had?'

'Huh. And two: won't it be weird to have the conversation while Luke is actually there? Like, I think this should just be a friend-to-friend thing. I'd hate for Stella to feel like we were cornering her.'

'Jessie, when has Stella ever felt like she was being cornered? She's the cornerer, if anything. She'll be fine. Besides, you can always ask Luke to give you two some time if you really want to.'

I consider this for all of one second before deciding that it's a great idea. Things definitely ramped up a few thousand notches between Luke and me last night and if I don't get this off my chest soon, I may well explode.

'Okay.' I exhale. 'I'll do it. And also, can we take a moment to appreciate how accurate Zodiac Girlie is for me? The only way out is through and I'm literally about to go through a maze on my quest for true love.'

Em is welling up as she looks at me fondly from across the table.

'I absolutely love this for you, Jessie.'

'Wait,' I say, not wanting to leave Em on her own at breakfast. 'Tell me more about what happened with Ryan first. Did you two have fun last night?'

'So much.' She beams. 'Ended up back at Ryan's.'

'Did he cleanse *your* aura?' I grin.

'Thoroughly. Now, Jessie, for Jupiter's sake, stop being polite and go and find Stella before you burst. Hang on, drink this first.' She pushes a shot glass in my direction.

'What's in that?'

'Ginger, vinegar, collagen.'

'That sounds literally horrendous, Em. I'm not necking vinegar for breakfast!'

'Don't argue, Jessie. Straight down the hatch. It'll do wonders for your pep.'

'My pep?'

'Exactly! You'll need a spring in your step when you're off to ravish Luke. You can thank me later.'

I eye the glass warily, and then neck it. It tastes even worse than it sounds.

'You're welcome,' says Em. 'Now go chat to Stella! I'm rooting for you, babes.'

I clatter out of breakfast and beyond the herb garden on the hunt for a maze, which I cannot believe I haven't spotted in the almost entire week I've been here. It's as if I've had my head in the clouds or something. Ahem.

And there it is. There's even a big sign that says the word 'maze' on it. From my vantage point I can see down into the twists and turns of the neatly trimmed hedges, all routes wending their way towards a circular clearing in the middle with a fountain in it. It doesn't look that big from up here, and in one corner I spot two heads walking through it together. Stella and Luke! I make a beeline for the entrance.

Once inside the maze, I realise that perspective has got a lot to answer for. What looked quite small from just outside the main building is, in fact, a big maze. I can't see over the hedges, for a start, and it's disorientating to be surrounded by thick, leafy bushes.

'Get a grip, Jess,' I mutter to myself, striking on.

One dead end. Turn around. Oh, this looks more promising! Wait, haven't I seen this bit of bush before?

Five minutes later and, exasperated, I consider shouting out to see if Stella and Luke can come and find me. Where even are they?

I'm bustling through yet more pathways when Stella's voice comes floating over the tightly packed hedges.

'It's been a bit hit and miss with Fran recently,' she's saying.

'I thought something was playing on your mind,' replies Luke. 'Are you two okay?'

Sounds like they're having an important chat and I freeze, not wanting to interrupt or eavesdrop. I cast around, looking for a

230

route towards them when the time is right.

'Fran really wants kids,' Stella says. 'And you know she's like a dog with a bone. When she wants something, she wants it yesterday.'

'Where do you stand on that?' Luke asks.

'I don't know. When we first all got here, I was feeling really quite stressed about it but Jess and Em have been so good. They've helped me to acknowledge that it's okay to not have made my mind up yet. I ended up having a big heart to heart with Fran last night.'

'Is that why you didn't come to the staff party?'

'I did come! But then I had a work thing to clear up and once that had been sorted I just had this yearning to try and clear the air with Fran. How was the party, by the way? You look knackered.'

'Yeah, it was . . . ' Luke pauses and I can hear the smile in his voice. 'It was awesome.'

'Sounds like Em spent the entire night flirting with Ryan. Did you see Jess? I hope she was okay and not left on her own.'

'Nope. I mean, yeah, she, ah, looked like she was enjoying herself too.'

Oh *god*. I'm actually quite pleased they can't see me right now. I think my cheeks are having their very own tomato girl summer.

'So' – Luke clears his throat – 'the chat with Fran went well, then?'

'I definitely feel better for having had it,' Stella says. 'I explained that we're not even thirty yet, and that hopefully we've still got plenty of time to make these decisions.'

'It's difficult when you're coming from different perspectives.'

'Yes,' Stella agrees. 'We haven't exactly resolved things, but then I don't know how we can resolve it because I just haven't made my mind up yet.'

'And that's okay, Stell,' says Luke. I like how reassuring he's being and I do not like how I am accidentally eavesdropping on this situation. 'All you can do is be open and honest with each other.'

'When did you get so wise?' she asks, as I cast around for a different exit. There must be another route which will lead me to them, surely? And why are mazes so leafy and confusing?!

'Maybe this whole time? You'd probably have enjoyed some more of my wisdom if you let me get a word in edgeways when we were younger.'

'There was nothing wise about your Bermuda shorts years.'

'You never did have any style.'

I'm laughing as I listen to the two of them bicker, picturing Stella's face after Luke dealt this no-style blow.

'Ouch! Don't punch me,' complains Luke.

Thought so.

'You deserved that.' Stella laughs. 'Remember when Fran and I came out to America to stay with you guys and Brie turned up at the airport in a latex boob tube? I thought Fran was going to have a heart attack.'

I pause, unsettled, my mind snagging on Stella's last words. Who is Brie? An ex-girlfriend, maybe? I try to breathe normally, even though self-confidence-destroying thoughts are now niggling at me. The spectre of an ex who wears latex to the airport and looks so good that she induces palpitations.

I finally find another path I don't think I've tried yet and make my way down it.

Stella and Luke's voices are still clear, slightly louder even, so I must be walking towards them.

'How *is* Brie?' Stella asks. 'You haven't said anything about her since you got here.'

'I haven't had much of a chance to—' Luke's saying, but Stella interrupts him.

'When does she land?' she asks.

I feel a strange pulling sensation in the pit of my stomach. A sense of foreboding, the sudden appearance of a ton of red flags all waving directly at me. My body's itching to get out of here.

'I'm assuming she's got a job at the hotel here too,' Stella says.

'Will you be her boss or vice versa? Ha, could be awkward.'

'Stell—'

'I know I haven't spent all that much time with Brie,' says Stella, 'but you two are cute together. Like peas in a pod. Listen, I know I can take the piss sometimes but, real talk, I really like Brie. It's amazing that you have the tennis background in common. Look at me and Fran right now. It's important to have that good foundation for when the shit hits the fan. Anyway,' Stella finishes, finally taking a breath, 'it's been, what, four years for you two? You must be missing your girlfriend like crazy, little bro.'

Girlfriend.

Present tense.

The word hits me like a sucker punch.

I think I'm going to be sick.

Chapter 20

I turn on my heels and run. Only, I'm in a fucking maze and the more desperate I am to get out of there, to unhear what I just heard, the more lost I get. Tears cloud my vision as I stumble through the narrow pathways, my legs feeling heavy, and I trip over a loose shoelace on one of my trainers.

I tumble into a hedge, a painful, slicing sensation across my face as a sharp edge of bramble cuts into my cheek.

'Argh,' I shout, angry now as I push myself back up, force myself to carry on. I touch my face and there's blood on my fingertips but I don't care. I keep going.

I run down one dead end after another and every time I turn a corner, I'm petrified I'm going to bump into them by accident. The last thing I need.

Eventually I find the exit and I don't look back.

I don't look back even as I pull my phone out of my bag, dial the only number I can think of that will help right now. Carl Vomitorium on Wheels. I'm so focused on getting out of here, so relieved that taxi driver Carl says he isn't that far away. He can be here in ten. I can't face walking back through the main hotel, can't even deal with seeing Em right now. I don't want to have to explain, or talk. Suddenly the hotel feels too cloying, too claustrophobic. All I can see are perfectly manicured gardens, the smiling faces of guests in towelling robes. All I can smell is that luxurious hotel scent that seemed so inviting at first. All I can hear is the gentle sound of jazz music being piped through the speakers in the grounds. And I need space from everything.

'Alreet, pet,' says Carl as his shiny blue car screeches to a halt outside on the drive. 'No sick stains today, you'll be pleased to know!' he adds cheerily, his face falling when he sees the state of me. 'Christ alive, what happened to you?'

I slump into the backseat.

'Sorry,' I sniff, swiping at my face with the back of my hand, which comes back covered in blood.

Carl hands me some tissues.

'No need to apologise, pet, although if you get that on the leather there will be a surcharge,' he says, with a note of guilt in his voice. 'But don't worry about that. Where to?'

God, where do I want to go to? Home isn't home anymore. Besides, Otis might not even be out of my flat yet and even if he were, I definitely can't afford a taxi ride all the way back to Carpston. All of my stuff is here, my friends, my . . . No, *not* Luke. It doesn't matter about him anymore.

I think about the drive over here, how we wended our way through that pretty little town, how it had a pub in it. Somewhere I can hide for the day and drown my sorrows.

'That town we drove through on Friday, the one where you grew up?' I say, my voice sounding heavy, sluggish through sadness.

Carl nods, eyeing me in the rear-view mirror.

'What happened to your opponent, then?' he asks.

And that's when I burst into tears.

I cry all the way to town where Carl drops me off. I walk along the clifftops first, looking out over the sea, the wind buffering my body. And when the local pub opens, I remember what Carl said about their whisky selection so I order a whisky on the rocks and cry into that too.

Only when the astringent heat of the alcohol hits my bloodstream do I stop crying, and that's when I start to get angry.

Because, *oh my god*, what a total a-hole, I think as I sit slumped in the corner of the pub, nursing my drink. What a complete jerk. Did Luke think we were just going to, what, hook up behind his girlfriend's back? Absolutely URGH. I cannot believe him! I'm so cross I could scream, only the bartender's already giving me a wary look so instead I ball my hands into fists and press so hard that my nails leave little crescent moon imprints on my skin.

Trust me to fall for yet another inappropriate man. What is wrong with me? I knew, I *knew*, this was a bad idea. I can't trust my own stupid feelings, can I? This is cold hard proof of that. I've got no clue. How silly of me! Of course someone like Luke wouldn't actually, properly like someone like me. I knew, deep down, that it didn't make sense. Only I let myself believe it for too long and now I feel completely gutted, and foolish, and hot tears are falling from my eyes so fast I can't see straight.

Dita was right. Poor, stupid Yessica.

No doubt to Luke I was just some low-hanging fruit. Easy to pick off, just as easy to throw away.

I peel the corners away from the beer mat, feeling so foolish.

For a while there, I'd dared to hope that Luke was going to be a part of my new chapter. There he was, all beautiful like a Roman god with kind eyes and nice words and, bloody *fireworks*. No one has made me feel that way before. And I took it as a sign that Em was right, that this Saturn Return thing maybe was happening for me. A chance to start afresh. Instead of living my life for other people – Mum, Dad, my boring ex-boyfriends – I was going to live it for me.

But no. Steel-eyed boys are where danger lies. The man I cannot take my eyes off has a girlfriend in America, who Stella thinks is perfect for him, whom he's loved for four years, and who wears latex to airports and is called *Brie*.

URGH.

I can't believe he invited me back to his after the barbecue, and how much willpower it took for me not to go. But I wanted to do the right thing, to talk to Stella first. Meanwhile, he couldn't have been less concerned about doing the right thing; he was too busy cheating on his partner. It's almost laughable, when I think about it. Almost. I'm sure, in time, I'll come to see this as a lucky escape. Thank god I didn't sleep with him. But right now it's all so raw.

I spin the whisky tumbler around in my hand, running a finger over the hard glass edges. Maybe Bryan was right. Maybe I should put this silly pretence to an end and get back to the real world. Go back to my job, make the most of the new salary he's offered. I wince when I think how much I spent in the hotel shop on beautiful clothes just to impress Luke. What an idiot I am. I cringe hard at that thought, furious with myself for making so many stupid choices.

So, should I go back with my tail between my legs? I could go back to the flat. Who am I to be making such grand gestures, anyway? I should have started smaller. Maybe dyed my hair or got a tattoo, not quit my entire life and fall for a heartbreaker.

I order another whisky.

Head outside to sit on a picnic bench in the beer garden, looking out to sea.

The beauty of the day jars hard against my mental state. The waves are peaceful. The sound of seagulls carried on a gentle breeze. I look down at my white T-shirt, drops of cherry red blood seeped into it from the cut on my face.

Here I am, covered in stains again.

Only this one looks much harder to wash out.

The pub starts to fill up at lunchtime and I find myself being taken under the wing of a group of retired people who've just finished a long coastal walk. Despite the warm day, they're wrapped up in layers and start discarding their coats as soon as they find a spot in the pub garden, which is shaded from the wind, the sun beating down on us.

'This looks like heartbreak to me,' a kindly woman wearing a sweatband around her head calls over. 'Would you like to sit with us?'

I'm at the why-not stage of drinking so I shuffle over to their picnic bench and they introduce themselves as Anita, Peter and his wife Rita.

'We know our names rhyme.' Peter chuckles when he spots my confused face.

'Oh good. I thought I was more drunk than I actually am for a minute there,' I say. 'I'm Jess.'

'Would you like to talk about it, Jess?' asks Rita, the one in the sweatband. 'The heartbreak?'

'How did you know?' I whisper, sitting down under a parasol. 'Are you psychic?'

Rita smiles. 'No, love, I'm just very wise.'

'Very old, you mean,' says Anita, chortling. 'I can make that joke because I'm older than Rita by a year,' she adds to me. 'Eighty-one!'

I hope I'm still wearing sweatbands in my eighties, I think vaguely.

'You're right,' I say. 'I met this guy a few days ago and I really liked him. Like, a lot. I even bought a beautiful new swimming costume so we could go for this midnight swim, and then things seemed to be hotting up, and then this morning I overheard him talking about his American girlfriend,' I add with a long sigh. 'So, he's been cheating on her, with me, which does not make me feel great, Anita, Rita and Peter.'

Peter nods sagely.

'You can't beat a new swimming costume,' says Anita. 'Did you go for a high leg? I used to love those, always made your legs look incredibly long. These days I buy costumes with depressing

238

things in the title like "tummy control" but I look back fondly on those high leg days.'

'Erm, it *did* have quite high legs,' I say, about to launch into a full description of the costume.

'Anita!' snaps Rita. 'Now is not the time for waffling on about swimwear! Poor Jess is in romantic turmoil!'

'It's okay—'

'Poor love,' Rita says, taking a sip of her sherry. 'How are you feeling?'

'Very sad, and cross with myself, and cross with him, and also a bit tipsy now,' I admit.

'Understandable,' says Peter.

'Maybe you shouldn't jump to conclusions,' suggests Anita.

'Maybe she should,' huffs Rita. 'They are all at it, men.' Peter looks a bit miffed at this.

'Well, hang on, Rita. Jess said she overheard him talking about his girlfriend,' Anita says, turning her attention to me. 'Could you have heard him wrong? This might be a lot of fuss for nothing, after all. No big deal.'

'Hmm,' I say, mouth now on fire thanks to many midday whiskys. 'Maybe you're right, maybe this is not a big deal. I let myself be ruled by my heart for a week and I got in a pickle and that's . . . fine. A valuable life lesson, right? You know, the hotel we're staying in advocates a "whole life cleanse".'

Peter scoffs at the words 'whole life cleanse' and I offer up a watery smile, trying not to feel too silly. The things is, though, the hotel has got the right idea. I'm meant to be getting rid of complications, not adding them in! I literally already knew this and I'm so cross with myself for getting distracted by Luke, and bitterly disappointed that I misjudged someone again.

I mean, seriously, what is wrong with my good human-being radar? Did I just get lucky early with Stella and Em? Maybe this is the cosmos's way of telling me I'm extremely fortunate to have two beautiful humans in my life already. Not to mention Mum and

Dad, of course. I should be counting my blessings, not crushing over boys who are actually quite mean, when you think about it. Why would Luke lie to me like that? And why, when I think about him, do I feel this longing to be in his presence even now that I know what he's done?

YUK.

This is why I don't let myself develop feelings for beautiful boys. Or any boys, if I'm being honest. This is precisely why I'm doing just fine on my own.

'Eff you, Luke,' I mutter darkly, as Peter pushes a plate of chips my way.

'Chips always help,' he says kindly, as my phone begins to ring.

'Where are you?' barks Em, who is not usually a barker so I immediately know that something's wrong. Thankfully my good friend whisky has taken the edge off so I don't flinch too hard as she starts talking with some urgency down the phone.

'I'm with my new friends Anita, Peter and Rita,' I reply, head swaying a little.

'ARE YOU DRUNK?' Em is shouting now. 'Stop that immediately, Jessie, and tell me where you are. Luke is here.'

'Nope.' I hold my palm out wide, even though she can't see me, in the ultimate 'stop' move. 'Not Luke. Never again.'

'Jessie, wait! You need to listen.'

'I've done enough listening, Em,' I snap. 'I've listened to you going on about this Saturn Returns like it's an exciting thing to happen and I got all buoyed up and thought it would be great and now bloody look at me! Drunk and sad and eating chips, Emerald!'

There's a long pause and I brace myself for some sharp words in response.

'Jessie? You're breaking up . . . Where are you? Luke . . . in the maze . . . WRONG, JESSIE!'

'I know I was wrong! You don't need to give me a lecture

about it.' I huff.

'What? Did . . . hear that? Can . . . back, Jessie. Where . . . '

'I can't hear you!' I shout back. 'There's no reception.'

'Wait . . . coming,' she replies. What does that even mean? I wonder, flinging my phone down on the table and stuffing five chips into my mouth all in one go.

Anita watches me with concern.

'I think she's going to need a parmo as well,' says Rita mysteriously.

I look up with a raised eyebrow. What *is* she talking about?

Chapter 21

Every day's a lesson and today, as well as learning that I've fallen for a total wanker and developed a taste for swearing, I have also discovered that a parmo is something of a local delicacy. A piece of breaded chicken topped with béchamel and cheese.

'Get stuck into that.' Peter, who has fluffy white eyebrows, smiles, and I end up apologising profusely for being a vegetarian.

'The kids of today!' He tuts good-naturedly, taking my plate and tucking into it himself. 'Let's get the poor thing some more chips then.'

I drop my head on the table and bang it lightly. What am I doing here? I wonder. Hanging out with a bunch of kindly pensioners and burying my head in the sand, I guess. Much like our coastal location, I feel all at sea. I've tried so hard to embrace this new me and it hasn't worked. Should I text Bryan now and tell him I'll see him on Monday? Just the thought of that fills me with dread. Trudging back into work to spend the day putting out fires before trudging home again to watch a documentary about biohacking your health or that gameshow where families compete to build the most impressive playdough sculptures. I'm way too old for their target audience btw, I just can't help myself.

What once seemed like a sensible path now seems quite bleak.

Despite everything I've learned today, and the fact that it makes good sense to retreat home with my tail between my legs, I just don't want to. But what's the alternative? I feel like this past week has offered me a taste of something new and exciting and now I want more. Or is it just that I want Luke? I'm so confused and the beginnings of a headache have started to pulse at my temples.

I push my drink around, a sudden and overwhelming yearning to talk this through with someone. The girls are my go-to for advice, but obviously I can't turn to Stella with this, tied up as she is within the fabric of this drama. And Em seems to be using her scant reception to shout things at me. So my stupid brain flies straight to Luke and I tut at myself. How did he make it into my top three people in a matter of days? I've known Stella and Em for a decade and suddenly Luke's right up there with them, the person I want to share big stuff with, the person I want to lean on for support. How ironic, then, that he's also the person I need to get as far away from as possible.

What I need, right now, are my parents. When Otis and I were breaking up, I spent hours round at Mum and Dad's house drinking sherry and talking through my problems. Maybe I could get hold of them, I wonder as more chips arrive. Even though they are halfway around the world, with a bit of luck they might still be up.

'Just going to message my parents,' I tell the gang.

They all bob their heads up and down, making 'good idea' noises.

Hello

Are you free for a chat? Xx

Mum is typing . . .

Hello love!

243

Your father's just in the bathroom

He's having a bit of bother with his digestion but a week of eating only grilled meats will do that to a man

Shall I call?

I'm calling!

Mum is calling.

I get up from the picnic bench and head over to the edge of the beer garden, leaning against a fence and looking out to sea as I take the call. 'Mum,' I answer, relieved, the soothing sound of her voice already making me feel marginally better. 'How's the trip so far? You're already making the most of that photo-sharing app, I see.'

'Did you see the picture of me with one of those little marsupials?'

'I loved it.' I laugh to myself. 'That little guy looked so cute and weirdly like it had a smile on its face.'

Mum chuckles. 'They're so friendly. ANDY, WHAT ARE THOSE LITTLE MARSUPIALS WE MET ON THAT ISLAND CALLED?'

I can hear the muffled voice of my dad in the background.

'FOR HEAVEN'S SAKE, ANDY, IT'S THE MEAT! YOU'LL NEVER HAVE A SUCCESSFUL TRIP TO THE TOILET IF YOU DON'T EAT SOME FRUIT AND VEGETABLES.'

Mum continues to give Dad, presumably still on the loo, a loud lecture about his digestion and for some reason I find it comforting.

'Oh, here he comes now,' Mum says as the sound of a door opening and a flushing toilet come down the line. 'SHUT THE DOOR, ANDY, THE STENCH! Our Jess is on the phone.'

'Oh hello, love!' Dad calls amiably.

'I was asking what those little marsupials were called Andy,' Mum says.

'Quokkas,' says Dad. 'Delightful little things and so friendly. They live on an island just off the coast of Perth, declining population apparently. Your mother fell madly in love and wanted to bring one home in her suitcase.'

'I think that sort of thing's frowned upon,' I say and it makes me smile. 'Anyway, you've only just started your trip. You're not actually coming home for ages.'

'Now then, how are you, luvvie? How are the girls?'

It doesn't matter that we're all about to turn thirty, Mum will still never not refer to me and my friendship group as girls.

'Oh . . . ' I begin, and I don't even have to get another word out for Mum to sense that something's wrong.

'What is it?' she asks. 'Wait, don't tell me yet. I'm going to video-call you so I can see you too.'

A minute later and Mum, Dad and their hotel balcony have filled my phone screen.

'You look so well!' I cry, taking in their holiday glow.

'Never mind that,' Mum says dismissively. 'What is wrong?'

'I'm in a bit of a pickle.' I sniff, and inevitably I pour out every single thing that's been going on, from the Luke crush to the discovery that he has a girlfriend and everything in between. Well, not everything in between. They *are* my parents and I skip a lot of what happened by the bonfire. But by the time I've finished, Dad has folded his arms and looks positively mutinous.

'If you want me to fly back and give him a talking to, Jessie, I will,' he says.

'Don't be silly, Andy.' Mum tuts. 'Our Jessie is perfectly grown up enough to sort this out by herself. Even if it seems awful right now, she'll be fine, won't you, love?'

'I guess so,' I say, wavering, not feeling quite so confident in myself.

'I had a holiday romance once,' says Mum.

'Did you?' Dad and I ask in unison.

Mum turns to Dad and gives him an exasperated look. 'It was you, you daft bat.'

Of course. I've heard a few stories of when Mum and Dad first met over the years and I'd forgotten that they were on holiday at the time.

'There I was, living my best life as a Butlin's holiday rep, when your father turned up with his family for a break.'

'I couldn't take my eyes off you,' Dad tells Mum.

'I remember' – she chuckles – 'your mum kept telling you off.'

'Nanny Jane always said it was rude to stare.' I smile at the memory.

'I know.' Dad shakes his head. 'But you were breathtaking, Pam. You were back then and you still are now.'

'You two!' I sniff, almost welling up.

'Of course, it wasn't all plain-sailing,' Dad explains. 'There was a long line of young bucks hoping for the chance of a date with your mother. She'd perform a song on stage each night and then there would literally be a queue of lads waiting by the stage, hoping she'd stop and chat to them.'

'I think you're exaggerating there.' Mum chuckles.

'I am not!'

'So how did you win Mum's heart then, Dad?' I ask.

'Well, thankfully we were there for two weeks for a start,' he recalls. 'Because I spent the first week mooning after your mother and telling myself that I would never be good enough to date someone as beautiful as her.'

'Honestly, Andy.' Mum tuts. 'You're making it sound like I was Cindy Crawford.'

'I told myself I was stupid to even consider it. What had I got to offer that all the other lads hadn't? I tell you, luvvie, I was a right grumpy bugger for that first week. Then I saw a flyer for a poetry writing competition and thought I'd enter, just for something to do.'

'That's right.' Mum smiles. 'You were the only boy in the competition! And your father won! He stood up and read this lovely poem he'd written and I remember thinking, "Who is this handsome, sensitive soul?"'

'Of course, I didn't think it was very macho to be writing poetry, let alone entering it into competitions. But I trusted my instincts and look where it got me,' Dad says, proudly taking Mum's hand.

By now, I'm in bits. I wipe a stray tear from my cheek and beam at the image of my folks on screen.

'I miss you so much.'

'Listen, love,' Mum says, 'you'll be just fine. I always say that honesty is the best policy. You need to go back, in your own time, mind, and tell him you know he has a girlfriend. But give him a chance to tell you what's happening. Don't make any rash decisions before you've got all the facts in front of you.'

'Yes, and don't make any decisions at all after a few whiskies,' chips in Dad. 'I learned that lesson the hard way. That's how I got roped into starring in that production of *The Full Monty* at the local. That was after a night on the sauce. Let me tell you, the drunken idea of getting naked on stage and the actual reality of it are two very different things.'

'Yes, half of Carpston have seen your father's you-know-what,' adds Mum cheerfully, before peering into the screen again. 'Let your thoughts percolate, Jess. Give yourself time. We love you and we support you.'

'Thanks, Mum. Thanks, Dad,' I say shakily, before hanging up. I weave through the picnic tables on my way back to Rita, Peter and Anita's table, now strewn with empty sherry glasses, half-eaten bowls of chips and crisps packets ripped all the way open. For octogenarians, these guys are hungry.

'Come on, we're going inside,' Rita says, frowning at a solitary cloud passing overhead, shrugging her coat back on. I follow my new friends into the pub, still slightly wobbly after three whiskies, and we find a table inside.

'You all right, love?' asks Anita as we settle in.

'Just had a nice catch-up with my folks. That's what I want'– I sniff – 'a relationship like Mum and Dad's.' (Maybe minus the toilet chat.)

'And what's to stop you having it?'

'I'm not exactly having much love at the moment,' I point out, motioning towards my frazzled, blood-stained, whisky-smelling carcass. 'It's not screaming romantic heroine, is it?'

Rita is still chuckling as the front door swings open in dramatic style and Gary, the barman, mutters something about its poor hinges. That's not what I notice. It's Em who is barging in.

'There you are!' she huffs, looking at me like I have caused her a major inconvenience. 'Finally.'

'Aye, aye, aye.' Dita Ortiz follows shortly after, eyeing me with concern. 'My darling Yessica. What on earth is going on?'

'What are you two doing here?' I sniff. The whole pub falls silent, and it takes me a moment to remember that Dita is a Hollywood superstar who has just bulldozed her way into the pub. The last time I saw Dita she was very much incognito at the barbecue. Today she's not remotely low key – blood red lipstick, voluminous hair and a pearlescent blazer thrown over a lace-trimmed dress. And then there's the fact that her bodyguard Viktor is loitering behind her, a slab of muscle scoping the joint.

'How did you find me?' I press, hopping out of my seat.

Taxi driver Carl is the next to barrel through the doors, which pretty much answers my question.

'Can we *please* mind the hinges!' huffs Gary.

'That'd be my fault, pet,' Carl says, nodding his hellos to every single person in this pub and sending an apologetic look to Gary.

'Carl!' I tut. 'Isn't there such a thing as, I don't know, driver–traveller confidentiality?'

'Don't be cross with Carl.' Dita rests a manicured hand on

Carl's shoulder. 'He's a good boy.'

'Our Dita can be very persuasive,' he adds.

'But—' I'm so confused I stagger back and collapse onto a bar stool.

'Babes, it's actually thanks to you that we found you,' Em explains, looking at me with a mix of fondness and exasperation. 'Remember how you made us take down Carl's number in case of emergencies when we first got here?'

'Oh yeah.'

'Well, you'd been awol all morning and when I couldn't find you at the hotel, I started to get worried. It's not like you to just disappear into a black hole.'

'I think you'll find our little town is no black hole,' Anita points out, perturbed.

'We've got our own outdoor gym, don't you know?' adds Peter.

'Absolutely no shade on this place,' Em says sincerely. 'It's a beautiful town. Dita and I were admiring the bunting decorating the town square on the drive here.'

'I sewed some of that.' Rita grins proudly.

'No way!' Em beams, before bringing herself back to the matter in hand. 'Right, where was I? Oh yes, while I was looking for you, I found Stella and Luke, who said they hadn't seen you in the maze. That's odd, I thought. I know your sense of direction is atrocious—'

'Hey!'

'But not even Jessie could get lost in a maze, I thought to myself. And I'd definitely seen you go in when I was coming out of breakfast. When I said that to Luke, his face clouded over, babes. He said, and I quote: "She must have heard."'

'Yes, I did hear,' I butt in. 'I heard him and Stella talking about his American girlfriend of four years. PRESENT TENSE.'

Dita puts a soothing hand on my shoulder, now.

'Yes, well, there's an update on that,' Em insists, not looking nearly as furious as I thought she would, on my behalf. 'But anyway, long story short, we realised you'd be having a paddy—'

'I'd hardly call this a paddy!' I say, indignant. 'I'd call it an existential crisis, Em. A bloody life-changing, why are all men such supreme *idiots* moment.'

'And historically, I've seen you storm off enough times when you've lost your temper,' Em ploughs on.

'Like when?' I ask.

'That time at uni when you got a 2.2 on a mock exam, then holed up in the library for an entire day, fuming. That time when—'

'Okay, okay, I get it.'

'We looked in the hotel library,' adds Dita. 'No Yessica.'

'No Yessica,' Em echoes with a shake of her head. 'And then I remembered that you'd made me store "Carl's Vomitorium on Wheels" in my contacts. And here I am! Viktor and Dita followed behind Carl and me, and Luke stayed back at the hotel because he and Stella needed to have a conversation.'

'We came straight to find you,' explains Dita. 'And to tell you not to panic. I haven't known you very long, Yessica, but I can tell already that you are quite a dramatic sort of person.'

I literally don't know how to reply to this so I just lean against the bar, staggered, while the person who has just accused *me* of being dramatic pulls her tiny bell out of her bag and rings it.

'Y'alreet, Dita pet?' Carl asks when no one appears to take her order.

Dita tries again. Gary the barman eyes her warily, arms folded across his chest, and yet he says nothing.

'Jesus H, would you like a drink, babes?' Em asks.

'Yes, of course!' Dita is struggling to compute what has just happened.

'We don't answer to bells here, not even Hollywood ones,' Peter says cheerily, his eyebrows taking on a new shape.

'This has never happened to Dita before and I find it . . . majestic,' she says breathily, grabbing her pad from her handbag and making notes. 'So powerful. Barkeep, I would like a glass of your Viña Tondonio please.'

Gary the bartender sniffs. 'I can offer you red or white.'

'Ay dios mio,' mutters Dita.

The next thing I know, Dita and barkeeper Gary are arguing over the correct pronunciation of 'rioja' (ballsy move on Gary's part), and Em is buzzing around me like a fly.

'Jessie,' she says firmly.

'Sorry to interrupt,' says Anita, who has shrugged off her own coat since coming indoors and, it turns out, is dressed like she's starring in a Jane Fonda eighties workout video. 'But we're going to have a game of beer pong, would you like to join?'

Beer pong? Em mouths at me, confused.

'Yes, you do look very stressed, deary,' says Rita, also resplendent in leg warmers, as she takes a stack of red cups from Gary.

'Obsessed that you guys are about to play beer pong,' says Em, 'but I'm afraid Jess and I really need to talk.'

'I'd love to play beer pong,' I say defiantly.

'Jessica,' says Em, as if addressing a naughty child. She knows I'm trying to avoid her.

'Emerald,' I bat back.

'I *need* to talk to you,' she insists.

My face falls. 'I just can't face it, Em,' I tell her honestly. 'Today has been a lot already and my mum said I should let it all percolate.'

'Pam is very wise, but—'

'And, sorry to butt in again, but I'm really not having a paddy. I feel totally blindsided, and hurt, and angry, and not a little sorry for myself if I'm being honest. None of that feels great, Em. I know I've got to face up to it all soon, and I will, but for now I need distractions.'

'But Jess—' Em says, brows furrowed.

'Please, Em. Just drop it. I've made my decision, okay? I'm going to give myself a bit more time and beer pong sounds way more fun than facing up to the real world right now. I'm already drunk and sad and my heart hurts and I now get to decide when I want to face up to this shitstorm.'

Em looks super upset now. 'But Luke—'

'Nope. I'm not talking about him now. Look, tonight's our last night at the spa and I just want it to be the three of us. I want to forget about all this emotional drama and have fun with you and Stell. I got side-tracked, I can see that now. And as of tomorrow, I won't have to see Luke ever again.'

Ouch, stab to the heart at that thought.

'So for now, can we just drop it and play some beer pong, please?'

I'm not sure I've ever been so firm in my life.

Emerald concedes, albeit begrudgingly, and we play. And right when my team is about to lose dramatically to a bunch of pensioners, the pub doors swing open again.

'The hinges! Mind the hinges, for Christ's sake!' shouts Gary, getting quite cross now.

There, leaning against the doorframe, is Luke.

Chapter 22

I can't help but stop, for just a moment, to drink him in, so mad with myself for the way I still feel when I see him, after everything that's happened. My pulse has quickened. My eyes have dilated. My fingers twitch with their need to reach out to him. I can see that Luke's are doing the same and it makes me think of those old Westerns, where the hot criminal walks into a bar, fingers itching to unholster his gun.

He scans the room, finally finding me. Eyes settling on mine.

You could hear a pin drop.

Rita's knitting needle actually does clatter loudly to the floor in the silence.

'Don't mind me,' she says amiably, motioning for us to continue.

I can't look away from Luke, because my stupid eyeballs are drawn to him like moths to a flame even after everything he's done.

He takes a step towards me.

'Jess,' he says, that low Yorkshire accent like a melody.

I take a step back.

'Nope. Not today, Satan. Off you pop,' I say, pointing back towards the front door.

'She gets lairy after she's had a few whiskys,' Em explains to the crowd.

'And several pints,' Dita adds.

'I'm not lairy!' I round on them. 'I'm owning my own worth,' I add, channelling my inner Zodiac Girlie.

'Is there somewhere private these two can go to talk?' asks Em.

'Oh sure,' says Gary, showing us an old-school saloon-type room off the main bar. 'Totally private in there.'

Everyone turns to look at me expectantly.

'I'm not going in there, with him!' I say, swinging back to glare at Luke.

He's edged further into the pub, his head hanging low as he looks up at me through dark eyelashes.

'Jessica!' sighs Emerald, who appears to be really quite exasperated by now. 'There's something you don't know. You've got to hear him out, *please*, babes. You know I wouldn't put you in a horrible situation if I didn't know it would be worth it, right? Now will you please get in the bloody saloon with Luke and hear him out?'

'No, Emerald, I don't want to,' I say, hands on hips, or at least near hips, it's quite hard to tell where they are after all this beer.

'I'll go.' Luke starts to back off. 'I just . . . I'm really sorry, Jess.'

'You're going nowhere.' Em rounds on him. 'Jess, stop being so stubborn, for goodness' sake. You've done quite enough "percolating" now.' She sticks her bottom lip out a tiny amount, a move that for some reason I always find terribly hard to stand firm to. 'Please,' she says, smushing her hands together and giving me a very cute face.

'Urgh, fine. Five minutes, but I'm only doing this for you.'

I've barely finished my sentence when Em practically bundles me into the saloon while Dita clicks her fingers and sends Luke in after me.

The door closes behind us and I look anywhere but at Luke, taking in the dark wood tables and scuffed velvet seats. I hitch myself up onto a table and lean forward with my forearms pressed into my thighs. Thank goodness I had the wherewithal to swipe a cup of beer from beer pong before I got strong-armed in here. Take the edge off.

'Jess,' Luke says again, and it physically hurts to hear him say my name like that.

'What?' I ask, and it comes out so harshly that I can *feel* Luke's reaction, the intake of his breath, and in that moment I like it. I want him to feel bad. To feel just an inch of how I've been feeling all day, before his American girlfriend flies in and they go back to being two peas in a pissing pod.

'I really need to explain this all to you, if you'll let me?'

'Oh sure, Luke, yes, please. I'd *love* to hear all about this. Actually just can't wait to hear more about your beautiful latex-wearing American girlfriend, so fit that she gives Stella's partner heart palpitations. Honestly, please do tell me more about her. Or maybe, more about how you lied to me. Made me feel like I was special—' My voice cracks here but I'm too angry to stop. 'Like maybe we had something special. When actually, you were just using me.'

Luke stands there by the closed door, taking this from me, his brows crossed above sincere eyes. He runs a hand through his hair.

'I don't understand,' I carry on, and it's more like a sob now. 'Why would you do this?'

'Fuck, please don't cry,' he says, pain etched on his face, his fingers fidgeting in the effort of staying still. 'I'm so sorry I've caused this whole mess.' He reaches towards me, thinks better of it, snatches his hand away again. His head is bowed low.

'You've been bleeding, Jess,' he says.

I swipe angrily at the cut on my face. Glare down at the floor.

'Can we just get this over with, please? I've got one last day of holiday with my friends before I go home, I don't want to spend it feeling like this.'

'You're going home?'

I shrug. 'Guess so. I've been offered a job.'

255

I glance up to see Luke using his fingertips to rub his forehead. I can hear him inhale. See the turmoil on his face as he tries to put whatever he's about to say into words.

'You're right,' he says eventually, shakily. 'I have been lying.'

'Ha,' I bark out a hollow laugh, kicking my legs out in front of me like a petulant teenager. 'Knew it.'

'But not to you. To Stella. I did have a girlfriend back in the States but we broke up last year, Jess. Almost twelve months ago. I just couldn't bring myself to tell my sister, so I kind of kept the lie going, which is so fucking stupid of me, I realise now.' He pauses, tips his head back until it thuds against the door.

My fingers reach for the table I'm sitting on, and I grip it.

Luke carries on talking.

'Stella practically raised me, Jess, you know that. She was mum and sister all rolled into one because our actual mum just couldn't handle it. Stella sacrificed so much of her own childhood to make sure that I had mine—' His voice breaks at this, and my heart breaks for him, but I fight with myself to push those feelings down. Away.

I watch as Luke composes himself. 'And when I got that scholarship to America, she was so proud. She also made me promise to look after myself, which I did because she can be absolutely terrifying.'

I let out the tiniest laugh at this, eyes returning to the floor.

'And we spoke all the time I was away. She was there for me when the pro career went up in flames, she was solid as a rock. And when Stella and Fran came over for my birthday one year, I could see just how happy she was that I'd found someone over there. Brie was great, she's a good person. We were together for a few years. I knew that Stella loved that, she found comfort in the knowledge that I had someone over there, I guess.'

Luke stops and I look up briefly to see him shake his head.

Neither of us says anything for a while. There's too much new information swirling around in my brain for me to talk. My mind keeps snagging on the crucial fact, that he's *not* with anyone else, but somehow it feels too delicate, too precious to reach out and hold on to.

I'm aware of Luke stepping further into the room then. Moving closer towards me. He crouches down so he can meet my gaze, his hopeful face directly in front of me now. I try to look away but I can't.

'Jess, I'm not with anybody else. Brie and I broke up a year ago and, you know, there was no dramatic end to the relationship. Nothing big happened. We'd just fizzled out, that's all. I think we both knew that we weren't right for each other in the long run. But I didn't tell Stella and I wish I had, so much, because it's brought you all this pain and I hate that, Jess. I hate it. I never ever want to hurt you. I didn't tell Stella because I thought, stupidly, that I was looking out for her by pretending it was still going on. I thought she'd found peace knowing that I was in a relationship over there.'

My head's spinning. My tear-stained cheeks feel tight. I want so much for this to be true that I can almost feel my need taking shape. And still I can't say anything, not yet. I can't vocalise this hope that's building deep inside me. It feels too fragile still, and I don't want to frighten it away.

Luke's on his knees in front of me. His brow knitted. He's looking at me so tenderly, with so much emotion behind those steel-grey eyes.

'I should have told the truth ages ago,' he's saying now, shaking his head. 'I fully understand that lying like this is not a good look for me, and that's why I stayed back at the hotel earlier. Jesus, when I realised that you'd overheard our conversation in the maze—' He shakes his head. 'I've never felt like that before. Furious with myself and desperate to come and see you so I could explain myself. But I also had to make things right with my sister because she deserved to hear the truth.'

The corner of my mouth twitches up at the thought of this.

'How did that go for you?' I ask.

'She was mad. Furious, actually. She couldn't understand why I'd felt the need to lie to protect her and made it pretty clear that she didn't want it to happen again. Usually when she's cross she'll just swear a lot but this time she was quiet.'

'That's when you know she's really mad,' I say.

Our eyes meet and I see a flicker of hope cross his face.

'Didn't help that she was armed,' he says with the smallest smile. 'She'd talked me into joining her for an archery class—'

I wince.

'We were in the middle of trying to hit the target when Em came to find me. She pulled me aside to explain and when I went back to the class, I was in a bit of a state myself thinking about you, what you'd heard, how you'd gone missing. My head was all over the place. So I blurted it out right when Stella was about to take a shot and let's just say neither of us is allowed back onto the range again.'

'Oh. Shit.'

'I'm definitely never lying to her again, that's for sure,' Luke adds with a soft smile. 'So here's the truth, Jess. I haven't been in a relationship for ages and then I met you. And I would move mountains to make this happen between us. To take away your hurt.'

And I know this is the truth. I can feel it with every fibre of my being.

'Luke—' I say, heart soaring. 'You don't need to move mountains. I'm right here.'

He quiets. Watches me like he can't quite believe what I'm saying.

Sensing that he's struggling to compute what just happened, I decide to spell it out.

'I'm going to need for you to kiss me now.'

He's up on his feet in a heartbeat, wrapping one arm around my body, pulling me closer to him. The kiss, when it comes, is so tender I could cry. His lips like soft feathers on mine, his finger stroking gently around the cut on my cheek. The way he murmurs my name like he can't breathe without it.

'I need to see you,' he says eventually.

'I'm right here.' I laugh.

But he pulls away anyway, looks at me so intently that heat pools throughout my body.

'Is this real?' he asks, fingers swirling around the pulse points on my wrists. 'Do you really forgive me?'

'There's nothing to forgive,' I say. 'I mean . . . your timing is awful and you could work on being more open with your sister but apart from that, we're good.'

A huge, thankful smile crosses his face and he looks like a weight has been lifted.

'In that case, we're going to need to get back to mine as soon as humanly possible,' he murmurs. 'Get you out of those' – he cocks his head– 'bloody clothes.'

'Yes,' I whisper, and that's when the whole of the pub erupts with the sound of cheering.

The saloon door swings open and there stands Em, whooping like mad.

Luke and I pull apart.

'Yes, babes! Go, go, get back to the hotel!' cheers Em.

I shift my position, wrapping my arms around myself.

'Did you hear all that?' I ask.

'Totally,' says Carl the taxi driver.

'Ooh yes,' Peter, Anita and Rita answer in unison.

'Aye, aye, aye,' purrs Dita.

Oh my god. My cheeks are burning as Luke wraps his arm around me protectively. I slot in perfectly, feeling the warmth of his body.

'All right, show's over.' He laughs.

Carl announces that he'll give us a lift back and makes an unmentionable comment about spilt bodily fluids costing extra

259

that I shan't repeat here. So I say my goodbyes to my pensioner pals while Dita signs some autographs before setting off with Viktor. Then Em, Luke and I pile into Carl's cab.

'Wait, Luke, how did you get here?' I ask.

'I ran,' he admits.

'What?' shouts Em. 'The hotel's, what, five miles away?'

'Yeah, I'm going to need a shower when we get back.'

'I'll join you,' I blurt out before remembering we're in company.

'Jeez,' groans Em. 'This is going to be a long car ride home.'

Chapter 23

It *is* a long five miles home. With my legs pressed up against Luke's in the backseat, I can't think straight, and Emerald is definitely not helping with all of the eyebrow pumping she's been doing from the front seat. She shoots back constant orders for us not to get frisky in the back of the taxi, which makes Carl laugh and is actually a pretty good distraction from all the thoughts of a hot shower with Luke. Finally we reach the turning for Gurnard Cove, and it strikes me that so much has changed since I last made this journey just under a week ago. I mean, sure, some things remain the same, like the fact that I am still accident prone and covered in stains. But I feel even closer to my best friends now, and I don't even know where to start on the man sat next to me. As Carl drives down the gravel pathway, we spot Stella waiting for us outside the entrance to the hotel and my stomach flips again. She looks . . . quite stern.

'Argh,' I garble. 'Time to face the music.'

Luke reaches across and squeezes my hand. I catch an intoxicating scent of cotton fresh fabric softener plus sweat.

'I told her everything,' he says. 'Not just about my ex, about how I feel for you too. About us.'

Us. We're an us! The butterflies in my stomach take flight.

I'm about to ask Luke how Stella took that particular portion of the news when she knocks on the window.

'Jessica, Jessica, Jessica,' she says, pulling a face.

And just like that, I'm one hundred per cent sober again.

Is she mad?

'Erm . . . hey, Stell,' I say as we all clatter out of the taxi, Dita and Viktor pulling up in a matte black mega car shortly after us.

Ooh great, an audience!

'Stella,' I begin, painfully aware that Luke is also hovering in the background. 'I, erm . . . Can I have a word?'

Stella folds her arms expectantly.

'Right,' I say. 'You know I love you more than anything in the world, and I value our friendship above pretty much anything else, right?'

'Right.' Stella's lip twitches like she's suppressing a smile.

'And I would never do anything to damage our friendship.'

'That's true!' Em chips in eagerly.

'But there is, erm, something I have to tell you.'

'Ooh!' says Em. 'Is it that you're going to flounce off in another paddy? Because I've booked a diamond blow-dry for 5pm and I don't really want to miss it, so Stell, you're going to have to deal with Jessie this time.'

'Emerald! It wasn't a paddy and can you please pipe down!'

'Jeez, Main Character Jess is kinda spiky.' Em rolls her eyes good-naturedly.

'It's about The Pact,' I plough on. 'And . . . my feelings towards Luke. Your little brother.'

Stella's left eyebrow spikes up. 'Yes, thank you, Jess, I am aware that Luke is my little brother. Are you talking about the pact that we made back at uni about not dating each other's siblings?'

'Yes, and, erm, the fact is, I've sort of developed *feelings* for Luke and I'm sort of wondering if you might consider lifting the pact so that I can maybe, erm . . . '

'She wants to smash your little bro,' Em cuts in.

'OH MY GOD, EM,' I squeal.

'That was unnecessary, Emerald,' Stella says before turning back to me. 'Jess, we made that pact when we were teenagers. I think we've already established that we all did some stupid things back then. Remember when I tried to crochet a crop top? Remember your recriminations over nothing? And we haven't discussed Em's biltong-curing phase yet.'

'Hey!' she protests. 'I made money from that biltong.'

'You had *meat* hanging in your wardrobe and the whole flat smelled revolting and you literally sold one biltong to a boy who fancied you,' Stella points out.

Em tuts.

I clear my throat. 'I've never felt like this before.' I glance at Luke. 'But obviously . . . '

I trail off, noticing that Stella looks like she's mulling this over. Meanwhile, Luke clears his throat, steps forward and takes my hand. 'Same,' he says.

My heart whooshes.

And suddenly Stella's face breaks into a huge smile. 'Oh my god.' She laughs. 'You should see the look on your faces! As if I was going to put my foot down on this just because of some pact we made before we were grown-ass women.'

She chuckles away to herself while I shoot Luke a look.

'Come over here, you two,' she says, bringing us in for a hug. 'I'm really happy for you guys because I love you both dearly and it's so obvious that you'll make the most adorable couple. But listen, if you ever do anything to hurt—'

'I won't,' I say in a rush.

'Not *you*.' She laughs. 'I'm talking to this little dickhead. Do anything to hurt my best friend again and I will hunt you down. Hunt you down, Luke.'

I'm terrified on his behalf.

'That won't happen,' says Luke.

263

'Then go forth, with my blessing,' Stella adds magnanimously. 'Just spare me the details please. Straight sex is gross enough without it involving a sibling.'

Em, Dita and Carl start clapping and I'm awash with an acute feeling of happiness. It brings a certain clarity, too. For a while there, I thought I'd got this all wrong. I'd quit my job and ditched my annoying ex and set off on holiday with absolutely zero idea what my future had in store and then Luke came along and it all seemed to make sense. And then so did the news of Brie, and I spiralled. I was so close to going back to work with my tail between my legs. Back to my old life where I definitely was not living my life to its fullest.

I think back on my friendship with Stella and Em, and my role as mum of the group, and I don't regret that. But it strikes me now that I have spent the past ten years living vicariously through them. Every phone conversation with Emerald, where she shares some little snippet of what she's been getting up to. The amazing career. The trips abroad. The men! And Stella too, with her success and her confidence and her joie de vivre. I've been living off their crumbs, through no fault of theirs, ever since we left uni.

It's time I made my own meal. No crumbs allowed.

It's time to start living my own life to the maximum.

It's time, I decide, to have at it.

I nestle closer into Luke, pressing myself up on my tiptoes so that he can hear me.

'I've a favour to ask,' I say.

He looks down at me.

'Anything,' he replies, which makes me swallow hard and briefly lose focus.

'There's something else I need to do, and I sort of need to do it now.'

'Now?'

'Mm hm. Can you wait for me? I'll only be a couple of hours

or so.'

'I would wait forever for you, Jess.'

'Jessica Jones, what the eff are we doing?' asks Em as I grab my two best friends and hurtle through the hotel, out past the outdoor swimming pool, along the side of the gym, back past our suite and through the woods.

'Follow me!' I call.

'Shouldn't you be smashing Luke right now?' Em asks.

'Sibling present,' barks Stella. Out of the woods, along the headland, down the thousand steps, across the sand where Luke and I first sat together, back when us seemed totally impossible.

I say 'back when', even though it was a week ago, but holy smokes a lot has changed in this past week.

'I have this overwhelming need to try something. I've just got to get it out of my system,' I say as we reach the beach hut, and find Ryan there singing along to old-school surf tunes.

'Ryan, will you take us coasteering please?' I ask.

'Sure.' He shrugs, giving Em a wink and heading out back to find three wetsuits.

'Babes, I had no idea that you'd be so into coasteering,' Em marvels as the three of us zip ourselves in.

'I'm really not sure what's happening,' says Stella.

'Let's do this.' I beam as Ryan leads us out towards the coast.

As we go, I think back to how crazy this break had seemed. Just a week or two earlier I'd been utterly dedicated to a job that didn't value me, busting my balls to prove myself time and time again. I never took time off, fearing that it would make me look unprofessional, which I can see now was total madness. The sense of freedom I felt from quitting, on my terms, has been incredible. Finally I am taking proper ownership of my destiny, I think, before realising I sound a lot like Emerald.

'I'm taking ownership of my destiny!' I call over to her as we scramble up a cliff.

'I love this for you, Jessie,' she calls back, the wind whipping her hair.

'Jesus wept,' mutters Stella. 'Am I the only one who hasn't lost it today?'

Holy moly it's hot. My aching legs drive up the steps and onto the headland which I didn't dare jump off last time. Sheer drops and Jessica 1.0 were not a happy combination, back when I was driven by a fear of everything. Fear of losing my best mates. Fear of telling Stella the truth. Fear of letting myself feel true emotions for an unbelievably handsome man. I look around at my two best mates, all three of us hot and sweaty, hair going crazy. We've been through so much together, I think, absolutely filled up with love for these incredible women by my side.

'I just wanted to say that I love you guys,' I puff.

'Aw, emotional Jessie is one of my favourites.' Em grins.

'Could we maybe have done that without the half-hour hike across challenging coastal terrain, first?' asks Stella.

'No, because I really wanted to do this,' I say, motioning to the cliff's edge.

'What, show us the sea?' Stella asks.

'It *is* very pretty,' Em says indulgently.

'I just . . . I need to prove one final thing to myself,' I say. 'And I wanted to do that with you two.'

'Omg are you going to jump this time?' Em cottons on.

I walk over to the water's edge, to where I couldn't make the jump last time. Down below, the glorious blue water.

'Yes!' I say happily. 'Will you come with me?'

'The things I do in the name of friendship.' Stella grins. 'Go on, then.'

And so the three of us line up in our wetsuits on the edge of the cliff. We take hold of each other's hands. I count down from three, and then we launch ourselves off the headland and into the water.

It takes nanoseconds to hit the sea (it really was not that far

266

after all) but that brief moment in the air feels so good. I can feel all the weight I've been carrying whip off me and disappear into thin air. The air swooshes past my ears and I think I'm shouting WHEEEE like a small child going down a slide.

Splash.

I'm in the water, air pockets bubbling around me. My head breaks through to the surface and a glorious sense of sheer elation floats through my whole body. Em and Stella come to the surface too, and we're all pushing our hair out of our eyes, hooting with laughter together as we come up for air.

'Now *that* is what I call a Saturn Return,' says Em, beaming, as we bob up and down in the water. I let my limbs stretch out, relishing the feeling of lightness. It's literal, but emotional too. So much has been washed away by these gentle waves, and I have a feeling that there are so many new things to come, too.

Elated, the three of us walk with Ryan back towards the beach hut and there, in the sand, stands Luke.

'I might stay at the beach you know,' Em says, and I see her winking at Stella.

'What?' Stella says, and then suddenly, 'Oh yeah, me too. Definitely hang out here for a while.'

I grin at both of them.

'I might not, if you don't mind?'

'Don't you dare stay here!' Em says, shoving me in the sand towards the waiting Luke.

'I could get the paddleboards out if you guys want?' I hear Ryan say, as I walk away, crossing the sand towards Luke, my heart in my mouth.

'You made the jump.' He smiles proudly at me.

'Did you see?'

'Yup. You looked amazing jumping off that cliff.' He laces his fingers through mine and we stand there, drinking each other in.

'Thanks,' I reply. 'It felt great. So, I was wondering if you're taking any more classes today, or if, maybe, you have some free time?'

'My classes are done for the day,' he says. 'And if they weren't I'd consider faking a hamstring injury.'

'Shame,' I tease. 'I was hoping we might teach each other a thing or two. But sounds like you're going to have to spend a lot of time in bed.'

Luke lets out a sigh that does major things to my insides.

'Yes, I am going to be doing that. And you're coming with me. Happy for you to teach me a thing or two. I think we're going to need to get you out of these wet clothes for these lessons.'

A thrill shivers through me.

'Sounds sensible,' I manage as he leads me back to his.

Chapter 24

A beam of sunlight pours in through the open window, the sound of birds tweeting and waves crashing in the distance.

I open my eyes, a blissful feeling washing over me.

'Good morning,' Luke says, rolling onto his stomach in bed next to me. 'Good sleep?'

I turn towards him, under the covers of his bed, and let my sleepy brain process where I am. Whom I'm with. I catch the alarm clock on his bedside table.

'Luke, the time! Shouldn't you be at work by now?'

A fire flashes across his eyes. 'Technically, yes . . . '

'Technically?' I laugh as he pulls me closer and covers me in kisses. I sit up, trying half-heartedly to push him away when really it's just an excuse to lay my hands on him. After last night, I don't think I will ever grow tired of touching Luke. Last night . . . oh, *last night*. Let's just say I didn't get much rest.

'I've got a better idea,' he says, planting several butterfly kisses across the bridge of my nose.

'Mmm?'

'Mm,' he murmurs. 'We stay here. Then, when we're ready, breakfast.'

Oh *god*, the temptation. I'd love to say that I stand firm, insist he goes to work, but the magnetic pull of sharing a bed with Luke is next level.

Afterwards, I try again.

'Luke,' I say. 'I really don't want to get you in trouble. Don't you have tennis class first thing?'

'I did have,' he concedes, fingers lightly running across my collarbone. 'But weirdly Croissants hasn't been so fussed about tennis since you sent her off on a wild Dita chase.'

'Oh no.' I chuckle. 'I feel bad.'

'Don't. Did you hear what happened?'

I shake my head, intrigued.

'One of the guys who works on the bar told me that Croissants bumped into Perry Carver last night, after she left the barbecue.'

'The footballer?'

'Sounds like it was love at first sight.'

'Stop it!'

'True story. Somebody sent a message round on the staff's WhatsApp chat to say they had breakfast together this morning and they've even gone Instagram official already. It's hot hotel gossip.'

'That was fast,' I say.

Luke looks at me. 'When you know, you know.' He grins.

'Agreed. I'm really pleased for her, I did feel bad about sending her off on that wild goose chase.'

'And thanks to you, my morning is now free and I would very much like to take you to breakfast.'

'Then it's a date.' I beam, rolling over to check my phone. Zodiac Girlie has been busy overnight.

Enjoy the ride, you're about to accelerate.

Ah, sweet Zodiac Girlie, I think fondly. She's been disquietingly accurate since I got to Gurnard Cove, I guess she was bound to get something wrong along the way. Because I have definitely done all my accelerating now. Just look at me! Naked in Luke's bed! Any more accelerating and I will definitely need a lie-down.

Luke leads me outside to the hotel's beautiful kitchen garden, where fruit and veg are growing in neat aisles and up trellising. There's a small patch of grass in the middle of the garden, and on it stands a wooden table packed with breakfast treats. Juices, pastries, racks of toast, jams. Two place settings have been made up and he pulls a chair out for me.

'This is incredible,' I say, eyes lighting up. 'How did you do all this?'

Luke watches my reaction. 'I have connections.' He grins.

I sigh happily as I tuck into a bowl of fruit and Greek yoghurt, suddenly famished after the world's most chaotic day yesterday. The maze injury. The girlfriend bombshell. The mad drive to a nearby town. Befriending the locals. Beer pong through the heartache. Luke and the truth. Coasteering with my best friends. Not to mention everything that happened afterwards!

'I can't believe today's our last day,' I say sadly.

'About that.' Luke looks deep in thought as he plunges the cafetière and pours me a coffee. 'Have you thought what you might do?'

'Go home, I guess.' I exhale, the sheer idea of it making my stomach sink. 'This holiday has helped me to realise that I don't need to be in Carpston anymore, but I've still got some admin to do before my next step. So I'm going to head back and tie up some loose ends. Hand in my notice on the flat. Take the time to figure out what to do with my career. The bookshop where I volunteer are always after more hours so I could throw myself into that for a bit while I work things out.'

I track my eyes over to Luke's and decide, there and then, to say exactly what's on my mind.

'And hopefully spend some more time with you?' I add. 'Because the thing is, Luke, I really like you. And that scares me a bit because I haven't felt like this about anyone before. But recently I've realised that I can't just sit back and let life happen around me. I need to take control of my future. And that starts with you.'

'I am very much willing to be taken control of.' He grins, genuinely licks his lips here which renders me speechless. 'But, to be clear, are you asking me out, Jess?'

'I believe I am,' I say, taking a bite of toast.

A smile plays on his lips as he says: 'That has never happened before.'

I refuse to believe that. 'Oh come on! Surely that's not right?'

Luke shakes his head. 'Nope.'

'Well then' – I beam – 'this really is a day of firsts. I've never asked anyone out, either.'

Luke's smile has stretched to a full-on grin that lights up his face.

'You know, you're going to have to answer me at some point,' I say. 'Can't keep a girl hanging.'

'Jessica Jones,' he murmurs, voice tantalisingly low. 'I've been yours since the moment I saw you on day one here. I think you're incredible. I was actually just about to ask you the same thing but you beat me to it. But, ah, there's one thing I have to tell you first.'

I take another bite of toast, chewing nervously. This sounds ominous.

'Oh?' I say eventually.

Luke catches my eye.

'There's something else I haven't been totally honest with you about,' he admits.

Oh *god*. My stomach lurches.

'My job here, it's not a permanent thing,' he begins, watching my reaction closely, 'I took it as a stepping stone really, a chance to get out of America and to do some soul-searching. Exactly like what you plan to do. But the truth is that I never really planned to stay in Northumberland for long. I want adventure, Jess. I want to travel and see more of the world.'

'You're leaving,' I whisper, heart stopping.

He holds me with his gaze and I almost can't look. It's unbearable to think that he's going so soon.

'There's a new hotel opening up in the Maldives – it's owned by the same people who own Gurnard Cove – and they're after someone to head up their sports department.'

'The Maldives? That's far,' I say stupidly.

'True. But it wouldn't be so far if you came with me. If we went together.' He reaches across for my hand now, hope etched across his face. 'Jess, the hotel are planning to trial a pop-up bookshop there and they are looking for a bookseller to take control of it all.'

'What?' I gasp, not quite able to compute all of this.

'That job is made for you!' he says, sounding excited, squeezing my hand. 'You've always wanted to own a bookshop one day, right? And you just said that you're planning on heading back to Carpston to volunteer at the local bookshop. Look, I know you wouldn't be owning this place in the Maldives, but, I don't know' – he runs a hand through his hair – 'it could be an incredible way to get you on the right path, maybe? It's a six-month contract, same as the sports job.'

My jaw is on the floor.

'Look,' Luke adds softly after a while. 'I know this is a lot to take in and I don't want to scare you off – I really hope you don't think I'm moving things too fast. And also, if you don't want to go then I won't either. I want to be where you are, if that's okay with you? I just . . . I haven't felt like this before.'

He stops to give me an adorably hopeful look.

'And the timing is perfect,' he continues. 'You've quit your job, you're looking for your next adventure. I think I've found it, Jess, if you're happy for that adventure to be with me. Maybe we could kickstart those Pocket Adventures we talked about.'

'Erm . . . '

That's literally all I can manage. All this information has sent my brain into overdrive. Luke wants me to move to *the Maldives* with him and run a bookshop? It's like fate just handpicked all of my favourite things and offered them to me on a plate alongside this morning's delicious breakfast. Almost too good to be true.

Luke's watching my reaction, trying to get a read on how I'm feeling, and goodness knows what my face is doing right now.

'It's too much,' he says eventually, clearly deciding that my lack of ability to express myself means that he's somehow broken me. 'I'm so sorry. Damn, I knew I'd mess this up. I'll stay here. We can do this the more normal, less a-hundred-miles-an-hour way. Date and hang out and not move abroad together after becoming official five minutes ago. Christ, sorry, what was I thinking? That is, if you even still want to date me after that.'

Finally, I process what's happening. Good things, that's what. And I realise that once again, Zodiac Girlie was right. The best is yet to come, all I need to do is put my foot on the gas.

I'm up and out of my seat then, walking around to Luke's side of the table. I place myself in his lap, set down the coffee cup he's holding.

'Where do I apply for this job, then?' I ask.

Later, once I've not even remotely come back down to earth, I skip back to the suite to find Em trying to get Stella to do some yoga. She's got yoga mats rolled out, calming water sounds playing in the background and is currently encouraging Stella to get into a downward dog.

'Oh thank god,' Stella says when she sees me, unfolding herself and sitting down on the mat. 'That's quite enough of that.'

'Jessie!' Em cheers. 'Finally! We're on tenterhooks. How did last night go? You need to spill, I want every last drop.'

'Woah, let's keep it PG please.' Stella grimaces.

I place a reassuring hand on her shoulder. 'For decency's sake, let's just say I had a lovely evening and leave it at that.'

Emerald eyes me then chuckles, delighted. 'YOUR AURA. I'll

say no more, for Stella's sake, but basically you get it, girl.'

My flushing cheeks are interrupted by the phone ringing.

'Hello?' I answer.

'Hello, madam, it's Santi from reception. Miss Ortiz has invited your party to lunch, are you free to join her?'

I cover the handset.

'Guys, Dita's asked us to join her for lunch. Are you up for it?'

'Lunch with a movie star? Why not?' Stella replies.

'That's great, we'll be there. Thank you!'

'Yessica has had the impeccable intercourse, no?' Dita has taken one look at me and is now addressing my friends.

Honestly. Am I a total open book?

Em claps gleefully as we grab a seat at Dita's table. 'She sure has, but we're not talking about it in too much detail for Stella's sake.'

'Sí, sí. So tell me, girls, have you enjoyed your spa break?'

I look between my best friends, and feel that familiar sense of joy to be in their presence. And for the first time in a long while, I realise I'm no longer living vicariously through Em's exciting life. I've started my own. And while I will always bask in their successes, I feel genuinely excited about what the new future may hold for me now.

'It's been the best.' Em beams at us. 'Properly wonderful to spend this time together.'

Stella nods. 'You guys have really helped me get some perspective on the whole Fran thing. We're going to have a proper talk when I get back but for now, I feel like we can just keep the conversation going, you know? I have decided on something, though.'

'Oh?' I say.

'I'm going to take some time off work and spend some proper time with Fran. There's no point discussing whether or not to start a family if we can't even find time for each other, right? Fran's been so patient with how busy I am at work, and now this trip.

I need to show her that she's my priority, too.'

'That's really sweet, Stell,' I say. 'Have you decided what you'll do?'

'Not yet, but I'm thinking somewhere sunny, maybe a beach, where we can just be together.'

'I have a little place on the coast in Spain for you,' says Dita. 'It's one of my houses. You two would be very welcome.'

'Seriously?' Stella splutters. 'Are you sure? That would be amazing, obviously, but—'

'It's done,' Dita says. 'I will get Viktor to organise it.'

Stella, for once, has been stunned into silence.

'Now what about you?' Dita points at me. 'How are you going to make things work with Luca?'

'Okay, I've got news,' I say excitedly, blurting out the Maldives plan. 'Luke's done all this research on the bookseller job and I really think I could be good at it. Obviously I need to apply, first, so I'm trying not to get too excited just yet.' I pause while my friends go wide-eyed with excitement. 'But the thought of something new and so positive and shiny! And sharing it with Luke . . .'

'Mate, what the hell? That sounds incredible,' says Stella.

Em simply has her hands in prayer position.

We're talking excitedly about selling books on the beach when Luke appears in the dining room.

'Hey,' he says, eyes settling on mine. 'I just came to say hi, I'm on my way to a cardio session.'

'Aye, aye, aye,' Dita purrs as Luke plants a brief kiss on my forehead. 'What a handsome couple you make.'

'If only you could see their auras.' Em grins as everyone looks at us.

'Better go.' He beams at me.

'Can't keep away.' Stella rolls her eyes good-naturedly.

'See you later,' I tell him.

'You know,' says Emerald as she leans back in her chair, 'this has been a seriously successful Saturn Return for you, Jessie. Banging new man, new career on the horizon, a little bit of lead character energy. You're shining bright, my friend.'

For some reason, this makes me well up.

'I love you guys,' I say, taking their hands. 'Here's to the next adventure.'

Epilogue

Soft white sand gives way beneath my feet, little footprints leading their way here. I look back at them now, marking out my route to the ocean. Next to them, much bigger footprints, almost twice the size of mine.

A woosh of foam reaches the tips of my toes and I turn my attention back to the turquoise sea stretching out for miles ahead of us. Another baby wave rolls gently into shore, leaving a fresh delivery of shells in its wake. This time, a pearlescent pink one is uncovered right by my feet and I resist the urge to pick it up because my shell collection is getting out of hand.

But Luke spots it, reaches down, turns it over in his hands. Slips it into his pocket and I just know he'll be adding it to the bowl I've filled with shells when we get home.

Home.

It feels strange and also completely familiar to call the Maldives our home. Even more so to say that I share that home with Luke.

I push my baseball hat further down on my head to shade my eyes from the setting sun. It's got the words 'book lover' written across it and no, I have not taken it off since we landed.

'This view will never get old,' says Luke.

'I know,' I reply. 'Tonight's sunset is pulling out all the stops.'

'I wasn't talking about the sunset.' He grins, and I realise he's looking at me. The sky, all purple and orange, is reflected in his gaze and not for the first time, I wonder if I should pinch myself, just to double check this is actually happening.

Because it's mad, really. I'm selling books to holidaymakers in the middle of the Indian Ocean. The white-washed bookshop is nestled in the hotel's grounds, surrounded by palm trees, just a short sandy walk from this very beach. Sometimes, on my lunch break, I'll dangle my feet over the nearby jetty, watching the marine life go about their business. Sometimes, if he isn't taking classes, Luke will turn up with a hamper filled with a picnic lunch under one arm and we'll eat together in the shade of a coconut tree.

Guests love the shop and my favourite thing is sitting down for a consultation, listening to their current reads and then recommending something I think they might like. It feels right, to be working here. Even on the crazy busy days when I'm racing from one customer to the next and lugging new stock into the shop. There's this feeling, deep inside, that I am finally doing something for *me*, something I've always wanted to do. I am finally following my dreams. And that is pretty special.

'Come on.' I pull on Luke's hand. 'Big day tomorrow.'

'Mm,' he says, nodding. 'Remind me exactly how many of your friends are descending on us?'

'Four.' I grin. 'And one of them is your sister so you can pipe down.'

'I think Stella's really looking forward to this time away with Fran,' Luke says.

'Naturally Dita's booked the presidential suite,' I add. 'I'm dying to see it.'

'You think it'll be nicer than our staff accommodation?' Luke smiles.

I consider this. Our little hut has a double bed, a small kitchen diner and a tiny bathroom. No bells and whistles. No shower where you can choose your mood, or voice-controlled coffee machine, or private plunge pool waiting just outside like at Gurnard Cove. But what it does have, is Luke. That week in Northumberland was going to be the start of my great big escape from life and I realise now, as we pad home across the sand together, that I wasn't actually escaping from anything. I was starting afresh.

'Come on.' I smile up at him. 'Let's go make the most of our last night before chaos descends.'

Fallen in love with *The Spa Break*? Don't miss *The Pick Up*, another hilarious and gorgeous romcom from Hannah Doyle. Available now!

A Letter from Hannah Doyle

Thank you so much for choosing to read *The Spa Break*. I so hope you enjoyed it! If you would like to be the first to know about my new releases, this is where you can follow me:

@byhannahdoyle
@byHannahDoyle
byHannahDoyle

I loved writing *The Spa Break* and if you loved reading it, I would be so grateful if you would leave a review. I always love to hear what readers thought, and it helps new readers discover my books too.

Thanks,
Hannah

Can love ever be as easy as ABC?

THE A TO Z OF US

HANNAH DOYLE

If you want to know the A–Z of love then it starts with Alice and ends with Zach.

Alice is a self-confessed cynic when it comes to love. She's never had a serious relationship and after supporting her best friend through a devastating break-up, she's not about to let down her barriers anytime soon. Relationships always end badly.

Zach is a romantic. Even after his parents got divorced, he still believes in love and is eager to settle down and have a family of his own. He just hasn't met The One yet.

After a chance meet-cute at an art gallery, Zach realises their names bookend the alphabet and suggests their next date begin with a B. Alice agrees to one date, pretty sure they will never get to 26 dates. But can love ever be as easy as ABC?

Available now!

Who needs real love
When you've got a fake romance?

THE PICK UP

HANNAH DOYLE

Sophie Rogers finds it easy to focus on the important things in life. Like her daughter, her job and her family.

So when Joe, another single parent at school, suggests they fake a romance to help them both out of a fix, she throws herself in.

But then Sophie starts to look forward to seeing Joe. In fact, she's thinking about his floppy hair, Irish accent and the way his lips felt when they grazed hers (her commitment to this is exceptional) more than their synced calendars and staged socials. And there is a reason the yummy mummies called him Hot Single Dad.

Sophie Rogers isn't silly enough to fall in love with her fake boyfriend. **Is she?**

Available now!

Acknowledgements

Writing books isn't easy (endless edits), or glamorous (working alone in yesterday's leggings) or indeed lucrative (hey streaming giants, call me!) but it is enormous fun and incredibly fulfilling. And somehow, I now find myself with quite a few books to my name. I know I wouldn't be in this lovely position without the help and guidance of a whole village of champions. (Not a literal village, although wouldn't that be fun?!)

Enormous thanks are due to Amanda Preston, as ever, for being the best agent in the business, and to the whole LBA gang. Similarly to Seema Mitra, thank you so much for your flawless editing on *The Spa Break*. To the stellar team at HQ Digital, including Kate Mills, Georgina Green, Lou Nyuar, Maren Landsnes, Eldes Tran and Michelle Bullock, thank you for everything you do, I'm incredibly grateful.

Grateful also to the fellow authors out there who are such a gorgeous, supportive bunch of legends. Thank you to Cress McLaughlin, Lizzy Dent, Lucy Vine, Hannah Tovey, Beth Reekles, Nicole Kennedy, Sophie Cousens, Olivia Beirne, Helly Acton, Anam Iqbal, Lisa Dickenson, Elizabeth Drummond, Isabelle

Broom, Kate Davies, Tom Ellen, Cesca Major, Lia Louis, Michelle Rawlins, Clare Swatman, Zara Stoneley and more.

When I told my husband that I was writing these acknowledgements he suggested: "To my husband, thanks for nothing." Thankfully this is very much not an accurate representation of his actual support. Prepare for sentiment. To my husband, thanks for *everything*. You're the best. Same goes to my mum, thank you for your limitless enthusiasm with the kiddos, you are a true angel. And to my best pals, including the aforementioned Loughborough Lads, thank you for being sunshine in human form.

This year I've been taking part in more author things and it has been so much fun, so another thank you is due to the brilliant people who have enabled me to cast asunder yesterday's leggings, and step into something more chic in the name of author panels and radio appearances. I've loved it.

And finally, most importantly, thank you to the glorious readers for taking the time to read and review my books. You really are the best. Hearing from you means the absolute world and I am forever indebted.

Thank you, Hannah x

Dear Reader,

We hope you enjoyed reading this book. If you did, we'd be so appreciative if you left a review. It really helps us and the author to bring more books like this to you.

Here at HQ Digital we are dedicated to publishing fiction that will keep you turning the pages into the early hours. Don't want to miss a thing? To find out more about our books, promotions, discover exclusive content and enter competitions you can keep in touch in the following ways:

JOIN OUR COMMUNITY:
Sign up to our new email newsletter: http://smarturl.it/SignUpHQ
Read our new blog www.hqstories.co.uk

https://twitter.com/HQStories
www.facebook.com/HQStories

BUDDING WRITER?
We're also looking for authors to join the HQ Digital family!
Find out more here:

https://www.hqstories.co.uk/want-to-write-for-us/

Thanks for reading, from the HQ Digital team